OLD SINS

Jane A. Adams

This first world edition published 2020
in Great Britain and 2021 in the USA by
SEVERN HOUSE PUBLISHERS LTD of
Eardley House, 4 Uxbridge Street, London W8 7SY.
Trade paperback edition first published
in Great Britain and the USA 2021 by
SEVERN HOUSE PUBLISHERS LTD.

British Library Cataloguing in Publication Data
A CIP catalogue record for this title is available from the British Library.

ISBN-13: 978-0-7278-9244-7 (cased)
ISBN-13: 978-1-78029-745-3 (trade paper)
ISBN-13: 978-1-4483-0485-1 (e-book)

All Severn House titles are printed on acid-free paper.

Severn House Publishers support the Forest Stewardship Council™ [FSC™],
the leading international forest certification organisation.
All our titles that are printed on FSC certified paper carry the FSC logo.

MIX
Paper from
responsible sources
FSC   FSC® C013056
www.fsc.org

Typeset by Palimpsest Book Production Ltd.,
Falkirk, Stirlingshire, Scotland.
Printed and bound in Great Britain by
TJ Books Limited, Padstow, Cornwall.

PROLOGUE

October, 1929

The cottage was remote, about a mile outside of the nearest village. It was stone built and had probably once been a tied cottage for the local farm. The garden wrapped around it on three sides, but the door of the cottage opened straight on to a narrow lane, little more than a farm track. Detective Sergeant Walter Cole had known this cottage all his life and had always fancied it. Like about seventy per cent of the Metropolitan Police back in the day, he had been recruited from a rural area – rural recruits generally being seen as being fitter, stronger, and usually having just enough brains to go with the brawn. He had retired from the force a few years early, but strangely had retained most of his pension. In retirement he had attained his dream of moving into this little cottage and tending to the large garden – this only being possible due to an unexpected windfall that had come his way. His roses were a sight to behold.

Walter Cole lived alone. He had never married, though he had dallied with the idea a few times. Getting a woman to put up with the long hours and low pay early in his career, before even the statutory day off a week became the norm, had not been an easy thing. When conditions improved after the Great War, and when Cole became a detective, he found that he was too set in his ways to consider the needs of another. A dog, he thought he might manage, but a wife, no. And so, since he had moved to this cottage, he'd had a woman who came in twice a week to 'do' for him. There was rarely much cleaning for her, Cole being a tidy sort, but she cooked the odd meal for him, and she took his washing and his ironing away and dealt with that, for which Cole was grateful.

He lived quietly. He could go an entire day seeing no more than a local farmer, and so when the knock came on his door at eight o'clock at night Cole was very much surprised. He was even more surprised when he opened the door and saw a once familiar face. Not a welcome face.

His first thought was what the hell was he doing here? He managed to voice, 'What—' before the knife plunged into his abdomen and he fell to the floor. The man with the knife leaned over him and Cole, vision fading fast, pain and the knowledge of death overtaking his body, blinked hard to try to keep him in focus.

'No more than you deserve,' the man eventually said. He placed a small bundle of papers in Cole's hand and then he was gone back into the night as quietly as he had come.

A few nights later Detective Chief Inspector Henry Johnstone received a knock at his own door but this was, by contrast, not just a familiar face but one he welcomed – even though he was surprised to see it.

'Mr Otis Freeland,' Henry said. 'What brings you here? Come along inside.'

Otis breezed into Henry's little flat and headed for the window that overlooked the river. Henry had acquired the flat because of that view: the coming and goings of ships and boats and the ever-changing colours of the Thames. Watching it soothed him.

'I often wondered what your view was like,' Otis said. 'I'd look up at your window think, "I wonder what Henry can see from there?"'

'Well, now your curiosity has been satisfied, perhaps you will satisfy mine. Can I offer you tea, or coffee . . . some whisky?'

'I can't stay long enough to be sociable,' Otis told him. 'But I've no doubt I will be in touch again within the next few days, or one of my associates will.'

Henry frowned. He had met Otis earlier in the year, when Henry had been investigating a murder and Otis a major currency swindle. Their paths had crossed and Henry, though he liked Otis, was still not sure exactly which government department the man worked for or even that Otis was his correct name. 'So what brings you here?' Henry said bluntly.

'Detective Sergeant Walter Cole was found dead three days ago. Stabbed in the abdomen. He managed to crawl out of his cottage and into the lane. A farm worker spotted him the following morning, by which time he was well beyond help. At first the labourer thought that Cole must have killed himself. He held a note in one hand and the knife that did the deed lay close by the other.'

Henry looked sceptical. 'A knife wound to the abdomen – that's an unusual method for suicide, at least here in England. But I see from your expression that you have no truck with that idea anyway. It's also an unusual and risky way of killing someone. It requires the assailant to be physically close to the victim and death is not usually instantaneous. There is the risk that the victim would be found still alive.'

'Not so much of a risk if you saw the cottage where Walter Cole lived. It's not a place anyone might pass by chance, the sort of location where a man can scream at the top of his lungs for help and no one will hear apart from the foxes and badgers. Believe me, I don't think you want the badgers investigating. They have sharp teeth, do badgers.'

'I've had no contact with Walter Cole in years. I worked with him that one time, that was it.' The tone of Henry's voice would have left no one in any doubt that he was glad of this fact.

'Once may well have been enough, Henry. You might also be interested to know that Detective Chief Inspector Hayden Paul was also found dead about a week ago. His death had initially been ruled as suicide apparently.'

Henry laughed in disbelief. 'Hayden Paul would never commit suicide. The man was a narcissist.'

'And bankrupt, thanks to our stock market crash in September. Though his wife and daughters had left him long before that. The surprise I suppose is that the man ever found anyone to marry him in the first place.'

'He could be charming on occasion. But I still don't believe the suicide. That man was like an oiled pig: nothing and nobody could grip on to him for long enough for anything to stick. He got away with—'

'No, it wasn't suicide,' Otis confirmed. 'It wasn't even particularly well staged. A single shot to the head, but the man was dead before the shot was fired. His neck had been broken.'

'It takes strength and a certain amount of skill to do that,' Henry said. 'And whoever did it must have realized that would show up in the post-mortem examination.'

'Presumably so. It seems that fact did not trouble them. Whoever killed these two is a man who likes to play games, to misdirect and confuse.'

'You know who the killer was?'

Otis nodded. 'We believe we know who is behind it and yes, in all likelihood who committed the murders. Hayden Paul also left an apparent suicide note, of sorts. Like the one clutched in the hand of Walter Cole, it was only two words. And given your past association with these two, you can see why we might be a little concerned about *you*.'

'My past association! Dozens of officers worked with them. I encountered them on one case a decade ago, and believe me that was enough.'

'Enough indeed, Henry. Enough indeed.'

'You suspect that their deaths are to do with that one investigation? With the Richardson case?' Henry's disturbance of mind at the memory of that case was revealed in the fact that he crossed to the sideboard and poured himself a drink.

'Richardson was released from prison not six months ago,' Otis told him.

'Released? He's lucky not to have hanged.'

'Maybe so. Anyway, he's gone to ground. But the coincidence . . . you must admit, is suggestive. As is the presumed suicide note, or should I say notes. The message that was written on the scrap of paper Walter Cole held in his hand was the same as the one found beside Detective Chief Inspector Paul. Just two words, Henry, two words. "Old sins". As they say, Henry, they cast long shadows.'

'Why had Central Office not been informed of these murders and called in to investigate? After all, these two men had once been serving officers in the Metropolitan Police.'

'In the case of Mr Walter Cole,' Otis told him, 'detectives have come up from Exeter. They have a complement of very competent detectives in that city and they are being assisted by members of my department.'

'And what department might that be, Otis?' Henry had asked.

Otis had merely smiled. 'Detective Chief Inspector Paul retired to Birmingham – you know, they are also well served for detectives these days. Again, they have been given assistance.'

'But I would have expected notices to have come through to Central Office, or for this to have been reported in the newspapers at the very least. Otis, is this being kept quiet?'

'In both cases, the local newspapers reported the deaths but in a circumspect way.'

'You slapped D-notices on them, didn't you?' Henry guessed. 'Why, what else is going on? You may as well have had that drink, you know – you've been here long enough.'

Otis paused, as though considering his response, but Henry knew this was a ruse. He was a man who usually had his story worked out fully already. 'Evidence was left at both crime scenes,' he said. 'Evidence that would show both the police force and government in, shall we say, a very unsatisfactory light.'

It was Henry's turn to pause. 'Ah,' he said. 'I can see how that might cause difficulties. May I ask what kind of evidence?'

'Documentary, a list of names, and evidentiary rather than simply accusatory. Suggestions that a miscarriage of justice had been perpetrated in the Richardson business and that he did not deserve the sentence he served. That the police were well aware of this and in fact manufactured some of the evidence against him. Evidence on which he was convicted. Henry, you and I both know that there were, shall we say, irregularities, but if any of this got out, well, there are still enough people from back then, now in positions of influence, whose names would be blackened, including your own.'

Henry was about to object that he had done nothing wrong but then he thought better of it. He had done plenty that was wrong, albeit for what he had believed to be the right reasons. At the time, he had been so certain, but he was certainly not proud of anything that had happened during his involvement with Paul and Cole – particularly the Richardson saga. Richardson deserved a far harsher sentence than he had served, but knowing what a man has done and being able to prove it could be two different things. At the time Henry had simply been thankful that the man had been locked away.

'And you fear that my life might be forfeit?'

'I'm worried about you,' Otis said slowly. 'But somehow I don't think Richardson will come after you in quite the same way.'

'Oh? And why is that?'

'Because, separately to what was left with both bodies, he's been in communication with, well, initially not my department, but his communications were passed to my department. He's also tried to get his manifesto and "complaint", as he called it, claiming that the evidence against him was manufactured, published by members of the Fourth Estate, but we had previously warned the press that this might take place, and have asked for their cooperation. This thwarting of his plans, eloquent as they were, is not going to please him. But I tell you, Henry, he really does not like you.'

'You've not yet told me why he was released. Surely he had not served his full term? In truth, the man definitely deserved to hang – you and I both know that.'

For the first time Otis looked uncomfortable. 'His release was not a matter that fell within my purview, I'm afraid. Let's just say that pressure was brought to bear, pressure which was given into, and those that gave in have now been removed from office. That man had many friends on the outside, many friends with long memories and investigative skills that frankly plenty in my department would envy. Men who it seems felt threatened by facts that Richardson could reveal about them and who therefore put money and resources into working for his release.

'Because of the importance, shall we say, of those involved in this, the hearing was held behind closed doors and it was deemed politically expedient for the man to be released with as little fuss as possible. Anyway, he is out of jail and looking for revenge.'

'Why now? Why after a decade? If he had this influence, this so-called evidence, why not make use of it before?'

'A good question. It seems most likely because external circumstances have changed. That those he had intelligence against have risen sufficiently for them to be of use. Put simply, Henry, they're now worth blackmailing.'

'But who would listen to a convicted felon?'

'Henry, you know as well as I do, a rumour spread about a powerful man, especially if that concerns a sexual or financial indiscretion, takes on a life of its own. Mud sticks, Henry.'

'And can I see these documents, this evidence left at the crime scenes, this manifesto or complaint, as you called it?'

'No. Afraid not. Regulations, you understand, but we would welcome your cooperation of course, and to that end, I am making all reports on the murders available to you, with instructions to my men on the ground and to local police that you are to be updated every two or three days. In the meantime, Henry, I'm sure you understand that this meeting has not taken place. I have men keeping an eye on you, of course, but I prefer that this conversation was not relayed to our friend Mickey, or to your dear sister. Henry, I know you confide in both of them, but on this occasion you must not, you understand that?'

Henry frowned and began to protest, but Otis quickly butted in.

'Henry, I don't doubt their loyalty or discretion for a moment, but the less involved in this the better. I will leave you means to contact me, should you have news or become unduly concerned about your situation. The plan, however, is that we will bring Richardson to heel and his associates with him, but we must draw him out first, and for that we need you isolated. Easier for our man Richardson to reach.'

It suddenly dawned on Henry what Otis was suggesting. 'So I am the bait,' he said.

'You are the bait,' Otis agreed.

ONE

The invitation had said that fancy dress was optional and, of course, Henry had decided to opt out. He looked to be in the minority, though, with most of the guests having raided the dressing-up box or hired something spectacular from Angels Fancy Dress, but despite this determined celebration Henry could perceive an air of desperation in the evening. A sense that every single one of the guests wanted to shut the world out for a time and pretend that the events of the past few weeks had happened to someone else, somewhere else, and had nothing at all to do with them. On 24 October stock prices on Wall Street had dropped precipitously. The press were now calling it Black Thursday. The following Monday stock prices plummeted again and Henry had read that some twenty five billion dollars, a figure he could barely comprehend, had been lost practically overnight. London had already suffered its own disaster back in September and Henry now wondered how many of those attending Cynthia's Halloween party, on that Thursday night, were now facing complete ruin.

'I thought you might cancel,' Henry had said to his sister, Cynthia. Cynthia's Halloween parties were legendary, but in light of events – more to the point in light of the death of recent friends – he had assumed that she might not hold it this year.

'I have to do this, Henry. One last bash. I will *not* be hosting another party, not ever, so you can see this as a farewell performance. But if I don't do this, I'll be sending totally the wrong message. We have to keep up appearances, now more than ever, my dear brother. If we look as though we are in debt, then the wolves will close on us and will tear Albert apart.'

Henry had been desperately concerned at that. 'How bad is it? I thought you'd taken steps to—'

'It will be all right. Yes, I did make certain of our basic security. But we have to pull our horns in and live quietly.' She laughed. 'At least by Albert's standards. The boys will be able to continue at their school, we'll keep the house in Bournemouth and live there permanently, but I'm selling the London property. We can take the staff with us, thankfully, but it's a waste of resources trying to maintain two properties when we live in neither full time. And, thanks to *my* foresight, both houses are mine – lock, stock and barrel – along with a few other small properties, which I'll sell when the market improves. And thankfully, the lawyers have tied up everything so tight that no one else can touch what I own, not even my darling husband.'

'And Albert's business?' Henry had asked.

'What business?' Cynthia had asked bitterly. 'Hocked up to hell, overstretched to breaking. As you know, he's made some stupid investments in the last year.'

Henry nodded. It was this tendency of Albert's towards risk taking that had caused his sister to take action and pressure her husband to sign over some of his property and investments to her. Cynthia had seen which way the wind might be blowing, but Henry knew she had taken no pleasure at all in being proved correct. 'Thankfully we pulled out of the German manufactories in time. Have you seen the latest news out of Germany?'

Henry had. None of it looked good. But then no economic news looked good, whatever bit of the world you happened to be examining.

And so this was Cynthia's swansong. The last big party at the London house before it went on the market in the new year. She would spend the time between now and then shifting everything of value, including her staff, to the Bournemouth residence – the three-storey townhouse with a little garden behind that Cynthia loved. He was profoundly glad that she had managed to hang on to that.

Not that you would think she is worried about anything to look at her tonight, he thought. Cynthia was holding court, standing close to one of the big fireplaces, a glass in one hand and a cigarette in a long holder in the other. She appeared to be dressed as an Egyptian princess, complete with black wig, winged scarabs and asps. She had worn the costume before, three or four years ago, he remembered. Beside her stood Melissa, her middle child, now thirteen and dressed as some kind of Greek goddess. This being the 'last big party', she had been allowed to stay up for a little while and her elder brother, Cyril, who'd come home from boarding school for the party, had been promised that he could remain until ten. Little Georgie, having protested very loudly that he should be allowed to go to the party too, had been permitted to greet the earlier guests and to raid the buffet table before being packed off with Nanny. It was Melissa who saw Henry first and came dashing over.

'Uncle Henry, Uncle Henry! I'm so glad you're here. Why haven't you dressed up?'

'Because Henry never dresses up,' Cynthia said fondly. She leaned in to kiss Henry on the cheek. 'Are Mickey and Belle able to come?' she asked him.

'They'll come along later. Belle doesn't get offstage until about half past ten. I expect she'll stay in costume.' Henry laughed. He glanced around the room, recognizing earls and lords and businessmen. Any other hostess would never have dreamed of inviting Detective Sergeant Mickey Hitchens and his actress wife into such company, but Cynthia had a deep love for Henry's sergeant and for Belle. The two women were close friends, and it would never have occurred to Cynthia to leave them out of this 'last big bash', as she called it.

'Melissa, go and get Uncle Henry a drink. He's going to have at least one glass of champagne.'

Henry watched fondly as Melissa, long red hair flying out behind her, dodged through the crowded room to the buffet table.

'Is Albert around?'

'Lurking in his study. So you have my full permission to go and fetch him out.' She lowered her voice and said, 'In fact, please fetch him out, Henry. He's been in the deep blues this last week or two, you know, especially after Ferdy died. That was a terrible business.'

Henry nodded. Ferdy Bright-Cooper had been Albert's best friend since they were schoolchildren, and two weeks ago he'd taken his own life. Whisky and a service revolver. The so-called gentleman's way out, Henry thought. Ferdy Bright-Cooper had not had a Cynthia to protect his interests, and the London Stock Exchange's crash back in September had taken just about everything from him. This latest disaster on Wall Street had, from what Albert had told Henry, finished the job. Ferdy would have been declared bankrupt by Christmas, his family losing their home, business and standing in society.

'What's happened to his family?' Henry asked quietly.

'Clara, his wife, has gone back to her parents' home. Taken the children. She left their family home three or four days before . . . Albert says that Ferdy told her to go, but I'm not sure whether it was pressure from her family urging her to go or whether he really did just tell her to leave. Either way, she now has nothing, poor love. She comes from old money, of course, so I'm certain that her family will protect her and the children from the worst of the scandal. The last I heard she was going to go abroad for a while.'

Melissa had returned, carrying a glass of champagne carefully cupped between both hands. 'Here you are, Uncle Henry. Mother, Mrs Ellington wants a word with you. Mr Robertson wants me to get him a whisky. Can I do that, please, Mama? I know how.'

'If you're very careful,' Cynthia told her. She smiled at Henry. 'I'd better go and see what Mrs Ellington wants. You go and find Albert.'

Henry watched as the two women in his life disappeared and then he abandoned his champagne. Albert would have whisky in his study, and Henry was not a big fan of fizz.

He made his way through the dandies, flappers, penguins and clowns and knocked on Albert's door, not waiting for a response before opening the door just enough to slide inside. Albert was dressed as a Stuart nobleman, his periwig cast aside on the floor and a very large glass of whisky in his hand. He sat in one of the comfortable and ageing leather armchairs, staring into the fire. He glanced up sharply as Henry came in.

Henry helped himself to a drink and came and sat in the chair opposite. 'I've been sent to find you and lure you out into the party,' he said. 'But I doubt we'll be missed for the next half-hour. Everyone out there seems as intent on getting drunk as you are in here.'

Albert laughed harshly. 'I'm at that stage, old man, when I can't seem to *get* drunk. I reach a certain level and then . . .' He took another sip of his whiskey anyway and then set the glass down with exaggerated care on a little side table.

'I won't ask how you are – that seems such a stupid question. But I will ask if there's anything I can do?'

Albert closed his eyes. 'Thanks, old man. I know you mean that. And I wish there was something you could do, or anyone could do, but I think I have to fight through this one on my own. It just seems so bloody, you know. Ferdy came through the war without a scratch on him. You know that – we all served together.'

Henry nodded.

'And now, to die like that. In peacetime. He used his service revolver, you know. Well, the war's over for Ferdy, isn't it?'

He reached for his glass again and Henry waited for Albert to take a big slug before he said, 'Cynthia said things were going to be tough, business-wise. How bad is it, Albert? Have you told her everything?'

'Just about. For God's sake, Henry, you know how that sister of yours is – she'll wheedle anything out of a man. Anyway, she understands the business better than I ever did, and that's the truth of it. It doesn't do my pride any good, Henry, but I have to admit that if it wasn't for Cynthia we really would be up Queer Street by now. As it is, when all of this is done and dusted, I should be able to start again with something. Though this house is going, did she tell you that?'

Henry nodded.

'But that's not going to be public knowledge until we have everything tidied up as best we can elsewhere. The solicitor tells me that no one can take this house, that it's not going to be an asset seized by creditors or anything like that, that any money that comes out of it will go into the trust that Cynthia set up, but she still doesn't want them closing in too fast. She is insisting that we keep up appearances, at least for now, and I see the sense in that, Henry, but it's bloody hard. Especially when I see men like Ferdy going under.'

Henry didn't feel that there was anything he could say. What comfort could he offer? Cynthia had done everything she could on a practical level to protect her family, but he could see how much Albert was hurting. Business acumen was meant to be a male domain; wives were not supposed to have wisdom that their husbands did not. And he could see that even though Albert was grateful, a little bit of him was also resentful. He hoped that Albert could get over it, that their marriage would not suffer because of this.

Henry drained his glass and stood up. 'Come on,' he said, 'this is your party too. You are the host. You must at least put in an appearance. One hour and then you can escape again. And Mickey will be here later, so you and he can talk about cricket and crime, and I happen to know he's made up some more microscope slides for you.' Henry knew that he was clutching at straws in his effort to bring cheer; he had rarely seen Albert look so utterly defeated.

Albert brightened just a little, clearly making the effort. He pointed to a little table set up in the corner of the study on which was set a brass microscope. Melissa was fascinated by all things scientific, and Cynthia had brought her daughter a microscope on her last birthday. Mickey had taught her how to make slides and Albert had been intrigued. He now had a device of his own and was building his own collection, though he was actually quite clumsy when it came to dissecting and mounting a specimen, so his daughter or Mickey usually did it for him. He was clearly thinking that he could manage an hour of being sociable, if he could then escape to his study later with the promise of company more suited to his mood and interests. Albert usually enjoyed parties, taking pleasure in seeing other people eating, drinking, dancing and making merry at his expense, but Henry realized that this was a bitter pill to swallow now.

'She is right, you know. It's important to put on a show just now, look confident, keep the wolves away.'

'I know she's bloody well right,' Albert said. 'But knowing she is right and that I got it so wrong doesn't help. You know that, Henry?'

'I know that,' Henry agreed. 'Come on, old son, put that smile on and don't forget your wig.'

Grumbling, Albert picked up the periwig and plonked it on his head, tugging it into some rough approximation of straight. He refilled his glass and then followed Henry out into the maelstrom.

Henry mingled, Melissa and then her older brother were sent off to bed, and the orchestra played in a second room that had been cleared for dancing. Albert seemed to have hit his stride, Henry noted – he stayed out for more than an hour playing the part of generous and welcoming host. Cynthia cast a grateful smile in Henry's direction.

Henry, of course, found himself questioned about the latest crimes, about 'any juicy murders' that he might have been involved with. Henry had realized that there were only certain murders this set was really interested in. The truly scandalous ones that happened rarely but explosively within their own society were of interest, of course, but Henry was not one of their own and would not, therefore, have been included in those particular conversations. Those violent crimes involving the middle classes were usually considered beneath them, bank clerks and doctors being of little interest – too bourgeois and too banal. Gang fights and the deaths of prostitutes had a strange appeal, Henry had learned; a woman who was no better than she should be, being slashed to death by her pimp, was sufficiently distant from their everyday experiences for it to be exciting without requiring any emotional response.

Henry, therefore, tried to avoid being questioned. Women usually thought that they could wheedle things out of him, but they were usually disappointed, and men would discuss the facts they had seen in the local newspapers with grave concern, clearly hoping for more gossip under the cover of manly exploration of the morals of others.

Mickey was far better at playing this game. He could chat for hours, giving the impression that he was taking the listener into his confidence but, in fact, disclosing nothing that wasn't speculated about in that morning's newspaper or already in the public domain.

Mickey and Belle arrived just after eleven, and a half-hour later Mickey had disappeared with Albert, and Belle was in deep conversation with two elderly ladies, one of whom Henry recognized as Lady Lydia Forsyth, and who had evidently mistaken Belle as being something of her social equal. Belle, Henry noticed, just looked amused.

A little later she sought him out, bringing a plate from the buffet table to the corner of the room where Henry was perched on the windowsill. She dug a fork into a piece of smoked salmon and asked, 'So how are you, my love?'

'I'm well, thank you, my dear. Mickey tells me that you will be in London for the foreseeable future, no more touring for the moment.'

'Being on the road all the time gets tiring. I've a good home to go to and a good man to be with. There are plenty of theatres in London, and I have enough of a reputation now to be confident of getting work. To be truthful, Henry, I've had enough of it. It suddenly struck me a few weeks ago that I'm not getting any younger, and that I have all of these slips of girls snapping at my heels, and I just thought to myself, Belle, what are you doing? Go home, stay home.'

'Well, Mickey will be happy.' Henry smiled at her. 'And how is the new show?'

'Mr Wilde knows how to write women, I'll give him that.' Belle grinned. 'Aren't you eating anything? You'd better get in quick – they're like vultures this lot.'

'I'm not terribly hungry,' Henry told her, 'but I'll tell you what, I can fetch us both a plate of something and you can eat what I don't want.'

'Oh, you know me so well, Henry Johnstone.'

She was right, Henry thought. These guests were like vultures. They had fallen on the buffet table, devouring the food as though they hadn't eaten for a week. More comestibles appeared as dishes emptied but, looking at them, Henry knew that none of these people had ever gone hungry, and he felt a sudden resentment. Henry and Cynthia both appreciated what it was to go without, and some small part of him – not a malicious or malevolent part but just a little whisper at the back of his consciousness – felt that it was about time some of these with privilege knew what it was like to have their sense of entitlement threatened.

He was on his way back to Belle, plates in hands, when a young woman swayed into him. She was dressed in an elaborate flamenco costume, her hair dressed high on her head and held in place with the tortoiseshell comb. A lace mantilla draped from the comb and hung elegantly down her back. She also wore a lace mask, obscuring the upper part of her face and framing very blue eyes.

'Excuse me,' she murmured. 'I hope I didn't knock you.' She appeared to do a double take then and look more closely at Henry. 'You must be the famous detective. Inspector Johnstone, isn't it?'

It was 'Chief Inspector', but Henry wasn't about to correct her. Eager to avoid another interrogation as to what spectacular crimes he might be investigating, he acknowledged that this was who he was, but that he was taking the plates to somewhere . . . And could he be excused?

The woman glanced across to where Belle was sitting and she smiled, deep red lips curving into what Henry thought of as a lascivious smile. 'But of course,' she said and drifted away.

Reaching Belle, Henry set the plates down on the deep windowsill and reached into his pockets for the cutlery that he had placed there. He found to his surprise that there was also an envelope.

'What's that?' Belle had registered his confusion. 'Well, open it – it's addressed to you.'

Examining the envelope, Henry realized that was the case. *Detective Chief Inspector Henry Johnstone* was inscribed in a very elegant, cursive hand.

'Good evening, Inspector,' said a familiar voice. The woman was smiling and was soon swept into Belle's embrace. 'Malina, my darling, don't you look wonderful.'

She did indeed, Henry thought. Malina was his sister's secretary and general assistant. Malina was, like Cynthia, also in pseudo-Egyptian dress: pleated silk nipped in at the waist with an elaborate sash and a heavily braided black wig covered her own dark hair.

'Malina. It's good to see you. You are looking very well.'

She stood on tiptoe and kissed his cheek and, a little self-consciously, Henry returned the greeting.

'Not in fancy dress, Henry, or are you disguised as a chief inspector?' Malina said.

Henry smiled. He was very fond of Malina. Originally she had come to Cynthia's house in need of protection during an investigation in which Henry had been involved, but she had stayed on as an employee and had become a friend. Henry knew her to be immensely loyal on both counts.

Belle's plate was empty, so she exchanged it for Henry's fully laden one. Henry opened the envelope. Inside was a single sheet of paper, on which was written a single name and a brief sentence. *Don't believe the obvious.*

Belle leaned in to look. 'Who on earth is that? "Robert Cranston Esq.". Do you know him, Henry?'

He shook his head. He turned the paper over, but there was nothing else. He folded the paper back into the envelope and stuffed it in his pocket, his eyes scanning the room for the flamenco dancer, but she was nowhere in sight. 'Belle . . . Malina . . .'

'Run along with you,' Belle said, smiling. 'Malina and I can catch up – we've not seen each other for, oh, at least a week. Go and find whoever it was that slipped that into your pocket. You obviously have some idea of who that might be. Be warned, Henry – if you don't come back soon, I'll eat your supper as well.'

Henry headed back to the buffet table, trying to remember in what direction the young woman had lurched away. He'd assumed she was inebriated, but now he wasn't so sure. With hindsight, the moment seemed staged. He searched the buffet room and then looked into the next room, where the musicians were now playing something ragtime and bodies gyrated and swivelled and collided, but he could see no one dressed in flamenco costume.

He went out into the hall where two young women in Cynthia's employ were waiting to fetch coats, take cloaks and point people in the right direction. Neither of them had seen a flamenco woman, but one of the kitchen girls, coming through with another plate of food, overheard and told Henry that she'd just seen a woman of that description heading towards the kitchen. She assumed the woman was lost and directed her back upstairs. She'd been too busy to notice where the woman had gone after that.

Henry ducked beneath the staircase and down the back stairs towards the kitchen. He knew the layout of Cynthia's house well, and he also knew that there was a small passageway just beyond the kitchen that led into a little yard. From there, via a delivery gate, it was possible to get out into the neighbouring street. He arrived to find the gate was open, but of anyone resembling flamenco dancer, there was no sign.

Henry walked up and down the street for a while, asking passers-by if they had seen a young woman in fancy dress, but she might have vanished into thin air for all the good it did him. He wandered back, returning to Belle, knowing she would be curious as to what had been going on. She had not yet started on his plate of food, and she handed it to him and told him that he must tuck in.

'Have you been taking instruction from Mickey?' he asked. His sergeant was always urging him to eat; Henry did have a tendency to forget, and it was only when he was ravenously hungry that his body reminded him.

'Did you find her?'

'No, it looks as though she left through the back door. It makes me wonder if she actually had an invitation in the first place.'

'Was anyone actually checking?' Belle asked. 'I imagine if you turn up in fancy dress and look confident then nobody is going to challenge you.'

'True,' Henry conceded. 'Let's find Mickey. He's holed-up in the study with Albert, I imagine.'

'I'll take your plate – you can fetch us both some champagne. I'm fully aware that you won't drink yours, but that's all the more for me.'

TWO

The days following the party were busy and Henry had been unable to put the note he had received at Cynthia's party out of his mind. He had sent it to the fingerprint department and they had, of course, discovered Henry's prints upon it, and a few other smudges but nothing very useful. Both paper and envelope were ordinary – Basildon Bond, the watermark declared – and they could have been purchased at any decent stationers. Henry was intrigued by the handwriting itself. It was neat and fluent and quite distinctive. But that was the *only* distinctive thing. He was convinced that this note related to Richardson in some way, but he wasn't sure how.

He had attempted to find out who this 'Robert Cranston' might be. Cynthia didn't recognize the name, and neither did Albert, and those they remembered who attended the party dressed as Spanish dancers were easily discounted. It seemed it was a popular costume.

Cynthia had set to and begun her own investigation. She had spoken to her own staff, and then, under the pretence of trying to locate a guest about some lost property, contacted the agency who had provided the extra serving staff for that evening. Her query was soon responded to. One young woman remembered the flamenco dancer in question. A young woman in a red dress and wearing a lace mask had come with a crowd of guests, about a half-dozen of them, all arriving at the same time. Cynthia asked if she could speak to the young woman and the agency sent her posthaste to Cynthia's house.

'You don't have to be nervous,' Cynthia told her. 'You're not in any trouble at all. In fact, I'm very, very happy that you remember this particular guest. This group of people that arrived . . . can you remember how any of them were dressed?'

The young woman wrung her hands anxiously, as though this was some kind of test. 'There was a penguin, and he was escorting a lady in a tall white wig and a big dress. And then there was somebody dressed like a lion, and he was with somebody who I think was meant to be Julius Caesar. Everyone kept saying "Hail Caesar" at him. I'm not sure about the rest, but the lady in the flamenco costume was with them. She had a lace mask and a lace scarf on her head, one of those big tortoiseshell combs and a very frilly dress. A red dress.'

Cynthia rewarded her with the delighted smile and a few coins for her trouble. The young woman left much happier than she'd arrived, and Cynthia, absently, realized that she had probably tipped the girl a full day's wages.

She recognized the costumes and knew who had been in that

group. Within minutes she was on the telephone asking her friends if they remembered this flamenco dancer arriving with them and if they happened to know who she was.

She wasn't entirely surprised when they drew a blank on this. They remembered her, and that she had come into the hall looking round as though for a friend, and then disappeared into the melee that was the buffet room.

Meanwhile, Albert had been attempting to track down 'Robert Cranston', questioning his business friends and within a couple of days coming up with an address. Albert and Cynthia had invited Henry for supper and relayed all this intelligence to him. Henry had the impression that this had been a welcome distraction for both of them, and that they would be only too glad if he could find some other task for them to undertake.

The following day Henry and Mickey called upon Robert Cranston at his lodgings not far from the Inns of Court. It seemed that Mr Cranston had originally set his thoughts on becoming a lawyer, but then business and trading had beckoned and he had become a stockbroker instead. His lodgings were comfortable, if a little cramped and old fashioned, the walls panelled in dark wood. However, he was clearly not comfortable with the arrival of two policemen at his door.

He was incredulous when Henry told him about the note and that this was what had prompted their visit.

'A prank,' he said, his mouth twisted contemptuously. 'I would have thought the police had better things to do than to act on what is obviously a practical joke.'

'It's a very specific joke,' Henry told him. 'And a very strange one. The tone of the message is perhaps somewhat threatening. But if you are certain there is nothing untoward, no one who might wish to harm you?'

Robert Cranston frowned. 'Why would anyone wish me harm?' he asked sharply. 'Now, gentlemen, I am rather busy . . .'

'Then we will leave you to your day,' Henry told him.

'Mr Cranston, may I ask, how have you fared with all this chaos that is going on, on the other side of the Atlantic?' Mickey asked cheerily. 'It's a right to-do, isn't it? What with the crash on Wall Street, and the fall of our own financial markets back in September.' He laughed heartily. 'It's a wonder any of you lot are still in business.'

Robert Cranston's expression darkened. 'Some of us have managed very well, thank you. Now, gentlemen, if there is nothing more?' He crossed to a side table and poured himself a drink from a cut-glass decanter.

'Nothing more for now,' Henry told him, 'but if there is anything that you remember, which might be causing you concern, please don't hesitate to contact either one of us.'

'You will be not hearing from me again,' Cranston said airily. 'There is nothing in my life to concern the police.'

Henry and Mickey left then but, glancing back at the lodging house, Henry said, 'I hope he's correct, but this concerns me, Mickey. And it's obvious that something concerns that young man. He was altogether too flip with us.'

'And there were creditors' letters on his desk,' Mickey said. 'I took a quick peek while he was pouring himself a drink. A little early in the day for strong spirits too, don't you think? I suspect this young man has not fared nearly as well as he would like the world to believe.'

It was 9 November, a little more than a week after the party, when Henry's deepest fears were confirmed. He was called to a sudden death. The man in question had been found by his housekeeper. He had been discovered slumped over his desk, a hole through his head, and the weapon that had inflicted it on the floor beside his chair. The police surgeon had already attended, judging it to be a simple case of suicide and firmly expecting the police officers involved to agree with him. After all, the weapon was there, the man was known to have been in financial difficulties and there was no sign of suspicious entry or exit or of anything missing.

Henry, however, declared himself unsure of this particular interpretation. His reason being, purely and simply, that the dead man's name was Robert Cranston. *Don't believe the obvious*, the mysterious note had said. And looking at what appeared to be a simple case of suicide, Henry was very disinclined to do so. The fact that this might turn out to be something else reminded him of the deaths of Detective Sergeant Cole and Detective Chief Inspector Hayden Paul. On the face of it, there was no reason to believe this latest incident had any connection whatsoever, but the letter, with its apparent warning, had unsettled Henry. As had news that Richardson was now out of prison and his whereabouts unknown – though he tried hard not to let this interfere with his life, day to day he found himself wary and on his guard. The fact that six months had passed since Richardson's release did nothing to reassure him. Richardson had always been a patient man and thorough when making his plans. It was in character that he'd wait, take his time and ensure all preparations were exact before taking his revenge.

'We treat this as a potential suspicious death,' Henry told the shocked and somewhat irritated police surgeon. And then he had sent for Mickey Hitchens and notified St Mary's Hospital that they should expect Mr Cranston later than morning and that he was to be prioritized on their post-mortem list.

On his way home that evening Henry sent a carefully worded telegram to the contact Otis had given him – but, as instructed, he made no mention of any of his thoughts and anxieties to anyone else, not even Mickey Hitchens.

THREE

'And he was right to be suspicious,' Mickey told Belle as he walked her to the theatre a couple of evenings after the body had been found. 'The hyoid bone had been fractured and there were clear indicators of haemorrhage in the eyeballs.'

'So he was strangled.' Belle had been around police officers long enough to understand what Mickey was referring to.

'Manual strangulation, from the look of it. That's usually the case if the hyoid is snapped.'

'The police surgeon will be kicking himself for not seeing that,' Belle said. 'Surely there would have been bruising on the neck?'

'Well, yes, but you see, the victim was wearing a quite ridiculous paisley cravat and that initially hid the signs and may be enough to spare our doctor too many blushes. Though, to be frank, I'm guessing he took one look at the bloody great hole in the man's head, another look at the gun lying as though the dead man might have dropped it post-mortem and drew the most obvious conclusion. And that might have been that. Suicide, straight to the mortuary, family notified and everything kept as quiet as possible to spare their public embarrassment.'

'I do feel for the family,' Belle said. 'There have been too many unfortunates doing away with themselves of late. You'd almost think it was an epidemic, that they'd caught the urge from one another.'

'You would indeed,' Mickey agreed.

'So what caused Henry to be called if it didn't look like anything but suicide?'

'Suicide still has to be ruled by the coroner. The scene must still be examined. If nothing else, the doctor would want to cover himself, just in case the family try to claim that the death couldn't possibly be suicide. For some it's so much worse if a loved one has taken their own life – it's worse even than murder. Most will try to claim it must have been accidental. I've seen enough letters pleading with the coroner to find any way but suicide.'

Belle squeezed his arm. 'It must leave them feeling so helpless,' she said. 'So what happens now?'

'Well, Henry is examining the background of our Mr Cranston and, as soon as I've dropped you off, I'll be joining him. We finally got the paperwork from his solicitor this afternoon, and the results of the post-mortem mean that this is now formally being treated as a murder enquiry. Then I thought I might meet you after and we could go and have ourselves a spot of supper somewhere.'

When he arrived back at Central Office at New Scotland Yard, Mickey found his boss alone, surrounded by files and folders and solicitors' notes, bound in red tape. Deducing that Henry hadn't had a chance to look at these yet by the fact that the binding was undisturbed, Mickey picked up a stack and took them over to his own desk. An hour later, he made tea and set both enamelled mugs down on Henry's desk, together with the notes he had made.

'So, what do we have?' Henry asked.

'Our man was not so much down on his uppers as worn through to the soles of his feet,' Mickey said. 'He'd been effectively wiped out in the London Stock Exchange's crash back in September – for which we have, among other factors, our old friend Clarence Hatry and his associates to thank. But there's one thing in his financial transactions that is very puzzling.'

'Oh?'

'As near as I can make out, just before his financial disgrace was made public, he opened a new bank account and deposited just under five hundred pounds in cash. Then there are three payments, also in cash, into that account in as many weeks and to the total of eight thousand pounds.' He passed the relevant paperwork over the desk and Henry examined it.

'And this was in the paperwork that came over from the solicitor dealing with the bankruptcy proceedings,' Henry confirmed. Enright and Baines had been all too happy to help. They had been retained by the courts to deal with what was left of Cranston's business affairs and assign dues to his creditors. Now that their client was deceased, they were, too, numbered among those creditors; they had seemed relieved to hand off this now unprofitable matter to the police.

'There's a note to the effect that the clerk dealing with the case asked Mr Cranston where this money had come from. He was told it had been a loan from a benefactor, but Cranston seems to have been unwilling to name said benefactor and declared it to have been a gentleman's agreement and therefore no paperwork existed relating to said loan.'

'It's a great deal of money for one person to lend to another, especially without any kind of written agreement or security.'

'I doubt he had anything left to offer as security,' Mickey said quietly. 'But it's an odd state of affairs, if you ask me.'

Henry nodded. 'And withdrawals?'

'Ah, now there's the other thing,' Mickey said. He found the relevant pages and turned the statements so Henry could see. 'Look, there are a series of small withdrawals, a few pounds here and there, the sort of amounts a man might draw to give himself some walking about money. But then there's this here, drawn as a cheque made out to funeral directors, Messrs Alfred and Dunn.'

'Funeral directors . . .' Henry scrabbled among the paperwork on his side of the desk. 'A sudden bereavement,' he said. 'Cranston's father died. The death notice and the programme for the funeral service were in his desk drawers.'

'So, how did the father die?'

Henry shrugged and then looked at his watch.

'That should wait until morning,' Mickey said. 'It's too late to contact either the family or the funeral director tonight.'

Henry frowned but accepted his word. He flipped back through the statements. 'Oh, but then—'

'Then he withdraws the whole damned lot,' Mickey agrees. 'On the morning of his death. Except—'

'Except he cannot possibly have done. The housekeeper

discovered the body a little before nine. No bank would have been open at that time of the morning. Someone killed him earlier that morning, or even late the night before, presumably after the housekeeper had retired for the night. And then they withdrew the money. In what form, do we know?'

Mickey shook his head. 'We only know as much as we do because Cranston was compelled to have copies of all his transactions sent to his solicitor. And the solicitor then sent everything they had to us.'

'So, tomorrow, we contact the family, the funeral director and the bank,' Henry said, reluctantly conceding that they had done all they could for the night.

Henry opened the door to his small flat, picked up his post and dropped a half-dozen matchbooks into a glass dish sitting on the sideboard. He went through to his living room and turned on the electric fire, still in his coat, waiting for the room to warm up. It was 11 November and many of his colleagues had attended remembrance services that morning, or had made their own personal act of remembrance, but this was something that Henry never did. There were too many remembrance days in his year for this to be in any way a special one. Too many haunted moments. He went through to the kitchen and turned on both gas rings, hoping that they would speed the heating of his small apartment, and then, still in his coat, he sat down on his favourite chair and stared out of the window watching the boats on the river.

After a little time, he took his journal from his pocket and began to write.

On my way back tonight, I passed a matchbook seller. I always use my lighter, but no doubt the matches will come in useful for lighting the gas ring. I bought six books from him, although I was a little afraid he might see such action as patronizing. He was not an old man – I doubt he had seen more years than I have, but he must have had less good fortune. He stood in the doorway, leaning against one wall so that he could dispense with one of his two crutches in order to serve customers. He had but one leg – his trousers were folded and pinned neatly where the second ended, just above the knee. And so I bought the matches and we exchanged a few words, and then I left him, counting my own blessings and wishing blessings on him.

Henry paused and looked once more out of the window.

11 November in the year of 1929. So much time has passed and yet it seems like yesterday. There are too many who have already suffered too much who have not managed to lift themselves out of poverty in this past decade. I'm afraid that with the situation first with our own economic importunities and now with those rippling across the ocean from America, that those who are already poor will suffer even greater ills and now be joined by far too many more. There are only so many books of matches that any man can buy.

He set down his pen and his journal. The room was a little warmer now, and he decided that he would make himself some tea before bed. He thought about his sister, about her family, about the way that Cynthia had protected them and would continue to do so. About the way that Cynthia had protected him when they had both been little more than children. This set him to thinking about Albert's friend, Ferdy, and the nature of his death, so like that of Robert Cranston with the single gunshot wound. Cranston's staged suicide barely stood up to even the most cursory examination, like those of Walter Cole and Hayden Paul. Was it possible that Ferdy had not in fact killed himself? Was it too much of a stretch of the imagination that these deaths could be linked?

Detective Sergeant Cole and Detective Chief Inspector Paul – well, there was no doubt in Henry's mind that Richardson was behind those. The notes left at both scenes were absolute confirmation in Henry's mind. But Robert Cranston and Ferdy?

Henry acknowledged that he was probably overreacting to the most tenuous of connections in the case of Geoffrey Cranston and no connection at all in Ferdy's. Mickey was right – the suicide rate had risen and because many of those suicides had been violent, they had required police attendance to verify that they were indeed death by the victim's own hand and not by another. But Henry was troubled. He decided that he should look again at the death of Ferdy Bright-Cooper, the small doubt now taking seed in his mind. Could there be something more suspicious about this death too?

Henry took up his pen once more. He was thinking now of Walter Cole and Hayden Paul. Men he had disliked intensely and whose honesty as police officers he had quickly learned to question.

1919 was not a vintage year for the Metropolitan Police, Henry wrote. *As the war ended, recruitment offices were sent to the front, to enquire among the rank and file and the officers if any would wish for employment in the police service and many signed up. I suppose they were dreading coming back, fearing the lack of jobs and security. Afraid that they would walk out of the trenches and into the unemployment queue. I've heard tell as many as forty per cent of these new recruits were turfed out of service within the first eighteen months. Drunkenness was rife, corruption too, and the selection process does not seem to have been particular or thorough.*

More troubling, though, were the police officers who returned to service having left their moral code back in the mud and filth of war. I understand men who came back disillusioned and angry – indeed, I could be numbered among them, but I came back to my work with relief, it has to be said. Easier to catch one murderer at a time than to survive day to day with the knowledge that this was what we had all become. For what else is war but mass murder? Although this is not an opinion I would readily share with anyone.

Detective Sergeant Walter Cole and Detective Chief Inspector Hayden Paul were two of those whom the war had changed. Perhaps it had not changed them, merely heightened and exposed those characteristics that were most venal but already a part of their make-up. I do not believe that men change so completely from their core substance. These two were corrupt before the conflict – the war simply accreted further levels of corruption.

I was a newly made inspector, less sure of myself than I could have been. The investigation was a complex one, and at first it was easy for them to tell me that my inexperience was preventing me from fully comprehending. Detective Sergeant Cole was beneath me in rank, but I had to acknowledge that he was by far my superior in terms of experience and that he had not risen in rank because, he believed, his background and education slowed his progress. I came to realize that he resented that, and I understood his reasons, even sympathized, until it became obvious that this was not the root cause. Cole had hung on in service, despite the accusations of members of the public and the disquiet of his superiors, because he was in many ways seen as a good detective. He got results and in those difficult times just after that terrible war results mattered more than method.

But, slowly, I came to realize that the two of them sought only profit and did not care who might be destroyed in the process.

I do not doubt that Richardson deserved to be imprisoned; in fact, I believe the man deserved to hang. Neither do I doubt that the offences for which he was eventually confined were not his own. The man was guilty, but so were they, and so, I fear, was I.

So how much did Otis know? Henry wondered. Otis Freeland was a man who could read the guilt in another's eyes, much as Henry himself had learned to do. He was also a man that Henry respected, and he found himself hoping that he had not lost Otis's esteem because of this matter.

Henry had come back from the Great War a broken man. For the first year or so back in the police service he had coasted, relying on instinct and good luck as much as any investigative skill, and it was only because the police force at this point in time was in such a dreadful mess that he had survived. They needed bodies on the ground, investigators who had proved their worth before the war, and so his promotion had been swift. But it was Mickey, arriving unexpectedly and seeing immediately what a funk Henry was actually in, that had enabled his survival and recovery.

He knew that Walter Cole and Hayden Paul had exploited his weakness, but that did not make it easier to bear.

My behaviour was beneath my standards, Henry wrote. *And now it seems it is time to pay for that behaviour. Though what form that payment will take, I cannot guess. Will it be a knife man come out of the dark or will it be something more subtle? Will I be found one morning with my throat cut, or having taken Veronal with my whisky? In my heart of hearts, can I really blame the man for his anger? His last words when they took him from the dock reminded those of us watching that old sins cannot be buried, that they do indeed cast long shadows.*

Though he did deserve to be jailed, Henry thought. When all was said and done, Richardson deserved even more than he had got in terms of punishment. He had extorted and murdered and led others to take their own lives. But did that mean that, when those investigating were unable to discover definitive proof for these crimes, he should have been imprisoned on the basis of manufactured evidence and the greed of others? At the time, Henry had told himself that the ends justified the means. Did he still believe that?

FOUR

The first step the following morning, 12 November, was to visit the bank with which Mr Robert Cranston had opened his new account and speak directly to those who had dealt with him.

The bank manager, Mr Hambledon, remembered the day almost two months previously that Mr Cranston had come in to open his account. He had good references, he assured Henry and Mickey. He opened the account with five hundred pounds and appeared to be 'a most affable gentleman'.

'As he did not seem concerned about anything, you would not have described him as a worried man?' Mickey asked. 'And I'm assuming that you looked into his finances before allowing him to open the account, especially in light of recent events?'

Mr Hambledon looked offended. 'As I said, he had the most excellent references. He was referred by a long-term client of ours, and if a man comes personally referred, then why would we look further?'

'And the name of this client?'

Mr Hambledon frowned, clearly put out. He consulted his notes again. 'It seems that it was Mr Cranston senior who referred his son.' He smiled, clearly relieved that the answer was a simple one. 'All perfectly regular, Chief Inspector.'

Henry's grimace told Mickey that he had better distract his boss before he said something unfortunate, so he asked if Mr Hambledon had dealt with the man directly, and if he would have recognized him if he saw him again.

The bank manager looked a little vague then. 'I dealt with him on the day he came to open his account, of course. My chief clerk introduced him and showed me the references he brought with him. Then I shook him by the hand and told him yes, of course, we would open an account for him. I checked that he had the deposit, five hundred pounds being more than adequate as I'm sure you'll realize. A man who has money worries does not open a bank account with a deposit of five hundred pounds.'

'And did no one think it strange,' Henry asked coldly, 'when he came in and asked to close his account and withdraw the amount in full? It is surely a large amount of money to have withdrawn. Eight thousand pounds is far more than the initial deposit of five hundred pounds. Would notice not usually have to be given?'

'Of course, as with all large withdrawals. Should he have wished to withdraw this in cash, it would have been more complicated, but he did not.'

'And so how did he withdraw the money?' Mickey asked quickly.

'Why, in bearer bonds. As you say, he gave us notice in advance, of course, because they do take a little time to prepare, especially as he wished them to be in a series of denomination. He gave us three days' notice, which is adequate, and then he arrived just as the bank was opening. My chief clerk dealt with him. Everything was in order.'

'And in order to withdraw that amount, did he need to show identification?'

The bank manager laughed. 'But of course, he had the letters of recommendation that we had seen when he opened the account, and he also had his passport and a letter from his solicitor, explaining that the money was required quickly for investment purposes. But in any case, my chief clerk knew him – he had been in on several occasions, you understand, once on the sad occasion of his father's death, when he drew a cheque for the amount of the funeral expenses.'

Mickey took from his pocket a picture of Robert Cranston. It was a mortuary photograph, but his injuries had been carefully concealed by a folded cloth. 'And is this Mr Robert Cranston?'

The bank manager looked confused. 'I suppose so, but it's hard to tell. A man dead does not look as he would in life. You should speak to my chief clerk; I will send for him.'

A few minutes later the chief clerk had expressed his opinion that yes, this was probably Mr Robert Cranston. That it certainly looked like Mr Robert Cranston. Then, when asked if he would be prepared to swear on oath that this was Mr Robert Cranston, he was a little more hesitant. 'He looks a little different. But I suppose that's on account of him no longer being with us.'

'So,' Mickey said as they walked away. 'Was it Mr Robert Cranston who opened the account or was it whoever withdrew his money after he was dead? This is a muddle, Henry, and no mistake.'

'Was the man who opened the account really Mr Robert Cranston, or someone pretending to be him? The only thing we do know for certain is that Robert Cranston did not empty his own account – that was done after he was dead. But what is most intriguing is that the notification of withdrawal was given three days before. Was he the one that gave it?'

The notification had been given in writing; a letter sent to the manager of the bank on notepaper headed by the name and address of the solicitor who had been dealing with Cranston's legal and financial affairs. Henry now had this letter in his possession. He took it from his pocket as they crossed the road and then read a section out loud. '"The withdrawal to be bearer bonds to ease the progress of various investments that Mr Cranston intends to make". Strange wording, is it not, Mickey?'

'Doesn't sound like any solicitor I've ever had dealings with,' Mickey decided. 'Not a "heretofore" or "therefor" to be seen anywhere. So do we go to the solicitors first, or do we keep to our original plan and interview the family?'

'We have made an appointment with the bereaved family,' Henry said. 'It does not seem fair to put them off. The solicitor can wait. We can get the driver to take us there when we return this afternoon.'

They had arranged for a police driver to take them a few miles outside the city to the seat of the Cranston family. Henry had done a little research and found that Robert's mother's side came from minor nobility. His father was from yeoman stock, farmers and small land-owners for as far back as anyone could count. Agriculture was still at the foundation of their fortune, such as it was. Robert's mother had brought a little money with her and more had been settled on her after the death of her own parents, but the family was not rich.

Comfortable, Henry thought as their car drove up the short driveway towards a square, brick-built house with an orchard on one side and a stable block on the other. A quick glance told them that the house needed attention – nothing major, the roof was still sound, and the chimneys looked as though they had been recently repointed. But it had that slightly rundown, tired appearance of a house that has been in the same family for so long that they no longer noticed defects.

The driver was told that if he went round the back to the kitchen, he would be accommodated, and Mickey and Henry were taken through into a small parlour. A fire burned in the house, crackling happily, and Henry caught the scent of applewood. The room was small and set out with three easy chairs, a small desk by the window and bookshelves that were filled with old volumes and pretty, rather feminine ornaments. This was a ladies' room, not a gentleman's study, and he guessed it been chosen for their interview because it was easily heated.

Two women entered – an older lady dressed fully in black and an equally ageing lady in a dress of navy blue with a small brooch at the neck. They looked enough alike to be sisters, and this turned out to be the case. Nora Cranston had been Robert's mother, and she had lost her husband and her son within a matter of weeks. She looked exhausted and pale, and her hands trembled as they pulled at the lace handkerchief she held. Bridget, the sister, laid a gentle hand on her sister's and stilled their movements, then stood beside her chair, one hand resting gently on her sister's shoulders. 'Would you like tea?' she asked. 'I've asked Cook to send in tea and biscuits and cake. I think we have cake.'

The door opened again and a young woman dressed in a servant's uniform came in carrying a tray. From the resentful look she cast Henry and Mickey and the concerned look she cast the ladies, Mickey gathered that this was not a household where upstairs and downstairs were harshly delineated.

'We are very sorry to have to call on you at a time like this,' Mickey said. 'Grief following grief weighs a person down, I know that all too well.'

Bridget thanked him with a faint smile, but Nora seemed so sunken in sorrow that Mickey wondered if they were going to get any sense out of her whatsoever.

'I'm sorry to have to ask you these questions,' Mickey began again, addressing Nora, 'but how did your husband die?'

The two women exchanged a puzzled glance. 'I thought you were here to speak to us about poor Robert,' Bridget said. 'What does this have to do with Geoffrey?'

'We are here to ask about Robert, but we do have other questions and other concerns,' Henry told her. 'You are aware of the results the post-mortem. That your son did not take his own life?'

Nora moaned softly and lifted the handkerchief to her eyes once more. 'Why would anyone want to kill my boy? Why would anyone want him harmed?'

'That's what we are trying to find out, Mrs Cranston,' Mickey said quietly. 'We know that your son paid for his father's funeral service, drawing a cheque that covered the expenses.'

Again, the two women looked at each, but this time it was not puzzlement so much as anxiety.

'Was there something that troubled you about that?' Mickey asked.

'We did not expect him to do it,' Bridget said hesitantly. She flushed slightly, looked embarrassed and said, 'We knew of his difficulties, you see. That he had lost so much money. Robert had always done so well, invested so wisely, managed his business so efficiently and yet . . . and yet . . . So we were surprised, you see, when he said that he would cover his father's expenses, that he would pay for the funeral.'

'It must have been a relief to you, though?' Mickey pursued. 'It must have given you thought that he was not so badly off after all. That perhaps his losses had not been so great.'

'We *were* comforted by that,' Bridget agreed. 'Not that any of that matters now. But you asked about the death of my dear brother-in-law. What concern is that of yours?'

'How did he die?' Henry asked brusquely.

She glared at Henry, not liking his tone. 'It was a tragic thing . . . he's always had trouble with his stomach, you see. The doctor said he'd had an ulcer for many years, which he'd been treating him for. All the worry of the farm, of everything else. And the loss of Robert's older brother – the war took him, you see. Took my husband too. He had gone as a medic, you see – he was a doctor and he felt he should do his bit.' She sighed, then seemed to shake herself. 'Geoffrey seemed fine when he went to his study after dinner. He liked to smoke a cigar and the doctor said it would do him no harm to smoke a cigar, but he must forego the brandy. We know that occasionally he did *not* forego the brandy but, what can you say to a grown man? Usually he would sit for an hour, then he would come back and join us and we would often play cards for a while. We live very quietly, very peaceably here. When he did not come back, Nora went to see if all was well. Sometimes he would fall asleep, and on one occasion he had fallen asleep and dropped the cigar on to his leg, only waking when the cigar burned through his trousers. When I heard Nora cry out after she went to check on him, I went to look but I could see immediately that it was too late.

Poor Geoffrey was no longer with us. We still sent for the doctor, of course. The doctor believed this his ulcer had burst and that the poor soul had bled to death.'

'Was there a post-mortem?' Henry asked.

'He was under a doctor's care,' Bridget said. 'And had been so for a long time. He was not a well man, Inspector. There were times when he vomited blood, and the truth is we counted each day that he remained with us a blessing. His death was no surprise, but it was still a shock. Poor soul, his lips were so blue. What really disturbs us is knowing that he died in pain and that there was nothing we could have done to alleviate it. Had we gone and checked on him sooner, perhaps . . .'

'In pain?' Mickey asked gently. 'Surely he would have cried out?'

'His study is on the other side of the house – we would not have heard him,' Nora said. 'But one look at his face and you could see how much agony he had been in before he died. That makes it so much harder, you understand?'

Mickey said that indeed he did. 'Could we see his study?' he asked.

Again that exchange of glances. These two women were obviously used to doing everything in tandem. 'Well, I suppose it would do no harm,' Bridget said uncertainly, 'but I'm not sure what you hope to learn.'

'Was Robert close to his father?' Mickey asked. 'Would Robert have confided in him, do you think?'

'They got along very well. Geoffrey was very proud of Robert, and Robert was sure to always write at least once every week. A letter to me,' Nora said, 'and with an enclosure to his father.'

'A private enclosure?' Henry wanted to know. 'Or just something for you to read out to him?'

'Sometimes one, sometimes the other. Geoffrey knew I had no real interest in Robert's business matters, and Robert knew that too, though I knew approximately what he did, and of course we are all very proud of him. It takes skill to invest, to work the markets.'

Nora broke off then, clearly aware that Robert's skill had failed him.

Henry stood. 'So if we may see the study? I promise we will not make a mess.'

Bridget led them through the house, from front to rear and into a room that was diametrically at the opposite end of the building to their little sitting room. She reached above the door, taking a key from the ledge, and then opened the door and stood aside. 'Please lock-up after yourselves, and if you wouldn't mind excusing us both and seeing yourselves out.'

'Of course,' Mickey told her.

'Is a key always left there?' Henry questioned sharply.

'Geoffrey was always losing track of it, so it seemed easier just to leave it above the door. He liked to keep his door locked – in my experience, men often do. They like to feel that they have a private space, but the truth was none of us were really interested in going into his study. Why would we be? But he said that if you left the key in the door, then it tempted people. We had a butler, years ago, that liked to help himself to the port. Not that we've had a butler in many years, but I think that was why perhaps . . .' She trailed off.

Mickey thanked her, but she was already walking away, going back to where she had left her sister.

'It's as well he was not cremated,' Henry said. 'We will need an exhumation order. In fact, we will be needing two.' He had already confided his anxiety about Ferdy to Mickey.

Mrs Cranston and her sister would not like that, Mickey thought.

The study had evidently been locked and left after Geoffrey Cranston's death. It was cold and beginning to feel damp, no fire having been lit for quite some time. Henry shivered.

'How long are we going to be here?' Mickey asked. 'There's coal and kindling. I could start a fire if you think it will be a while.'

Henry nodded assent, his eyes already scanning the room. The chair in which Geoffrey died sat behind the desk, and the desk was close to the window so that natural light could fall upon it. There didn't seem to be electricity in this part of the house; there was no light switch and a variety of oil lamps had been dotted around the room. It was not a bright space even in the middle of the day like this, and Henry lit the lamp on the desk.

'Account books,' he said, looking into the first drawer and withdrawing a set of ledgers. He examined them while Mickey set about making a fire. It seemed that the farm was doing well enough, there were rents from outlying properties; as he had initially judged, the family were not rich, but they were probably comfortable enough. Henry searched the other drawers and finally found what he had been looking for: the letters from Robert to his father.

Mickey had the fire going now, though Henry sensed that it would take a long time for it to make any difference at all to this chill, damp space. It would do the books no good, he thought. The shelves held books on farming and geology and history; all factual titles, and many of them a century or more out of date. Geoffrey, he guessed, was not much of a reader, but he probably liked the look of his library.

While Henry read Robert's letters, Mickey began a systematic search, slow and careful, unsure of what he was looking for as yet. Drawers were opened and books removed from shelves and shaken gently for anything that might be concealed within. He spent about an hour in this activity but found nothing much apart from dust and spiders. Returning to the table, he flicked through the ledgers that Henry had first taken from the drawer and then turned his attention to the letters that Henry was reading.

'Anything of interest?' he asked.

'There was evidently a fondness between father and son. Some of these are mere notes, like that one.' Henry pointed to a letter that described a trip to the theatre and a conversation with a mutual acquaintance. 'Others have more to do with his business dealings and, as you'll see from the more recent ones, with his worries about his finances. He seems very concerned to make sure that nothing he has done will impact upon his family and their home. He tells his father on several occasions that his debts are his own and not theirs to worry about.'

'Let's hope he was right about that,' Mickey said.

'But it's this letter that is of real interest. It seems to have been received by Geoffrey three or four days before he died. His son is urging him to go away for a while, to go up to Scotland to visit relatives there. It seems there has been a conversation between the pair of them before, suggesting his father do this, but this letter has a real urgency to it.'

Mickey took the sheet of flimsy and read it through.

I promise you it will be only for a time. I have this under control, but I would prefer for you and Mother to be out of the way. Aunt Bridget too. It seems I have been dealing with lice, rather than responsible men, and I am now very much afraid, I will admit to this. Father, please do as I ask. It will only be for a short time, but I would feel happier in my own mind if you were not there. Imagine, anyway, how mortified Mother might be if men knock on the door

speaking about my debts. They have no right to come and visit you,
but that does not mean they might not.

'Do you think that he is simply worried about potential
embarrassment or is in fact worried about mortification in the true
sense?' Mickey asked. 'The timing is suggestive certainly, and he
admits to being afraid. Was that simply fear for his reputation? Or
do you suspect the father was poisoned?'

'The wife mentioned blue lips. Cyanosis is often a mark of poison,
as you well know.'

'Administered in the cigars? Or in the brandy that he is not
supposed to have?'

'We will need both for analysis. Mickey – will you make your
way to the kitchen and see if the cook can be persuaded to part
with a small bottle so that we can take a sample of the brandy? The
rest should be tipped away, just in case anyone is tempted. They
may no longer have a butler, but they have staff who know where
the key is kept, and now *we* have been inside the study, it might be
said to have set a precedent.'

Mickey nodded and went off to find a sample bottle.

Henry sat for a few moments staring at the letters. He shivered
and went to stand by the fire. The truth was it was quite a meagre
fire, burning in a small grate, and he doubted this room was ever
really warm. Or maybe it was Henry who was never really warm.

When Mickey had returned and the brandy had been decanted,
Henry gathered the letters together and, on a sudden impulse, the
ledgers, and they prepared to leave.

The maid who had welcomed them was waiting in the hall with
their coats. She eyed the ledgers anxiously and reluctantly took a
piece of paper that Mickey had prepared, a receipt for items taken
away by the police. 'Give this to your mistress,' he said. 'The papers
will be returned in due course.'

The look she gave him would have frozen anyone less inured to
such looks. Being a policeman, Mickey thought, you had to learn
to ignore the anguish and anger of others to a certain extent.

'Why the ledgers?' Mickey asked as they settled into the car and
Henry pulled his coat tightly around his chest and legs.

'I don't know. On the face of it they are correctly kept and carefully made out, but there was something about them that rang bells
in my head. What the bells mean I'm not yet sure, but I think they're
worth another look.'

FIVE

Messrs Enright and Baines had apparently been established in 1763 and occupied a tiny set of offices just off the Inns of Court. They were accessed via a narrow alleyway, a rather ornate door and a dark flight of stairs, the paintwork of which could well have been the 1763 original. Their offices, however, were surprisingly large and surprisingly airy and Mr Enright, who greeted them, quite surprisingly rotund.

He seemed to be taking all of this very personally, Mickey thought, that a client appears to have been murdered, and that the police were now involved.

'It was all very unfortunate, of course,' Enright said. 'He'd been a very successful man, a very astute businessman, but even the most astute can be caught up in nefarious actions. Unfortunately, he made the wrong investments, and he wasn't the only one, as I'm sure I don't have to tell you.' He waved a hand towards a stack of papers on the side table, all bound in red tape. 'Soon to be bankrupts,' he said. 'Twenty or so in the last month alone that we've been dealing with. All gentlemen who have run their businesses well and efficiently but are now facing complete and total disaster. Their families too, more's the pity.'

'And what about Cranston's family? Will they be impacted by this? I know the father has died recently, but what about the mother and her sister?' Henry wanted to know.

'Fortunately, no. I've had to fend off several of his creditors, who believe that the family business was actually a family business that included him, but no. Robert Cranston's dealings were his own. The family estate is safe, but it would not surprise me if the ladies wished to liquidize the assets and move somewhere more comfortable. Have you seen that house? Great barn of a place, and most of it is never heated.'

Henry had to agree with the sentiment. 'I have here several letters from Robert Cranston to his father and one of them speaks of Robert's anxiety about creditors going to the farm.' He handed it over to the solicitor. 'Though in light of what happened, I do wonder if Robert had anxiety about something else. Did he ever mention whether more physical threats had been made? Did he ever mention that he was worried about his parents?'

The solicitor scanned the letter and frowned. 'Robert was a bundle of anxiety towards the end, which is why I was not so surprised when I heard about the suicide. Though, of course, it has turned out not to be a suicide. He had always been a robust man, but this last month . . . You have to understand that he was my client long before all of this mess, so I knew him well. I managed to appeal to the courts to allow me to handle his affairs, I knew that would be the gentler way of doing things. Having some stranger coming in and probing through his business dealings and his life – Robert would have found that unbearable. He was a nice man, Inspector. A good businessman and, for the most part, he dealt fairly and honestly. The business he was in, no one deals fairly and honestly one hundred per cent of the time. But Robert was better than most.'

'But did he speak of receiving threats?'

Enright pursed his lips and thought about it. 'He said nothing directly, you understand, but he was definitely anxious. I didn't think about it at the time because he had enough to be worried about, but perhaps . . . perhaps there was more to it than that.'

'You knew that he had opened another bank account?'

'Of course. I had to authorise it. His father lent him five hundred pounds. As you can appreciate, that is a considerable amount of money and I don't think the mother knew about it. Robert's assets, of course, were frozen after this nasty business with the stock markets, but I managed to get permission for this account to be opened so that at least he had money for living expenses. You understand, I'm trying to do the best for my clients. It *will* all end badly, but if I can mitigate the journey, if you see my meaning, then I do what I can. The agreement was that I would administer this account but that this money was, in fact, not Robert's. It remained his father's. This was a loan, the money was there for his use, but it could not be touched by his creditors because it remained in his father's name. I had paperwork drawn up to that effect. When his father died, I gave permission for him to draw some of this account to pay for the funeral expenses. It seemed the decent thing to do. I can show you all the paperwork. In fact, most of it should be with the bundle that I sent over to you today. I did tell you when I sent the first material over that there would be more.'

Henry nodded. He had indeed. 'But did you know about these other deposits?'

'What other deposits?'

'They were in the statements you sent over to me. Someone in your firm added a note that this was a loan from a benefactor. That he did question who that benefactor was, but that Robert Cranston said that this was a private dealing.'

He produced the paperwork he was referring to and placed it on the desk. Enright studied it carefully, a frown creasing between his eyes. It was clear that this was unfamiliar information. 'I cannot deal with everything single-handedly,' he said impatiently, but it was obvious that he was more annoyed with the clerk that had written the comment than he was with Henry pointing out his lack of knowledge. 'You may be sure that I will be looking into this. This is a large amount of money.'

'And the account was emptied on the day that your client died. Withdrawn as bearer bonds by a man claiming to be Robert Cranston, but we know that it was not because Cranston was dead by then. However, this letter, on notepaper with the heading of your firm, was sent to the bank some three days before the amount was withdrawn. As you can see, the bank believed that you had given permission for this to happen.'

The frown deepened, becoming a deep fissure between his eyebrows. 'This is totally out of order,' Enright declared. 'No permission came from our firm for any of this.'

'And the clerk who dealt with this, who wrote these comments?'

'Is inexperienced and should have sought advice,' was the terse response. 'You may be sure I will be dealing with him in short order.'

'And how difficult would it be for an outsider to lay hands on your headed notepaper?' Henry asked.

'Truthfully, I suppose anyone visiting my offices could obtain a sheet if they put their minds to it. We don't exactly feel the need to lock it in the safe . . . though on reflection perhaps we should.'

'Mr Enright,' Henry said, 'you mentioned that you are dealing with a substantial number of such cases. Businessmen finding themselves in difficulties and losing all they have. No doubt you know of other legal practices in a similar position?'

'Of course.'

'Can you think of any other cases – your own or that you might have heard spoken of – where the individuals involved have, on the face of it, taken their own lives?'

The solicitor grimaced. 'We now know that Mr Cranston was not a suicide,' he said coldly.

'Indeed we do,' Henry returned. He watched as the implication of his words were processed by the law man.

'You can't possibly think . . .? Oh, my word, that is a terrible thought.' Frowning, he picked up his pen and tapped it gently against his blotter. 'I can think of one other suicide. A young man who threw himself into the river. There were witnesses to the action, but the body, I believe, has not yet been found. Other than that . . . no, I think not, but I will, of course, ask my colleagues. I can assure you that I will be discreet. We don't want more panic, do we, gentlemen?'

He had promised to send details of the man presumed drowned and they were about to take their leave when Enright said, 'Of course, there was that terrible accident. Sir Ralph Helford, the surgeon. You remember?'

'He was one of yours?' Mickey was genuinely shocked. 'But he was a surgeon. How did he come to be—'

'He overreached himself, I'm afraid. Invested too much and too quickly, looking for a swift return. Unfortunately, he was also part of that set that were influenced by Hatry and his ilk. Instead of using their common sense, they were swayed by family name and reputation and no doubt the desire to emulate their betters. However, Sir Ralph's death, that was a nasty business, but I don't suppose it is of concern to you?'

'The car that hit him has still not been traced,' Henry said. 'Unfortunately, at that time of the morning there were few witnesses. Most reports speak of hearing a car. All reports speak of the sound of a powerful engine, the noise making it evident that this car was going at some speed. Then the shout and the clash of something being hit. The sound of a car being driven away.'

'Those that went down to investigate found Sir Ralph already dead,' Mickey added.

A tragedy, they all agreed.

Henry paused with his hand on the door. 'Mr Enright, perhaps you might send me all you have on Sir Ralph Helford's troubles?' he said.

'Oh, but you can't think . . .?'

'In my business, you gather detail before you allow yourself to think,' Henry told him. 'It's not a good idea to reach conclusions before you have the facts.'

It was, he reminded himself, a lesson hard learned a decade ago. Hard learned from his dealings with Walter Cole and Hayden Paul – men who reached their desired conclusion first and then sought only evidence that supported those desires. On the day he was convicted Richardson had reminded them that old sins cast long shadows. There was, of course, as yet nothing to connect the death of Robert Cranston or anyone else – apart from detectives Cole and Paul – to the Richardson business, but . . .

The Richardson case had taught him some bitter lessons, Henry thought. It had shaped his career in ways he was loath to acknowledge. Richardson's conviction had certainly done his career no harm. Though he hoped fervently that the more lasting and pertinent lesson had been in what he wanted to avoid. That he had acquired painful understanding of the kind of detective he did not want to be.

SIX

'So, what do we have?' Mickey asked, setting a cup of tea down on his boss's desk. Central Office was busy on the morning of 14 November but as neither he nor Henry was listed as on call that week, they were unlikely to be summoned urgently away. Mickey felt relatively relaxed.

He and Henry had an intriguing set of puzzles to solve, Belle was home for the foreseeable future. Life, Mickey thought, was pretty fine.

'I need to understand the business side of all of this,' Henry said. 'I have never held stock, never been tempted to gamble on the exchange, and although I have discussed such matters with Albert, I must confess much of this is still mysterious.'

'So you'll be going to see Cynthia, then?' Mickey joked.

'I think that might be my best plan,' Henry agreed. 'In the meantime, we have the murder of Robert Cranston. The possibly suspicious death of his father. The suicide by drowning – presumably – of a' – he paused and checked his notes – 'Mr Ansel Peach.

Is that an invented name, do you suppose? And the death of Sir Ralph Helford, which to my mind is murder.'

'You'd need to prove the intention to kill,' Mickey pointed out.

'The car was driven at unreasonable speed. The driver did not stop to see what he'd done or if he could render assistance.'

'Drunk, probably,' Mickey said. 'Likely woke up the following day with a thumping head, a dent in his fancy car and no clear memory of any of it.'

'Which excuses nothing,' Henry said firmly.

Mickey sipped his still scalding tea and nodded agreement. 'What more can be done today?' he asked. 'I've prepared the paperwork for the exhumation requests, but nothing will happen with that until tomorrow. There will be a few days before the exhumations are carried out anyway – supposing we gain permission. You should warn Albert about Ferdy,' he added. 'It will be upsetting for all family and friends to know that their loved one's rest is about to be disturbed.' He paused. 'Henry, do you believe we might be overreaching ourselves? Robert Cranston's death could have many solutions. Because he met a violent end at the hand of another does not mean that the others have.'

'As I told our solicitor friend, I am not yet drawing conclusions. I am gathering information. If that detail becomes irrelevant, then I'll be happy enough to cast it aside. Believe me, Mickey, I've no desire for more murders than we already have on our collective plates.'

'But those bells are ringing in your head,' Mickey said.

It was the most natural thing in the world for Henry to go and speak to Cynthia when he had a problem. He and his sister were incredibly close – they went through so much together as children, and their father's death when Cynthia was only fifteen meant that she had taken charge of raising Henry.

This time, however, he knew that he was on sensitive ground. He knew something of what Albert had lost and the investments that had gone wrong because Henry was aware of the criminal activities that had, in part, led to the crash of the London Stock Exchange back in September, but he had deliberately not asked for details or sought to discuss this too much with his brother-in-law. He liked Albert, knew that his pride was hurting as much as his bank account, and had no wish to rub fresh salt into the wound.

Henry was therefore quite relieved to find that Cynthia was alone. Albert had gone to his club and even Malina, Cynthia's trusted assistant and secretary, had gone to the cinema. The children were in bed by the time he arrived and so it was just the two of them, resting beside Cynthia's fire in her bright little sitting room and enjoying a rather good single malt.

'So,' Cynthia said. 'What is it you need to know? Albert lost over twenty thousand on a single investment.'

'Good Lord!'

'His friend Ferdy lost even more. Albert will recover.'

'Largely due to your foresight.'

'In part. In part because his reputation is also solid. He is known to be a good and honest businessman, Henry. One who is careful and considered, and fortunately he gambled with his own money, not the investments of others, so the losses affect no one else.'

'It must have impacted on his capital worth, though?'

'It has, and that can't be kept secret. His investment and his losses were far too public for that, and it won't go unnoticed that we are selling property and tightening our purse strings. Handled properly, though, this will eventually just be seen as sensible precautions, I hope. He has quietly let it be known that he settled certain properties in my name when we married, that he thought it right that I should manage my own affairs and those of the children and that these properties will be in trust for them, and that now the children are getting older I wish to free up funds for travel and education.'

'When in fact . . .'

'When in fact I had him sign those properties and those accounts over to me last Christmas, as you well know. The world does not need to know that, however. A man's reputation in business is as precious to him as a woman's good name. Albert will recover because I am prepared to do all it takes for him to maintain his reputation. Oh, it is not sentiment, Henry, but good sense. I have my children to think of. And I have the life we have enjoyed together to think of. I consider myself fortunate, you know that. My marriage to Albert isn't a particularly romantic one, but he is a good man and we have become great friends and he is an excellent father. You know that to be true.'

Henry nodded. Albert was indeed a very loving father, and Henry also knew that he regarded Cynthia with a great deal of fondness and that he too considered himself fortunate. He considered himself especially fortunate that though Cynthia had more brains in her little finger than her husband had in his entire head, she never rubbed his nose in that fact. It would not be true to say that Cynthia existed in Albert's shadow – she was far too much her own person – but it was certainly true that Cynthia was discreet when discretion was required.

'Ferdy could have survived this too. True, it would have been painful for him, and for his family. But they still had land they could have sold, pictures that could have been disposed of, the sale of his wife's emeralds alone would have cleared most of their debts, but no, sadly he was like so many of them – he must keep up appearances. And I suppose, in fairness, I have been doing my best to keep up appearances too, so I can't be too hard in my judgement. But we *will* be making a tactical withdrawal where necessary. As I told you, no more parties and only little extravagances – just enough that those Albert has dealings with in his business world feel assured that we have the capital to back up whatever project he has in mind. In that regard, appearances do matter.' She sighed and tapped at her glass somewhat impatiently.

'Cynthia, how do you think Albert would feel if I have Ferdy's body exhumed?'

'If you do *what*? Henry, are you serious? He would be appalled, as would Ferdy's family. Henry, I know for you to say this you must have good reason, but—'

'How certain were they that it was suicide? Did they have a post-mortem?'

She stared at him as though this had never occurred to her. 'Why would a family declare that a loved one had committed suicide if there was any chance of it being otherwise? You know how painful this is – they can't even bury him in the family vault.'

Henry considered that. 'And what if he was murdered?'

'Oh my God, Henry. Are you serious? Why on earth would you think that?'

Henry shrugged. 'Cynthia, I'm not certain, but I'm investigating a murder that had been staged – very badly I might add – to look like suicide. I was called to the lodgings of Robert Cranston a few days ago. Sadly, he's been murdered.'

'Henry, that is dreadful. So that note you were given, do you think it was from someone trying to protect him, or someone who meant him harm?'

'It was certainly sent by someone who wanted me to look into the potential harm that might come to Mr Cranston. How they knew this or whether they actually considered murder, I don't know. His housekeeper found him, with a bullet through his brain and the gun nearby. But he had, in fact, been strangled. And there were some very unusual financial dealings. He appears to have received a loan from person or persons unknown, the amount paid into his bank account and then withdrawn, by someone claiming to be Cranston, several hours after his death. Withdrawn as bearer bonds, so not something we can trace.'

Cynthia got up and refilled her glass and offered the decanter to Henry, who declined. 'He took out a loan? Henry, if this man was desperate enough that his killer thought his suicide might be accepted, was he also about to become bankrupt? Surely, if that was so, he could not borrow money? His name would already have been blacklisted, would it not?'

'His case had not yet come to court, so his name had not yet been listed in the newspapers. His financial difficulties were not yet completely public, though I imagine they would have been known to most of his associates. But this is not an ordinary loan. He told the clerk dealing with his case that it was a private transaction, a gentleman's agreement and therefore—'

'Oh my God,' Cynthia sat down hard.

'Cyn, what is it?'

'Henry, this may have nothing to do with your case, but you know that Ferdy and Albert both belong to the same clubs, they moved in the same circles . . .? Well, there are certain people within those circles who have been offering loans. "Gentlemen's loans", they called them, and some for quite substantial amounts. I'm not sure if Ferdy succumbed. Fortunately, Albert asked my advice first and I told him that he should not put his reputation in the hands of others. *Again.* We had a bitter argument about it, Henry, but he eventually came round to my way of seeing things. Though I think if Ferdy hadn't died he might well have given in to the pressure.'

'And do you know who these so-called gentlemen are?'

She shook her head. 'I know very little about gentlemen's clubs, for the very good reason that I am not a gentleman,' she told him, managing a slight laugh.

Henry could see how pale she had grown, could almost see her mind working its way through the problem that he had posed for her, and the relief for what must have now felt like another near miss.

'But if you want to bleed somebody dry, lend them money and then get it back at God knows what inflated rate of interest, why kill them?'

'Why indeed,' Henry agreed. 'We can only guess that Robert Cranston and perhaps Ferdy too are the tip of a much larger iceberg. That in those specific cases, and for some as yet unknown reason, something went wrong. Ferdy killed himself; Cranston may have threatened his lenders in some way. These are not street-corner schemers or our usual brand of loan sharks – the amounts are far too great. But we may be certain that they operate on a similar principle. They will seem to be helping, then, as you say, they will bleed their victims dry.'

Or was this all to do with Richardson? Henry thought. He had been directed to look out for Robert Cranston in that mysterious note. Cranston had duly been found dead and then discovered to be murdered. Richardson was a clever man and liked to display that cleverness. He was a master of extortion – and he enjoyed the game almost as much as he enjoyed the win. Had he been behind the note delivered to Henry at Cynthia's party? Was Richardson playing games with him? If so, then this was an elaborate game. A long game – but that fitted with Richardson's brand of patience, Henry remembered. Where was Richardson leading him? Or was this anything to do with Richardson, after all? Was he just jumping at shadows? Henry asked himself, suddenly impatient with his own anxiety.

Cynthia was thoughtful again. She sipped her drink, eyes slightly narrowed, and Henry, knowing that she was searching her brain for some very specific memory, remained silent and waited. Finally she said, 'Henry, what if those people didn't want to take the loan? What if they were forced to do so? What if someone threatened them, threatened to expose something if they didn't borrow the money? Made it impossible for them to say no?'

'Where did you get such a notion from?'

'Oh, just from a conversation I overheard. It was between Albert and Ferdy. I didn't actually realize Ferdy was here one day. I came to the study to rouse Albert from his desk – I think, if I remember right, we were due to go out for dinner. But anyway, I was about to knock when I heard Ferdy's raised voice. At first, I thought they were arguing – you know how unusual that would have been – and then I realized that Ferdy was just very distressed. He was saying something like, "You don't understand, Albert, old boy – if I don't do it I'm ruined anyway." I only caught a bit of the conversation, but Albert said that Ferdy should not allow himself to be threatened, that he should speak to you. That whatever problem they were discussing, it amounted to blackmail. Ferdy was almost hysterical by then, and he was getting very loud. I was afraid the servants might hear, and that would embarrass everybody, so I knocked on the door. Albert shouted to come in, and they both shut up. Henry, I admit it's a leap, but what if?'

'Some form of extortion,' Henry said. 'It is entirely possible. For those whose reputations matter to them more than almost anything else, fear of exposure, or fear of the extortionist harming their family or even their family name might compel individuals to borrow from the wrong people. Of course, it's not really borrowing, is it? It's leaving your last little step of firm ground behind and leaping off into the void.' Just as Richardson had done with his victims a decade ago.

'Henry, that is a terrifying idea, isn't it?'

'But it wouldn't be the first time it has happened, or the first time that it has led to murder.'

In fact, in many ways, he was reminded of the Richardson affair and the involvement of Cole and Paul. There had been related investigations, too, but Henry could not call all the details to mind; he had not been fully well at that time – much of it was still blurred and fuzzy, his brain still not back to its usual acuity. He would need to draw those cases from the archive and examine them fully. He was, however, certain now, feeling himself to be on firmer ground. When he had arrived at Cynthia's the idea that Richardson could be involved in anything other than direct revenge had seemed fanciful. He had killed Detective Sergeant Walter Cole and Detective Chief Inspector Hayden Paul, men he had reason to hate. He would come after Henry; Otis was certain enough of that to be frank about using Henry as bait. But simple revenge would never be enough for a man like Richardson, Henry knew that, and the echoes of a decade ago were sounding more loudly with every step. He must revisit the case files, re-examine the evidence, see what his then still-wounded mind had caused him to forget.

He was aware that his sister was watching him, clearly wondering what he was thinking about. It angered him that he could not tell her. Henry returned to present concerns. 'So will you warn Albert about the exhumation?' he asked. 'Or shall I do that?'

'No, it's better coming from me, I think. And I'll ask him about the people seeking to lend money. These so-called gentleman loan sharks.'

'Do that. But warn him to be careful about mentioning it to others.'

'But would we not be better to give warning? Henry, a lot of people are very desperate for money at the moment, very desperate to get themselves out of the hole they are in.'

'I understand that, but Cranston's death gives us reason to believe that they have killed already.' And at least twice more, counting the deaths of Cole and Paul, but he couldn't tell her that. 'We don't want anyone acting precipitously and bringing further trouble down upon themselves. Cynthia, did you know Sir Ralph Helford, the surgeon?'

'I've met him. He chaired a board that I was on, one of the homes for unmarried mothers. A man Albert knew from one of his clubs was on it too. We were raising money because the place where they were housed was in such a desperate condition – it was damp and insanitary. He was a nice man – it was such a shame.' Her eyes widened then. 'But Henry, that was an accident. He was hit by a car – the driver fled. But you can't think . . . surely? He wasn't in financial difficulties, I'm certain.' She looked at her brother. 'Henry, really?'

'His case is being handled by the same firm of solicitors who were handling Robert Cranston's. In fact, it was Mr Enright of Messrs Enright and Baines who drew my attention to the Helford situation. He has been uneasy about the so-called accident ever since it happened.'

'Oh dear God, Henry, this is a terrible thing. Henry, how far-reaching is it?'

Henry shook his head. 'I have no idea,' he said. 'My involvement began with what looked like a suicide. Actually, no, it began with the letter I was given on the night of your last party.' It had started before that, Henry thought, with Otis's visit, informing him of the deaths of Paul and Cole, but he could not tell Cynthia that.

'The flamenco dancer. But why the subterfuge? Why not send an anonymous letter to Scotland Yard? To bring a letter to my party seems so theatrical. I don't understand it, do you, Henry? Surely, if someone had reason to be afraid for Mr Robert Cranston, then there were other ways of informing you of this, simpler and less complicated ways. What if the flamenco dancer had been challenged? She was very careful – she entered with others and no one took much notice of her. But it could have been very different.'

'That's been bothering me too,' Henry agreed. 'It's almost as though someone wanted to involve me personally, rather than as a police inspector.' Henry's thoughts turned to Richardson again. 'It's a curious thing, Cynthia, but I will get to the bottom of it.'

'I've no doubt you will, but it begs another question, Henry. How many people know that you're my brother? True, our direct circle does, but I would imagine two-thirds of the guests that night would not know you from Adam, and would certainly not know that my brother is a detective – even if you are a chief inspector – just to look at you. Those are not the kind of circles our guests move in. Most of them were well-to-do and would assume that everyone else was of the same class. Of course, the dressing up means that everyone is somewhat more anonymous than they would usually be, but she must have known who you were, Henry – she must have known what you looked like. She approached you directly, even though she pretended it was an accident.'

Henry nodded, knowing that her analysis was accurate. 'Undoubtedly someone told her who to look for, and possibly even told her that I was not likely to be in fancy dress. As for knowing what I looked like, my face has been in the newspapers from time to time, so it would not be hard to get hold of a likeness. But the fact is whoever sent that message knew a week before his death that Robert Cranston was being threatened. If they knew that threat was as serious as it turned out to be, then they are also responsible for his death. Perhaps we could have protected him.'

'From what you said after you went to see him, he would have been a difficult man to protect. He wasn't taking any of this seriously.'

'True,' Henry agreed reluctantly. 'But it still rankles.'

'Of course it does.' Cynthia looked troubled. 'You know, Henry, lately it feels as though my mind is just too full. To be truthful, my dear brother, I am a little overwhelmed by it all and I will be very glad to get away from this house and down to the coast. The sooner we're packed and gone and this house is put on the market, the happier I shall be. We must wait until New Year – Albert has business dealings in the pipeline that must be completed first. Don't worry, Henry, I have vetted them.' She laughed, but there was no humour in it.

Henry got up to leave. He bent to kiss his sister on the cheek. 'You must take care of yourself,' he said. 'Things will improve, Cyn, darling. The worst, I'm sure, is over.'

'I hope so,' she said. 'I don't think I could deal with any more drama. I'm worn out with it. But I know we've been fortunate – there are many individuals who have lost every penny.'

Henry picked up his hat. 'What I don't fully understand,' he said, 'is how so many small investors could afford to buy stock at the rate they did. I mean, how did they raise the money?'

Cynthia laughed. 'Credit is cheap, or rather credit has been cheap. Besides, you don't need to raise all the money to buy the stock you want to invest in. You can speculate by buying on the margin. What that actually means, Henry, is that you borrow the bulk of the money to buy your stocks and shares. Your own investment is often just ten or twenty per cent of the full value. You keep them for a short while, you sell, you repay the original loan and you keep the profit.'

'Does that actually work?' Henry was extremely sceptical. It sounded far too easy.

'For the last few years it's worked exceedingly well,' Cynthia told him. 'But, of course, it only works when the prices are rising. Previously, if the price had dropped, then you simply held on to your stock for a little longer and the market rallied again. But suddenly the prices crashed. The world crashed. Lenders called in their loans with immediate effect and so many investors, big and small, crashed with it.'

'I prefer to have solid cash in my pocket,' Henry told her. 'I'm never going to grow rich in my particular chosen profession, but at least I know what I have in my pocket and that it is all mine.'

Cynthia hugged him. 'It is not a bad attitude to have,' she said. 'You know that *my* attitude has always been you should never gamble what you can't afford to lose.'

SEVEN

Early the following morning Henry dispatched Mickey to look into the death of Mr Ansel Peach while he himself went to the house of Sir Ralph Helford. Even before he knocked on the front door, he realized that the house looked and felt empty. The sound of the door knocker echoed through the hallway behind. Henry asked the neighbours and was told that Lady Helford had gone away before her husband's death and had not yet returned.

A housemaid from two doors down thought the remaining family might have returned as she'd heard a car pull round into the yard at the rear of the house where the surgeon always parked his own vehicle a few days after the doctor's passing. When she'd looked out into the yard from one of the open upstairs windows, she thought she had seen movement. She'd thought this was very strange because although the master of the house parked around the back, and often cut in through the kitchen, the mistress never did. 'And, of course, poor Sir Ralph was already dead by then, so I realized it couldn't have been him. And Lady Helford, she always came in properly by the front door,' she told Henry. 'The doctor often went out at strange hours – because of his job – and came in the back way, and parked his car, so as not to disturb people in the street.'

'Did whoever you hear park a vehicle in the yard?' Henry asked.

She shook her head. 'No. I heard an engine and I thought I heard the gate open, so I assumed . . . and then I realized, of course, it couldn't be the doctor's car. The poor man being dead and buried.'

'And you are certain you heard the gate?'

'I know the sound of it. The back door too. There's a creak to it you can't mistake.'

'And you heard the back door being opened?'

'I'm certain I did.'

The more she had thought about it, the more worried she had become, and so she had told her mistress what she had heard. Two of the male members of staff had been dispatched to check on the house, but though the rear gate had been unlatched, they had seen nothing untoward.

Henry asked her to point out the way into the rear of the building. Walking into the next street, he found a large archway and a wooden gate. This had clearly been a carriage entrance when the house had first been built. He pushed at the gate and to his surprise it was not locked. Cautiously, he swung the gate wide and stepped through. Initially, everything looked orderly and quiet and it was only when he went to look closely at the back door that he realized that the lock had been forced. If the servants from the neighbouring house had come into the yard in the dark, they probably wouldn't have noticed that anything was wrong, especially if, when they tried the door, whoever was inside had already shot the bolt. That would be a sensible precaution, Henry thought. Then anyone checking on the premises wouldn't be any the wiser to what had happened.

He pushed the door and it gave with a creak and a groan – the sound that the housemaid had reported hearing. He stepped inside and looked around – everything seemed as it should, but once he had gone through from the servant's quarters and into the main body of the house, he realized that it was anything but. The whole house had been ransacked.

Henry retreated, went back to the neighbour's house and asked if he could use the telephone. While waiting for his colleagues to arrive, Henry examined the empty house. With the exception of the kitchen, which probably held nothing of worth for thieves, the entire house had been emptied of valuables from attic to basement. Shaded areas on the walls showed where pictures had been removed – there was no silverware in any of the drawers in the dining room or on the sideboard where Henry might have expected it to be in a house like this. From his examination of the attic rooms he guessed there were normally three staff resident – probably a cook and a kitchen girl and a valet-cum-butler that would serve the needs of the master. Had the staff been dismissed after Helford's death, or had they gone with Lady Helford when she had been sent away? Sir Ralph had evidently expected trouble, Henry thought.

He had no way of knowing what Lady Helford had taken with her in terms of clothing and jewellery, but he hoped for her sake that she had prepared for a long visit, wherever she might have gone, and taken her personal possessions with her. A scattering of photographs lay on her dressing table, as if they had been removed from their frames. It was odd, Henry thought, that the thieves had taken time to do so. Yes, a photograph might be used to identify a frame, but they could have been removed later and burned in any kitchen fire. For Henry, this spoke of an unhurried raid on the Helfords' family home. They had entered the house, these thieves, and taken their time about ravaging it. Presumably because they had known that the master of the house was dead and gone and the servants away with their mistress or perhaps even dismissed from service.

He made a note to himself that he must track the servants down.

A shout from below told him that police officers had arrived and he called back, informing them where he was and who he was. And then he returned to the neighbours' house in the hope that they would have some idea of where Lady Helford or her servants might be.

Mickey Hitchens had spent his morning trekking from mortuary to mortuary, from hospital to funeral directors, but had not found any sign of Mr Ansel Peach among the unclaimed bodies. Nor did any of them have any record of a drowned man matching his description. This in itself meant nothing, but Mickey knew the tides and the moods of the Thames and would have expected a body to be washed up by now. Most did, becoming caught beneath the supports of bridges or drifting at low tide on to the mud, and police officers checked these usual locations on a daily basis. It was rare not to find at least one body on any given day.

A little frustrated, he went to the address given as the lodging house where Mr Peach had lived for the last few weeks of his life. Mickey, for whom London had always been home and workplace, knew there was not a street in the East End that had not been laid claim to by some criminal gang or another and this boarding house lay at the edge of the territory that was the domain of the Forty Elephants, owned and controlled by Diamond Annie. He was very aware that his movements would be reported back to her.

The boarding house was a rough kind. The landlady lived in the back room on the ground floor and rented out the others above and one at the front of the house. The door to this room was open as Mickey entered and he glimpsed a bed, a washstand, and a hotplate, with a scatter of foodstuffs, set on a small table beside it.

The landlady was not inclined to be particularly cooperative. ''Is room's been let,' she told Mickey acerbically. 'You can't be expecting me to leave a room empty. A dead man won't be coming back, will 'e? Neither will 'e be paying rent.'

Mickey agreed that he probably wouldn't. He asked about her relationship with Mr Peach and she glared at him. 'I mean,' Mickey explained, 'was he friendly? How did you get along? How did he get along with your other . . . tenants?'

She narrowed her eyes at him and cocked her head on one side, as though his question warranted a great deal of thought. 'Never seen him from one day to the next, did I? 'E came, 'e went. Paid his rent.'

'And work? Where did he work?'

''Ow the 'ell should I know? Spoke like a toff, didn't 'e? Lost it all, 'adn't 'e?'

And fallen very far even before he fell from the bridge, Mickey thought.

'Did he leave anything here?'

She disappeared into the back room and came back a moment later with a large brown-paper package. 'Never let it be said I'm not an honest woman,' she told Mickey, shoving the parcel in his direction. Then she retreated into the back room once more.

Mickey went upstairs and knocked on both doors but received no answer and found the doors locked. These residents had probably gone to work. The door to the front room was now closed, its resident obviously returned. He knocked and a young boy answered it and looked nervously at Mickey. He said his mum and his dad weren't there, and that he didn't know no Mr Peach.

Mickey made his way back to Scotland Yard and the Central Office carrying Mr Ansel Peach's belongings in the rather smelly parcel he had been given, wondering how Henry had been getting along.

EIGHT

Mickey deposited the pungent brown-paper parcel on his table and then went to find his boss. He discovered Henry down in the records office, discussing an ancient case and trying to be as helpful as possible to the clerk who was trying to find it. But Henry's version of being helpful seem to consist of issuing a string of instructions and half-remembered detail; Mickey had come into the end of the conversation, but even he could hear that they were contradictory.

Henry was obviously on to something, Mickey thought, and evidently frustrated that he couldn't find it himself. He exchanged a sympathetic glance with the records clerk and then suggested that Henry come back upstairs with him.

'I have a parcel of Mr Peach's personal effects,' he said. 'I thought you might like the pleasure of looking through it with me.'

Henry cast his sergeant a sharp look. 'Anything interesting?'

'I wouldn't know yet. The landlady had parcelled everything up and assured me that she was an honest woman and there will be nothing missing, but I've not had the pleasure of going through it yet. I thought I might wait for you. What are you doing down here, anyway?'

'I remembered something, an extortion case that I worked on back when I was still a sergeant. There are familiar features, but I would have to re-read the case to be sure there's any relevance.' He was aware of Mickey's speculative glance. 'It may be nothing, of course.'

Henry followed him back up the stairs and a few minutes later they were both regarding the brown-paper parcel, wrapped up with the rough twine, with a degree of suspicion.

'What's that smell?' Henry asked.

Mickey cut the string and drew the edges of the paper apart. 'Mouldy cheese,' he announced. 'So the landlady was true to her word – she *is* an honest soul.' He chuckled happily. 'Or perhaps she just couldn't stand the stink. What the hell kind of cheese is it?'

But Henry was peering closely at the offending article. 'Now this is odd,' he pronounced. 'This is not an English cheese, not even a very smelly Stilton. Look, it's boxed up, the top of the box is missing, but, there, it's still in the bottom half. If I'm not mistaken, it is a very ripe' – Henry brought his nose closer to the offending dairy product – 'well, a very *overripe* Camembert or something similar. Now what would a man as down on his uppers as our Mr Peach apparently be doing with a whole Camembert? Never having bought any myself, I couldn't tell you what it cost, but it's got to be more than the usual mousetrap Cheddar.'

Mickey was intrigued now. He peered more closely at the squishy and very pungent cheese. He glanced around, aware that they were getting some very raw comments from those in the office. 'The question is what should we do with it right now? Is it evidence? Should it be preserved? Can it be preserved?'

Henry left him and came back a few minutes later with an old biscuit tin. He scooped the cheese inside, put the lid on firmly and then announced that he was going to find a cold place in which to store it. Someone shouted across the room that he should stick it on the fire escape, and even though it was intended as a joke, that's exactly what Henry did.

'So what else do we have?' he asked. 'Nothing quite as noxious, I hope. I've eaten Camembert at Cynthia's on occasion and it's a pleasant cheese. But evidently those I've tried before were somewhat fresher.'

Mickey had laid out the items from the parcel on the tabletop, but he was examining the brown paper that they had been wrapped in. 'It seems the landlady even reused the brown paper that belonged to Mr Peach,' he said. 'Do we have an address for him, from before he went to live at the boarding house?'

'No doubt his solicitor has, so it will be in among the papers that arrived this morning. I've had no time to go through them yet. Why?'

'This parcel has a return address and this is certainly not one from the East End of our city. It seems not everybody turned their back on our Mr Peach.'

Henry picked up the brown paper and examined the stamps and the postmark and the return address. 'So it is from a Mrs Green, and the street address, if I remember right, is close by Chelsea Town Hall.'

Mickey produced a map. Henry, of course, was right. She lived on Camden Hill, a short walk from the town hall. 'So who is Mrs Green and what does she have to do with our Mr Peach?'

Henry was examining the contents of the parcel. A small silver propelling pencil and a blank cheap notebook with several pages torn out. Two pocket handkerchiefs, neatly pressed and three pairs of socks – one darned but the other two in good condition. They looked relatively new and from the feel of them Henry deduced that they were of excellent quality. Two shirts, both white and very clean and a pair of pinstripe trousers with deep turn-ups on the hem that Henry promptly turned inside out, dropping the inevitable cargo of fluff and gravel on to a sheet of clean paper. Mickey folded the paper to contain what might be useful evidence, but what might on the other hand just be fluff.

'And this was it, all he left behind him.' It was not a question; it was a statement and Mickey could see at once what was troubling his boss.

'He was previously a man of substance whose business presumably failed in September, when the London Exchange collapsed. I am making that presumption as he is a member of that group of bankrupts being dealt with by Enright, the solicitor. It is now only mid-November. Even if he lost everything in a very precipitous manner, he would still have had his clothing, and some small possessions that he hadn't pawned, sold or otherwise disposed of. The clothing in this package is of excellent quality and yet there is so little of it. He is a man who clearly cared for his clothes; cared for the quality of them, when he had the money to do so. It seems unlikely that he would have rid himself of everything else and just be reduced to three pairs of socks, one pair of trousers, and two shirts.'

'Plus whatever he was wearing when he died. What was he wearing when he threw himself off the bridge? Do we know?'

'I expect there was something in the witness statements,' Mickey said, 'but from what I remember, no one was particularly close to him when he jumped. It was early morning and the witnesses were a road sweeper, and a couple returning from a party that had lasted until the dawn.'

Henry was thoughtful. 'I suggest we go through all the documentation the solicitor sent to us, look at the witness statements again, and then we go and visit this Mrs Green and find out why she was sending parcels containing expensive cheese to this Mr Ansel Peach. And I'm betting that's what was in this brown paper originally, no doubt along with other consumables.'

Mickey nodded. He began to put the small collection of possessions into manila envelopes and brown-paper bags, noting down Mrs Green's address before folding the paper. 'And what did you learn from Sir Ralph Helford's house?'

'That someone had taken advantage of his death and his wife's absence to ransack the place, taking everything of value that might have been there.'

Mickey paused as he was about to drop the notebook into an envelope. 'When did this happen?'

'According to the housemaid two doors down from the Helford home, it was probably three days after Helford had died. The wife had already left – no one seems to know where she's gone to. She's taken her maid with her, they think. The cook seems to have gone away on holiday, taking the opportunity to visit family until such time as the Helford household need her back, though no one seems to know exactly where either. And as to Sir Ralph's valet, that is anyone's guess. I think Sir Ralph must have expected trouble and scattered his household in the hope that they would be safe.'

'You think he anticipated foul play?'

Henry shrugged. 'I doubt he anticipated being murdered and I am more and more convinced that's what happened, but, yes, I think he anticipated something and wished his wife out of the way. The mistress of the house next door suggested that she might have gone to see her sister, somewhere on the south coast, or it might be in the West Country. Sir Ralph and his wife had only lived at the house a few months and it seems they did not entertain a great deal. Sir Ralph, after all, was pretty much retired. He was approaching seventy and his wife not much younger. By all accounts, they seem to have lived very quietly. They had one child, a daughter, and there was mention of a grandchild.'

'So we have an afternoon of reading ahead of us,' Mickey said. 'All the paperwork about our Mr Ansel Peach and similarly about the affairs and misfortunes of Sir Ralph Helford. Do you have a preference for how we divide the task?'

Henry smiled wryly, knowing that his sergeant would much rather be out there hunting down leads than in here reading. 'I suggest while you make tea, I make a start on Mr Ansel Peach. You then examine what I have already seen and see what I've missed. That way the task is divided equally, and we can both be equally bored by the legal language and the minutiae that Mr Enright seems so enamoured of.'

The minutiae of which might just prove to be extremely useful, Mickey thought sombrely as he went off to fill the kettle. Often the devil really was in the detail, such as a half-eaten Camembert cheese and the address of a lady written on brown paper.

NINE

That evening Henry returned to see Cynthia. News had come through that the exhumations had been approved and he felt he should go and speak to Albert and explain the matter to him more fully. He had to admit that he was worried about his brother-in-law; Albert had been even more down in the dumps as of the last few weeks, and Henry had no doubt that this matter would take him into an even deeper blue funk.

News from the New York Stock Market was that things had rallied a little, but Henry had no idea whether this would be advantageous for Albert. He was just relieved that the trouble that had come to Cynthia and Albert was not worse.

He arrived in time to join his sister and her husband at dinner. Henry hadn't actually realized what the time was, and was reluctant to interrupt them, but Cynthia, of course, insisted, and Albert, much to Henry's relief, seemed equally eager for his company.

Family dinner at Cynthia's house was usually a very informal affair, the children sometimes joining their parents in what Cynthia referred to as 'the little dining room'. Tonight, however, it was just Cynthia and Albert and, as she usually did, Cynthia had dismissed the servants, telling them that she and her husband could tidy up for themselves. When they were dining alone, Cynthia and Albert liked to chat and to do so without being overheard. Henry was aware that some of their servants did not consider this quite proper, and that those with a more presumptuous attitude about what constituted gentlemanly and ladylike behaviour often didn't last very long in Cynthia's household.

Albert poured Henry some wine and then passed him the plate that Cynthia had laden with food. 'And how are you, old chap?' Albert asked him. 'Cyn tells me you've got your hands rather full.'

Henry admitted that indeed he had. 'Cynthia, if I wanted to buy a Camembert, what might I pay for it and where would be the best place to get one? A whole one, in one of those box things.'

Cynthia laughed. 'They aren't that difficult to get. As to what you'd pay, that shifts with the seasons somewhat. I must admit the only time we ever seem to serve it is when we have particular guests, but I can check the accounts for you after dinner.'

'And why would you want to know that?' Albert was clearly amused. 'Can't say I like it that much myself. Stilton or Cheshire are rather more to my taste. Or what was that lovely one we had while we were in Wales? It was all crumbly and white.'

Henry told them about Mr Ansel Peach and his rather smelly parcel.

'Oh, it's a clue, is it?' Albert seemed impressed by the idea. He took a sip of his wine and then said diffidently, 'So you're going to dig up old Ferdy. I'd ask if it was really necessary, but I don't suppose you'd do a thing like that if it wasn't. I saw his family today. Most cut up about it, they are, but they want to do the right thing. I told them you were a good sort, and you'd make sure it was done properly.'

Henry was a little taken aback, but he nodded and thanked his brother-in-law. 'It does have to be done,' he said. 'There are some strange things going on, Albert, and if there's the slightest chance that Ferdy did not kill himself, you understand that we have to know.'

'Of course I do. But it's a blow, coming on top of another blow. You know, Henry, I'll be heartily glad to see the back of this year.'

They ate in silence for a few minutes. Beef and cabbage with boiled potatoes – Albert liked his food simple. And then Albert said, 'I wrote some names down for you – fellows that were trying to loan other fellows' money. I said no, of course, I didn't see sense in throwing good money after bad, not when we look as though we can get out of this hole under our own steam, but there are others not so fortunate who might have succumbed, you know?'

Henry glanced at Cynthia, noting Albert's revisionist view of how he had come through this episode so unscathed, but she was looking down at her plate, determined not to catch his eye. If Albert's pride required that he modify his narrative, she was clearly not going to argue with him.

Henry turned his attention back to his brother-in-law. 'Do you think Ferdy was among them?'

'Damn sure he was. Made no sense to me, mind you, but damn sure he was. It started off with him saying he didn't want his family to know how deep in he was, and then his creditors started in on him, and of course he couldn't keep things secret after that and so he tried to make a good fist of it. Tried to tell everyone that his creditors were mistaken about what he'd lost, carried on like nothing was wrong. He even started planning for his races next year, you know he drove at Monte Carlo.'

Henry nodded. 'Which must cost an enormous amount of money. Did he still have his racehorses too?'

'Oh, you have no idea how much. Yes, indeed yes, everything must continue as it had, including the gee-gees. But you know, Henry, even the likes of Ferdy can only go so far on credit; bills must be paid eventually and it's when the small people begin to threaten to take you to court that you know you're truly sunk. The veterinarian and the feed merchant. When the local butcher will no longer supply you with meat, you have to understand that no one is fooled by whatever show you might be putting on.'

'Had things really got that bad?' Cynthia asked.

Albert shrugged. 'Not something a man likes to talk about,' he said. 'But yes, apparently it had. And then suddenly he was in the swim again. Swore he was getting things back to normal.'

'And he had borrowed the money,' Henry stated.

'I believe so. Yes. I don't see what else he could have done. But at what rate of interest, I can't imagine. I tried to raise matters with his family today, but, of course, neither his wife nor his mother knew much about the family finances and his brother, well, he more or less told me that it was none of my business. Politely, of course, but he pointed out that they were *old* money and could survive on their name and reputation alone and that I was new money and . . .' Albert shrugged. 'It's nonsense, of course. Half the old names in this country are poor as church mice, and half the reputations are sustained only by discreet marriages to the newly rich. An American heiress can mend your roof when an old name can't, and that's the truth of it.'

Henry was a little surprised at the bitterness in Albert's voice. He and Ferdy had been close since childhood and he guessed that the sudden realization that Ferdy's family had really only ever seen him as beneath them in status would have hurt quite brutally.

'Anyway, I have written down the names of those gentlemen I believe to be involved in all of this "refinancing", as they call it. It might be that they are perfectly legitimate, you know, Henry. And I'd rather my name didn't come into this, you understand that. Discretion. Business dealings call for discretion.'

'Of course they do,' Henry agreed. He would be sure to make it obvious that this intelligence had come through solid police work and not via personal connection – though he knew such subterfuge would not stand up to close scrutiny. He might not be a member of any clubs, but he was well aware of what a close and incestuous world they were. He was also aware that, in better times, Albert was quite happy to tell all and sundry that Cynthia's brother was a murder detective. Crime was glamourous only when viewed at a great distance; close up, it was sordid and unfortunate.

It was about a forty-minute walk from Cynthia's house to Henry's little flat, more if he took his time and loitered by the river. By mutual consent, conversation had wandered to other things, and Henry had taken time to look at Albert's latest microscope slides. Most of these, Albert confessed, had been created by Melissa, who was now a 'dab hand'.

It was close to midnight when Henry finally arrived home, and as he approached the entrance to his block of flats, he was aware of someone standing across the road and watching him. A tall woman and two not-so-tall men. The woman detached herself from her companions and came over to where he stood.

'Detective Chief Inspector Johnstone, a good evening to you.'

Henry concealed his surprise. 'And a good evening to you, Annie. What brings you here?'

She gave a wry smile. 'Don't worry, I don't expect you to invite me up. We both know that if I wanted to be inside your flat, then that's where I'd be.'

Henry acknowledged that with a slight inclination of his head. 'And so?'

The woman made a gesture with her right hand and the rings on every finger glittered beneath the streetlamps – she wasn't called Diamond Annie for nothing. Annie mainly ran gangs of young women who specialized in lifting stock from London's most prestigious shops. Annie selected her girls with care, ensuring they would look the part. Dressed much the same as the bright young things flitting about the capital, they frequented the most fashionable establishments, stole to order and then shipped their thefts out of London, often within the same hour. There were also much darker and more violent sides to Annie's operation, and Henry knew she kept tight control of all her dealings. One of the men came over and handed her an envelope. Annie held this out to Henry. 'Your sergeant came and visited one of my houses today.'

'One of *your* houses?'

She smiled. 'One of the houses in one of my streets. I consider them mine – you know that. But we ain't going to argue about that now. It so happens I didn't like the look of 'im, the man what took the room with Nellie Hayes. So I had him watched. You'll excuse the writin'. My lads ain't schooled, but you'll be able to make it out.'

'Why would you want to help me, Annie?'

'Like I said, I didn't like the man.'

She turned away, going back to her companions and strolling down the street as though she owned the place. But then, Henry thought, Diamond Annie walked everywhere as though she owned the place. For her to approach him in this manner, to have come herself – that suggested she was rattled. That suggested that the envelope she had given him was going to prove important.

Henry let himself in through the front door and went up to his flat, half afraid that, despite what she had said, Annie had already been there. The door was still firmly locked and a quick inspection suggested that nothing had been disturbed, though it bothered him somewhat that she knew where he lived, and he not only locked the door but fastened the deadbolt before settling down to read the papers she had given him.

They were in a form of a daily diary, written in several hands, some pretty illegible and others printed in clear capitals but with execrable spelling. A few were in a neat and rounded hand, and Henry guessed that these had been dictated later by someone, or several someones, for whom letters were still a mystery.

He was surprised to find that this record covered just over six weeks and, from the dates involved, it appeared that Mr Ansel Peach had moved to the boarding house only days after the stock market crisis in September. Henry thought back to the records that he and Mickey had perused that afternoon, certain that Peach's full losses had not become apparent until early October. The man had certainly lost a great deal on 20 September but his greatest downfall had come because he had invested what funds he had remaining into yet more stock – and Henry knew from other records he had read that afternoon that many of these purchases had not been made with Ansel Peach's own money – and these too had failed. This was a man that, towards the end of his investments, had definitely been buying on the margin, and, as Cynthia had explained to Henry, that meant putting up perhaps ten or twenty per cent of the value of stock in your own money and borrowing the rest. This worked well in a rising market, but if the market fell and the brokers then called their margins in, that meant you were liable for the immediate repayment of the whole loan. If you could not repay your loan in full, then your entire investment was forfeit and the broker could sell your shares on. Henry could understand how such a precipitate fall could render someone bankrupt quite literally overnight, not to mention all the money they had lost from other investors, forcing them to sell up and take refuge somewhere like Mrs Hayes's boarding house. But the fact was Peach had not been in that position when he made that move. He seemed to have moved some time before his financial situation necessitated it. His losses would not have become apparent immediately, and yet he had made speed to leave his address very shortly after the London Stock Exchange's crash. This compared so oddly to all of those who Henry knew were trying to carry on as normal, to maintain the appearance that nothing serious had happened . . . why would he have done that?

Glancing through the rest of the notes, Henry was surprised at the detail. Someone had watched Peach twenty-four hours a day. They recorded when he got up, when he went out, what mail he received. Henry seriously doubted that police surveillance could have been more thorough.

Intrigued, but too tired to read through all the documentation that night and also wary of handling it too much (he'd prefer for it to be dusted for prints first, so at least they had some idea of *who* was keeping this surveillance – they were almost certain to have a police record), Henry slipped everything back into the envelope and from there into his coat pocket, and then he took himself to bed. Thinking about it, Henry saw the hand of Otis Freeland here. Annie's excuse that she didn't like the man was probably true, but there was more to it than that. Otis had probably financed Annie's observations, he thought. Henry was not sure if that made him feel better or more anxious. Strange bedfellow, Otis, Henry thought.

That night he dreamed of Diamond Annie, her hands bright in the streetlight's beam, scattering flashes of light.

TEN

The following morning Henry handed everything over to the fingerprint department in their eyrie overlooking the river on the highest floor of New Scotland Yard. They had promised they would return the documents to him that afternoon once any fingerprints they had found had been photographed, but the cross-referencing could take a day or two.

He arrived back to Central Office to find that Lady Helena Helford had been tracked down and that she was not as far away as they had first thought. She had gone to stay with her daughter in Bedford. Within the hour Henry and Mickey were on the train, and very soon walking between the rows of red-brick Victorian houses, finding their destination was only a few streets from the station, on Preston Road. The house was a pleasant one, a three-storey villa with a tiny frontage and a large front door. Lady Helford had been told to expect them, but it was her daughter who answered the door and led them inside.

Dora Brown was a handsome woman, now in her late forties, and it was evident from the moment she welcomed them that she was deeply troubled. Her mother looked like an older and greyer version of Dora with a delicate, almost heart-shaped face, pale-blue eyes and a wealth of thick, wavy hair. A younger woman sat beside Lady Helford, and Henry immediately wondered if this was Dora's own child – the likeness was unmistakable. She held a toddler on her lap, fairer haired than her elders but with the same pale eyes and heart-shaped face. It was clear that the women were afraid and Mickey immediately responded to this.

'Hope you don't mind my abruptness,' he said, 'but what is going on here?'

The three adult women exchanged a glance and Dora sat down heavily. Then got up again. 'I should make tea. I'm so sorry, I don't know where my manners are.'

'Refreshments can wait,' Henry said quietly. Turning to face the oldest woman, he continued, 'We came to talk to you about the ransacking of your house, Lady Helford, and about who might have been threatening your husband. But I think there is more that you need to tell me.'

Dora Brown picked up a little tapestry bag. It contained wool and knitting needles and something else, wrapped in a piece of cloth. She glanced anxiously at her daughter, Alice, and at her grandchild, and then led the police officers over to a little side table and opened her bundle. Inside was a soft toy. It had once been a rabbit, Henry guessed from the long ears. But the toy had been shredded and mutilated with a very sharp knife. Or with a razor, Henry thought.

'There was a note with it,' Dora said. 'I'm so sorry, but Mother was so horrified she threw it on the fire. This was Violet's favourite toy.'

The little girl, hearing her name, looked up eagerly. Dora dropped her voice to a whisper.

'Two nights ago, we couldn't find it before she went to bed, and she cried herself to sleep, but this morning this was left on our doorstep. And the note said that next time it would not just be a toy rabbit. Detective Chief Inspector, they are threatening my grandchild. When the toy went missing, we assumed it must be somewhere in the house. Knowing how fond of it Violet is, we don't let her take it out with her, just in case it gets lost. This was her bedtime toy. We are all certain it was left on her pillow, which means that someone . . .' She swallowed sharply, clearly trying hard not to cry. 'Someone came into our home and took the toy and did this to it.'

'What time did you find the toy? Have you informed the local constabulary?'

'A little after nine. And they sent some stupid constable round, who kept telling us it was a child's prank. That this time of year around Halloween and Guy Fawkes Night, "youngsters get up to all sorts of tricks".'

'And the note had been burned by then?'

'I'm so sorry,' Lady Helford said from her seat. 'I read it and I cast it into the fire. I was so frightened by it.'

'And what did it say?' Henry enquired.

She pursed her lips as though she considered the query impudent. 'Threats,' she said. 'Threats to the child.'

He waited, then asked, 'And was there more?'

'Is that not enough? Chief Inspector, he threatened my grandchild. I did not commit the exact wording to memory. I was too shocked for that.'

Again he waited but it was evident that this was all she was prepared to say. 'And the constable was perhaps not convinced there was a note?' Henry said.

'But there was. We are not making this up, Detective Chief Inspector.'

'We don't think you are,' Mickey reassured her hurriedly. 'Lady Helford, Mrs Brown, is there somewhere you can all go to? Somewhere as far from here as possible? And is your husband in residence, Mrs Brown?'

'I was widowed in the war,' she said. 'Alice was only a child at the time. My husband went away and did not return, so I raised Alice alone, with my parents' help, of course. Alice came to stay only because she wished to spend time with her grandmother, after her grandfather's death. But they've already packed and will catch the train and return to her husband in Aberdeen this afternoon.'

'That will at least put distance between them and whoever has made these threats,' Mickey said. 'And will you go with them?'

'No, Mother and I plan to visit relatives in Cornwall. They were a little surprised when I telephoned this morning, but I explained the situation to them and that is where we will go. I think it best that we put distance between *ourselves* and Alice and little Violet.'

'Probably wise,' Mickey said. 'If you give us the address, where you will be staying and, of course, your daughter's home address then we'll inform the local police and ensure that they do take notice of your safety.'

Dora hesitated and then nodded briefly, but Henry sensed that the dismissive tone of the local constable had left her with little faith in the effectiveness of provincial police.

'When the toy was returned, was it wrapped in anything?' he asked.

'In butcher paper,' Dora said. She crossed to a roll-top desk and opened it, and took out a piece of white paper, handling it gingerly by the corners as though it might be contaminated. Mickey was quick to put this and the shredded toy into a large brown-paper bag that Dora fetched from the kitchen. Intending only to conduct an interview, he had not brought his evidence bag with him and Henry could see that his sergeant now felt himself sadly unprepared and very put out.

'Lady Helford, we need to speak with you before you leave,' Henry told her.

The older lady composed herself carefully. 'Of course, Detective Chief Inspector. But perhaps you'd allow my daughter and grand-daughter to continue packing – we would all rather be gone as soon as possible.'

'Of course. And perhaps you will allow my sergeant and myself to escort you to the station?'

Lady Helford hesitated. 'Detective Chief Inspector, we have decided that we are going to take a taxi and leave from Luton rather than Bedford. We think the station there might be safer. It's clear that we have been watched here, our habits observed, and whoever threatened us knows exactly how to strike. I must admit I was in two minds about whether I should speak to you at all, but I have never been a coward and it's too late in life for me to start now. So I *will* speak to you and I *will* answer your questions, and then we *will* get into a taxi and go away from here and hope not to be followed. There is no doubt whoever this is will know that my granddaughter and her child are returning home and that does trouble me. Therefore, I accept your suggestion that you notify the local constabulary. Dora and I will be going to a village where strangers will stand out and where we are well known. Frankly, I consider that will assure our safety far better than a local constable might.'

Henry nodded but refrained from comment. 'Did you have any suspicion that your husband's death was not an accident?'

'What sort of stupid question is that? Of course I did. Ralph sent me away believing that there was danger. I didn't fully understand what was going on, but I knew that he was a frightened man and believe me, Chief Inspector, Ralph was no coward either. I thought at first he was afraid of his creditors, that he wished to spare me the embarrassment of being at home when they came knocking at the door, but he assured me that he had paid his debts, and that I had nothing to worry about on that score. Which, of course, caused me even more worry as I'm sure you'll understand.'

'You worried about where he had obtained the money to pay his creditors?' Henry stated.

'Indeed I did. He assured me that he had borrowed from a friend, that this friend was an honourable man and could well afford the loan. He told me that he had secured the loan against our house, that he felt he had to do this but that his friend had not pressured him to do so, but that he felt it was also an honourable thing to do. That worried me, Chief Inspector, that worried me a great deal.'

'He risked leaving you homeless?' Mickey said.

'He did, indeed. Dora, of course, would have taken care of us, just as we took care of her when she needed assistance. I love my daughter very much, and I am proud to say that she loves me, but nevertheless, it would have been more than an inconvenience. We are of an age when we do not want to worry about where we shall die or where we will end our days. Of course, poor Ralph does not have to worry about those things any longer.'

She paused and dabbed her eyes and they held the silence for a moment longer before Mickey said, 'And in the days before he sent you away, how was his state of mind? What did he tell you about who was threatening him?'

'Very little. It was clear that there was something on his mind, but he told me that he could deal with it and that it was nothing for me to worry about. In itself, that troubled me. You see, we had a remarkably close and equal marriage. I had supported him whole-heartedly early in his career when he was just setting up in practice. I managed all his paperwork and his accounts. I kept house on very little. Those early days were lean times, as I'm sure you know they often are for medical men. But gradually he carved a path for himself. He was a great surgeon, Chief Inspector, a successful man and when the knighthood was bestowed I know he felt that his achievement was complete.

'We have had a long life together and I thought he would confide in me but with this, it seemed he wanted to keep everything out of my grasp. Chief Inspector, you can see how much that must've disturbed me.'

'This loan . . . did he not give any clue as to where it might have come from? Did he tell you the name of this friend?'

'Someone he knew from the club he went to. It was his habit to go perhaps twice a week, sometimes he would even spend the night there. I was never troubled about this because it had always been his habit to do so. I understand that sometimes men need to escape from domesticity just as much as women do, and I had my commit-tees, and my ladies' afternoons. He said it was someone he knew well, that he had known for a long time, but that for the sake of decency they would keep this as a personal transaction, one simply between old acquaintances.'

'And he used that term, "old acquaintances",' Henry queried. 'Not old friends?'

'No. I suppose it does seem curious, but to be truthful Ralph's old *friends* are mostly other medical men and while they were mostly comfortably off, they were comfortably off because they had worked lifelong not because they had inherited money or had any to spare. Ralph had been investing on the stock market all of our married life. Not big investments, you understand, and usually very sensible ones. As a result of that we had a little pot of money each year that we could use to help our daughter when she was younger, or to take a holiday or to put aside for after our retirement so we could maintain our independence. You understand that this was very important to us, that we should have savings so that we were not dependent on anyone else in our old age.'

'So your husband lost your life savings?' Henry said bluntly.

Lady Helford blanched and Mickey said quickly, 'I'm sure he had the best of intentions when he made those investments. Many have been caught out both here and in America, people who have invested wisely for all these years.'

'I will sell the house, of course,' she said, but her tone was cold. 'And I will retire to somewhere quiet. What has happened cannot be undone, but my husband is dead and my family threatened so rather than pass judgement on my husband's mistakes, I suggest you discover who killed him and why and who would have the indecency to threaten a small child.'

She stood then and told them both that she intended to finish her own packing and that she had nothing further to say. Henry hadn't finished with her, however.

'You had servants in your home. A cook, a maid and a valet, I believe.'

'What of it? We also had another maid, a child of sixteen or so, a relative of our cook.'

'And where are they now?'

Lady Helford frowned. 'The maid has found employment elsewhere, I believe. My cook, I hope, will return. I've paid her half wages for three months and I believe she is with her aunt in Margate.'

'I need the address,' Henry told her.

'And why do you need that? You don't suspect her, surely?'

'We need to check everything and everyone,' Mickey said gently. 'It's possible that pressure was applied to one of your staff. Pressure to provide information on your household. On who does what and when.'

She was still annoyed. Even more annoyed when Henry asked, 'And your husband's valet?'

'How would I know where Parks has gone to?' she demanded. 'He was my husband's valet. I'd no use for him. When my husband died, I gave him notice and ensured he had good references. He left. I have no idea where he went to.'

'And had he been with you for long?'

'Long? A year or two, I suppose. Ralph had a man that stayed with him for years but then grew too old to be of use. So this one came. His references must have been satisfactory, I suppose, but the employment of a valet was my husband's concern, not mine. I hired the cook and the maid. He, as was only natural, dealt with the valet.'

Henry nodded. He checked names of the servants and waited impatiently while Lady Helford found addresses for her cook's relatives. Their references, she told him, would still be at their London home.

She was clearly impatient, both for them to be gone and to have herself departed. The taxi for the station arrived just as Henry and Mickey left. Henry wondered vaguely how long the cab would be kept waiting while the women finished with their preparations and if he should be feeling guilty that he had caused their delay.

He decided not.

'A familiar pattern seems to be emerging,' Henry said as the detectives got on the train.

'Of you offending elderly widows?' Mickey asked. 'No, but you are correct. There is a familiar pattern emerging, a pattern of criminality that is thriving because all of those concerned are part of the same social class, perhaps. That they are all people who share the understanding that silence is a virtue, and they should not include the hoi polloi – including the police – in their troubles. I suppose when you have been used to living high on the hog it's not a comfortable feeling when you slide off and hit the ground. It does seem to me, though, that many of these failed investors are men who already have much but want still more. My pity I have to admit is for those who invested what little they had, hoping to improve their lot. Even so, it's a game I would never play.'

'No more would I,' Henry agreed. 'I wouldn't know where to begin. Though Cynthia assures me that for the last decade the trend has been upward and most of those who took the risk have profited.'

'But what goes up,' Mickey said wisely, 'must come down again. Gravity will win in the end.'

ELEVEN

Before they had left for Bedford that morning, Mickey had learned about Diamond Annie's visit to Henry the previous night and had gone up to the fingerprint department and glanced briefly at the notes to take a look for himself. However, the carriage on their train had been crowded, leaving Henry and Mickey unable to discuss the matter further, but finding that they were alone in the compartment on their return trip, they picked up the conversation in earnest.

'The landlady said that Peach came and went, and she had little to do with him, and that does seem to be true. He goes off in the morning as though he has a job to go to, comes back in the evening in much the same way,' Mickey said.

'And Annie's people would have to be careful about tracking him into the territory of other gangs. Though it seems they tried, and what I'm getting from the handwriting is that the job was given either to children or women, both of which can pass more freely than the men known to be in Annie's employ.'

Mickey nodded. 'The neater handwriting, the statements you think were dictated, were certainly written in a woman's hand, I would have said. Some of the other notes too. And others by a child or an illiterate. But the sense of it can still be made out. When we get back, we must plot his routes on to the map, but from the quick glance I had, he seems to have followed the river, crossing backward and forward by the bridges, rarely using public transport or anything other than his own feet. If I were a cynic, Henry, I would suggest that he wanted to be followed, that he sought to make it easy for them.'

'I thought *I* was the cynic,' Henry said. 'At least we have a list of addresses to follow up. Places he visited, though most appear to be cheap cafés and small shops, which is interesting in its own right.' He glanced at his watch. 'Will there be time when we get back to London, I wonder, to go and visit Mrs Green, the woman who sent him that parcel? Or will that have to wait until tomorrow?'

'My suggestion,' Mickey said, 'is that we plot the routes out as soon as we get back. We look also at Mrs Green's address, and we see what cluster of businesses was visited by our Mr Peach. Those and Mrs Green's we can take in one go tomorrow. And we also take the time to assess what else Mr Enright might have sent us overnight. I swear that man seems to be ridding himself of all the files and folders he simply did not want his own office.' He paused, straightened in his seat, and doing a passable impression of the solicitor declared, '"Ah, this one is dead too – send his files to the police officers and let them deal with it. Another dead bankrupt? Well, we all know what to do with that." He probably has a standing order to his clerks that if his clients die, they are to send the file to Detective Chief Inspector Johnstone and Detective Sergeant Hitchens for "further investigation".'

Mickey could feel his superior looking at him curiously.

'You *are* out of sorts today,' Henry said. 'What's bothering you?'

Mickey looked out of the window, reluctant to reply, but finally admitted, 'If you must know, it was seeing that torn-up rabbit. I know it was only a little toy, but it was done with such malice, and to threaten a child with the same. What people are we dealing with here, Henry?'

Henry nodded, his grey eyes cold, river-pebble hard. 'Soon the child will be far away,' he said, 'and if the family have any sense, they will keep her far away. Keep themselves out of reach too.'

'You consider that's possible?' Mickey asked. 'Some criminal organizations have a long arm . . .'

'I do indeed, but frankly, Mickey, this does not strike me as one of those. This feels more focused, more hastily composed than some of the long-established gangs that we have dealings with. I may be wrong in this, of course, but for blackmail and extortion to thrive, those who are being extorted must stay silent. They must not draw attention to themselves, and we both know just how long some people allow themselves to be fleeced before they come asking for help. Embarrassment has a lot to answer for, Mickey. And yet look at the cases we know about. True, the knowledge of one was brought about by chance. If *I* had not attended Robert Cranston's death, if I had not been warned beforehand by the letter given to me at Cynthia's party, then his death might easily have been passed off as suicide.'

'It's to be hoped that the broken hyoid would have been picked up at the post-mortem,' Mickey disagreed.

'And we both know how carelessly suicides are treated. They are passed through, usually without full process being observed, coffined up and shipped back to the families for a quiet funeral, and that's if the family will accept them back, or if a family even knows. So many suicides end up in paupers' graves. So many poor souls who take their own lives put themselves beyond the pale, and no one in authority cares. If they are from a good family, then the coroner might be kind and rule their deaths as accidental, even if the evidence shouts that they died by their own hand.

'Anyway, if we look at Robert Cranston's death from another angle, such a cover-up was crude and showed a distinct lack of knowledge – and, yes, I'm aware I'm being contradictory, Mickey. But then there's the mysterious death of Mr Cranston's father to consider.'

'We don't know yet that it *was* mysterious,' Mickey objected.

'True, but the exhumations will take place in the next few days, and then we will have a much clearer picture.'

'And you have absolutely no reason to be suspicious of the death of Albert's friend?' Mickey reminded him. 'Your suspicions are aroused only because the man shot himself, same as our Cranston fellow. But if you think about it, if this Ferdy Bright-Cooper wanted to do away with himself, that's going to be the obvious thing. A man of his class and breeding, what's more likely than he should blow a hole in his head with his service revolver, no doubt after wasting a half decanter of good single malt?'

Henry narrowed his eyes at his sergeant. 'Somewhat bolshie comments, Mickey. Don't you have any respect for the class of Mr Ferdy Bright-Cooper and his ilk?'

Mickey just laughed. 'You know the answer to that one. I realize that they're not all tarred with the same brush, but . . .'

'Then we have Sir Ralph Helford. I am more and more convinced that his death was murder.'

Mickey nodded in agreement on that one. 'And the threats to his family – threats which speak in a particular brand of nastiness.'

'And perhaps a certain desperation. Threaten adults, and other adults will as often as not close ranks and will stand defiant to that threat. But threaten a child, and that's the way to truly frighten the family.'

'Especially such a sweet little mite as Violet.'

'And which, in this current context, makes no sense. They

threatened the child, but they were warning the family to do what? Or *not* to do what? Not speak to the police? Lady Helford gave no indication that they had been told explicitly *not* to speak to us, though I suppose she implied as much. As she said, she's no coward. However, the remainder of what she told us was in itself not especially useful. What is it Lady Helford knows that she *could* have told us? What did Sir Ralph Helford do that could have led us to those who killed him? I would like to go and look at the house again, the Helford residence, to see if there's anything I've missed. I didn't have the time to do a thorough search, and you weren't with me to see anything I failed to see.'

Mickey accepted the compliment without thinking. It was a simple fact that the pair were a good team. 'They didn't tell us not to come,' he said. 'The Helford women seemed willing to speak to us. I just wish Lady Helford had not burned that note.'

'Ah, now I believe that is the crux of the matter. Why did she burn it? Do you, for one minute, believe that she was so overwhelmed with horror that she threw it into the fire? For that matter, does she strike you as the kind of woman who would do that purely on the impulse of momentary shock?'

'No,' Mickey agreed, seeing what his boss was driving at. 'She seemed cool and in control. Upset, of course, genuinely so. But no, the note said something, told her something, gave instructions as to what they should do if they wished to keep their child safe. If that instruction was to send the child and her mother home and for the widow and her daughter to remove themselves from our reach, then I suppose they are following those instructions. But what if it said something else? It's possible,' he laughed shortly, 'that there were even instructions for the handling of any police officers that came calling.'

'Well, she's not about to tell us, that's for certain.'

'No,' Mickey agreed. 'She struck me as a tough old bird. Let's just hope that Aberdeen and Cornwall are far enough away. Whether the local police will take the threat seriously, we've little evidence to go on. As the Bedford constable said, a chopped-up toy rabbit could look like a juvenile prank. Except, of course, they are right, these women. If that toy was taken from the child's bed then either the thief broke in or someone already in the house gave them the toy rabbit.'

'There were no servants in the house today,' Henry observed.

'No, I did ask about that. Dora Brown has a daily maid who comes in to help with the cooking and cleaning, and Lady Helford, as we now know, did not bring her own staff with her. The cook has gone to visit relations and the maid found other work, or so she told us.'

'Well, the local constabulary can make up for their dismissive attitude by interviewing Dora Brown's daily maid,' Henry said sourly. 'I suppose we can entrust that task to them and have her fingerprints taken, so that we can compare them to our records.'

They were nearing London now, and Mickey asked, 'What prints were found at the Helford house? Do any of the staff there have a record?'

'I've not been told that they do, but will double-check,' Henry told him. 'It seems, from what we learnt today, that the valet had not been with Sir Ralph for long, and it might also be worth tracking down the previous valet and establishing background information on the household. The cook, according to the neighbours – or rather, according to the neighbouring staff who can always be relied upon to know these things – has been with the household for some time, so she would also be a source of useful information.'

'Loyalty might keep her quiet,' Mickey observed.

'It might, but that depends on what terms her mistress parted with her. Keeping her on half pay for three months, just in case she's wanted back doesn't give the poor woman much to live on.'

'Especially as she would have had room and board with the doctor and his wife,' Mickey added.

'Especially that. Neither does it free her to look for work elsewhere, and I very much doubt that Mrs H would have given her the references until such time as she was definitely done with her. She didn't strike me as a particularly flexible woman.'

The train pulled into the station with a screech and a huff, and Henry fastened his overcoat and stared quietly out of the window.

He seems preoccupied, Mickey thought. 'You are troubled by Annie's visit,' Mickey guessed.

'Among other things.' Henry seemed to hesitate and Mickey had the sense that he was about to tell him something. Then the moment passed and Henry said, 'Annie and her gang would usually take matters into their own hands. If someone came on to their ground and made trouble, or their face did not fit, then they would be unlikely to stay for long. They'd either be driven out, forcibly removed or made to feel so uncomfortable that they left of their own accord. The Forty Elephants do not simply observe and then bring their intelligence to Scotland Yard.'

'She didn't, though, did she?' Mickey reminded him as they stepped down from the train. 'She brought it to *you*.'

Henry cast him a sharp glance, as though realizing that his sergeant had put a finger on exactly the point of irritation. 'She came to *me*,' he agreed. 'She sought *me* out, came to *my* home. Now why would she do that?'

When Henry returned to his flat that evening he found himself reflecting on the train journey. He'd been a bit short with Mickey, mindful of Otis's warnings not to involve his sergeant, but he felt uneasy about it. His sergeant had put a finger on the exact spot of his irritation when he'd pointed out that Diamond Annie had brought her intelligence to him. The previous evening he had sensed Otis Freeland's presence in this, but now he was even more certain. Otis had come to him because of the deaths of Walter Cole and Hayden Paul and because he said he was concerned for Henry's safety. What was Otis really concerned about? The answer to that was other people's reputations, those far higher up the social scale than Henry would ever be. Who were they? Henry wondered. Likely he'd not recognize their names even if Otis told him. Otis Freeland moved in much more rarefied circles even than Albert and Cynthia.

The desire to confide in Mickey was almost overwhelming. He felt no justification in keeping anything from his sergeant – or from Cynthia. As Otis himself admitted, their loyalty was unquestion-able . . . loyalty to Henry, anyway. Otis was probably far more interested in loyalty to the state, to the government, to those in power. He had admitted, freely enough, that Henry was simply bait.

It was an uncomfortable thought.

When he walked into his flat, he found two packages waiting for him. Both contained crime-scene photographs, post-mortem reports and initial observations from the investigating officers of the deaths of Detective Sergeant Walter Cole and Detective Chief Inspector Hayden Paul. Henry spread them out on his table and examined the two batches of photographs closely. Walter Cole lay face up, his feet on the threshold of his front door and his body lying across the narrow lane. Blood streaks on the ground showed where he had crawled, dragging himself across the quarry tiles of the kitchen floor and then outside, presumably trying to look for help. Perhaps he had stumbled back and fallen to the kitchen floor when he was attacked, Henry thought. His killer must have left the door open on leaving, for there was no way a man with that kind of wound, losing that volume of blood, could have stood up and reached the door handle.

Apparently the bundle of papers that Otis had been talking about, and which he considered so dangerous, had been grasped in the dead man's hand, and Henry found that strange. The officer in charge of the enquiry, Detective Inspector Bennett, had found it strange too. In his report, he came to the same conclusion that Henry now reached – that the killer had hung around, watching as Cole crawled out of the house into the open and had then placed the documents in his palm.

The farm worker who had found the body testified that Cole had been lying face up, and that he had not touched him. Neither had he looked at the letters grasped tight in the man's hand, rigour mortis fully established by that point.

'So,' Henry said to himself, 'you plunge the knife into his belly, you watch him fall, you walk away leaving the door open. You knew he would try to get outside – Cole was a strong man.' And even looking at him dead, Henry thought, you could see the muscular frame had not diminished even in older age.

'And you watch him die, and then you turn him over and you place your evidence or your manifesto, or whatever it is you're calling it, in his hand. How long do you wait thereafter, I wonder?'

Walter Cole had been stabbed but when Henry turned to the pictures of Hayden Paul he was struck immediately just how similarly the scene had been dressed, how identical it was to that of Robert Cranston. The same hand was at work here, he was certain of it. The post-mortem report, too, was very similar. Manual strangulation and then the bullet wound to the head, post-mortem.

Richardson had been a powerful man, a physical man. Was he still now? Henry did not, for one minute, think that Richardson would have delegated these killings to another person. He enjoyed killing far too much to allow someone else the pleasure.

TWELVE

The following morning Henry and Mickey decided that their first port of call should be with Mrs Green, the lady whose return address had been on the parcel containing the Camembert and the rest of Mr Ansel Peach's personal effects. Had she been a regular sender of food parcels to the unfortunate Mr Ansel Peach? And what had their relationship been?

They arrived at the address just after ten o'clock but were told that the lady was still not dressed and were asked to wait in the parlour. Mrs Green had a small but very plush apartment and a small, very neatly uniformed maid who answered the door, conveyed messages and eventually brought them both tea. The flat was decorated with antique furniture and pretty ornaments that seemed a little old fashioned; no deco or even art nouveau but a lot of Victorian, and thick rugs laid over the carpet, in some places two and three deep. Henry found himself wishing that he could remove his shoes and put on some carpet slippers; he would not have been surprised if the maid met their usual visitors – not police officers – at the door and insisted that they do so.

There were books, a lot of books, a mix of ageing hardbacks and modern romances. Mrs Green's taste – Henry didn't see any evidence of a Mr Green – seemed to be eclectic.

The lady herself appeared at ten forty-five, after keeping them waiting for around half an hour. Henry had expected someone older, given the decor of the flat, but Mrs Green was probably only in her late twenties. She was tall, slender, with dark, bobbed hair, and was immaculately made up, her lipstick a deep red and eyes lined with kohl. Henry thought that she looked as though she was going out in the evening and not simply prepared for having breakfast.

'Two policemen – goodness, how exciting. I will send for more tea.' She ran a little bell that had been set on the side table and the neat maid appeared once more, removed the tray and asked her lady if she was ready for breakfast.

'Can I offer you something to eat?' Mrs Green asked.

Henry and Mickey both declined. 'But tea is always welcome,' Mickey told her. 'And very good tea it is too.'

The lady smiled at him and gestured for them both to sit down again. 'So what can I do for you? I'm assuming it must be something serious to have both a detective chief inspector and a detective sergeant visit me.'

'We're here about Mr Ansel Peach,' Henry told her.

She pursed her deep red lips and tilted her head to one side as though considering this matter very deeply. 'A sad business,' she said. 'He was a nice little man – I was quite fond of him.'

'And did that fondness cause you to send him regular food parcels?' Henry asked.

She laughed, a deep, rich sound. 'Oh dear, is that how you tracked me down? I always put my return address on parcels. Now I see it is quite a foolish thing to do.'

'It's a particularly foolish thing to do when you are sending parcels to that particular region of our city,' Mickey told her quite sternly. 'More thieves per head than you'll find anywhere but Limehouse.'

She raised an eyebrow. 'I'm afraid I hadn't given it much thought. But yes, I did send Ansel food parcels. I felt sorry for him. It's hard to fall from grace, and he still hadn't landed, I don't think. The poor love didn't realize how deep in he already was and when things began to fail, I'm afraid he just kept digging.'

'So what was your relationship with Mr Peach?' Henry asked. The maid had returned with another tray of tea and Henry noticed the pinched look about her mouth when he mentioned Mr Peach by name and the glance of disapproval. She set the tray on a large Oriental ottoman between their chairs.

'He knew my husband, so I'd known him since I married, I suppose. When my husband died, many so-called friends just fell away. But not Ansel. He seemed to understand that once the funeral is over, a widow is very much left to cope on her own. Everyone assumes . . . I suppose everyone assumes that you want to be alone with your grief when, in fact, the opposite is very much the truth.'

'That must have been difficult for you,' Mickey said. 'When did your husband die, if you don't mind me asking?'

'Almost three years ago. We travelled a great deal, and he contracted a fever in Egypt. Sadly, he did not recover. I buried him there. It seemed appropriate, and then I returned here. I was left with enough to buy this little flat, furnish it, and Simmons and I rub along very nicely. Shall I pour the tea?'

Simmons, presumably, was the maid. 'Your maid lives in?' he asked.

'There's a small second bedroom. I suppose it was intended for use as a study, but I have little use for a study, and so Simmons has that.'

She sipped her tea and regarded them both expectantly. 'And so . . .?'

'Did you send Mr Peach a Camembert cheese?'

'Oh my Lord, is that illegal now?' She laughed. 'I sent him some cheese, socks, chocolates and some cigarettes. Various other things at different times. I thought it might cheer the poor fellow up. I thought it might tell him that his friends hadn't completely forgotten him, though I know that several had chosen to do so when he was no longer on the up. People can be damned fickle.'

'Indeed,' Mickey agreed. 'We have a previous address for Mr Peach. Could you perhaps confirm it for us, and could you perhaps tell us a little about these friends he might have had when he was, as you put it, "on the up"?'

'And why would you need to know any of that? Poor Ansel threw himself off a bridge. Presumably the disgrace became too great for him to bear. You know he lost everything?'

'His financial records indicate that he was in the process of doing so,' Henry agreed. 'However, it does seem odd to us that he chose to move from his home so precipitously when things began to go wrong, and yet he continued with his investments and, if I may say, his poor judgements. Would it not have seemed more sensible for a man of his financial experience to have stayed put and simply stopped investing? He could have recovered something.'

She shrugged. 'I don't know about that sort of thing. I've never really been interested. Ansel tried to get Oliver, my husband, to invest a time or two, but Oliver wasn't interested either.' She gestured towards the floor. 'He said he'd rather invest in rugs and antiques. Frankly, I doubt any of them are worth anything – I'm not sure he ever really knew what he was buying.'

'And yet you are left comfortably off?' Mickey asked her.

She pursed her lips again, this time in disapproval rather than thought. 'I suppose as a policeman you are paid to ask impudent questions, but I am not paid to answer them. My finances are my own affairs, not part of your investigation.'

'But presumably you would have no objection to giving us some background information on Mr Peach?' Henry said firmly.

'I have no objection, but I don't see the use of it. Ansel jumped off a bridge. The man couldn't bear his losses, that's all there is to it. It's not as though he was murdered or anything, so I don't quite see what your interest is.'

Henry had the sense that she was simply getting bored with them now, the novelty of having police officers in her little parlour wearing thin. 'Sometimes one investigation impinges on another, sometimes information overlaps,' he said. 'As you have noted already, it's our job to ask questions, impudent or not. So perhaps you could find pen and paper and write a list for us of any place where Mr Ansel Peach lived, any acquaintances or friendships he might have had, any trades you know about? Any loans he took out?'

She set her cup down hard on the saucer, loudly enough for Henry to be concerned about its survival.

'Very well, but you are very tiresome. I have not even breakfasted, and yet here you are, asking ridiculous questions about something which is really not *my* concern. And all because of a Camembert cheese!'

She crossed to a Davenport desk in the corner of the room and found paper and a pen. For several minutes she sat in silence scribbling on the piece of paper, occasionally lifting the pen to her mouth and chewing on the end, as a child might – and in a fashion that infuriated Henry, who felt that you should have respect for your pens. Finally she came back to them and thrust the sheet of paper at Mickey.

'Here, that's all I remember. Now if you've quite finished with me, Simmons will see you out.' She rang her little bell and then sailed off, leaving a trail of perfume and an air of ladylike annoyance in her wake.

Simmons ushered them to the door.

'And you did not think much of Mr Peach?' Henry said to the maid.

'None of my business, I'm sure, sir.'

'But it might be police business,' Henry told her coldly.

She looked slightly anxious and glanced back over her shoulder to where her mistress had gone. 'He weren't no gentlemen. No gentleman borrows money from a lady, sir.'

'He borrowed from Mrs Green?'

She didn't answer. The bell rang again and she turned away from them, closing the door as she did so. Mickey made to stop her to continue with the questioning, but Henry gestured to let it go. He led the way down the stairs, and when they were out in the street Mickey challenged him.

'Simmons knows more. We should speak to her.'

'And so we will. But wait.'

He led Mickey across the road, finding a place where they could watch the apartment block but not be observed.

Some twenty minutes later Mrs Green emerged, dressed in a grey, fur-trimmed coat and a neat little hat. She set off on foot and Mickey followed her at a distance.

Henry re-crossed the road and went back up to the flat. Simmons answered the door quickly, clearly not expecting the policeman.

'Have you forgotten something, ma'am?' she began, mistaking Henry for her mistress. 'Oh, it's you. The mistress isn't in, sir.'

'No, I'm aware of that. Where is she going?'

'I don't know, sir. I asked if she'd be back for dinner and she said yes, that's all I know.'

'But you know a good deal more about Mr Ansel Peach, don't you?'

'Why should I know about him? Like I told you, he weren't no gentleman. He might have dressed and acted like one, but he weren't one. Though my lady couldn't see that – she just saw that he was a friend of her husband's.'

She looked at Henry in exasperation, clearly realizing that he wasn't going to go away. 'You better come in, I suppose, better that than stand on the doorstep and have all the neighbours gawking.'

Henry wondered how all the neighbours were supposed to be gawking. Each apartment occupied a single floor with no other neighbours on this landing, but he supposed that Simmons was the kind of live-in servant who had become protective of her position and so also of her mistress and would be worried about possible scandal. He followed her through to the kitchen where she hovered awkwardly while he sat down at the table, and then she took the chair opposite.

'How long have you worked for Mrs Green?'

'Since she moved in here after her husband died. She bought the place, and she took out an advertisement for a live-in maid. Someone to take care of her, do her hair, run errands, do some light cleaning and cooking. She don't entertain very often and when she does she gets the caterers in and I just help out.'

'So you are both lady's maid and a maid of all work,' Henry stated. That earned him a scowl. Simmons obviously saw her position as far superior to that of a maid of all work.

'And so you must be aware of all the visitors that come here. Did Mr Peach visit very often?'

'No more than was proper, and never at night. A woman alone has to watch her reputation, even if she is a widow. People talk.'

'And you are happy in your position here?'

Simmons hesitated and then nodded. 'I've had worse. She is a little strange, but she pays well enough and I have my little room. Good food. I've had a lot worse.'

'And you answered an advertisement to get this position?'

'I did. She had interviewed at least a dozen already, but she took a liking to me and I moved in the next day.'

'And before this?'

She frowned at him. 'Why are you asking me all these questions? I've done nothing wrong. I have good references.'

Henry nodded. 'Good references matter,' he said.

She looked curiously at him. 'Most young women want to work in an office, or a typing pool, or even a shop. I tried shop work. Shop work is all very well, but I wouldn't go back to it now.' She stood then, dismissing Henry as effectively as her mistress had done earlier. Henry did not move.

'Mr Ansel Peach may not have visited at night, but I wonder, does your mistress have any night-time visitors?' he asked.

She stared at him as outraged as if he had slapped her. 'I don't know what you're suggesting, but I think you should go now, sir. My mistress isn't here, but this is still her place, and I won't have her badly spoken of.'

Henry retrieved his hat and left obediently.

Mickey had followed Mrs Green, a little anxious in case she should hail a cab and leave him behind. To his surprise and relief, she walked, making her way on to Horton Street, and then entered a building that looked as though it was given over to offices. He stood in the rather smart, recessed doorway and watched as she got into the lift, going up to the fourth floor. In the lobby, the signage told him the fourth floor housed a language academy, a typing school, a solicitors' and an investment advice service.

'Now let me guess which one you are headed for,' Mickey said to himself. He took the stairs, arrived at the fourth floor, but there was no sign of Mrs Green.

The language academy was opposite the lift, the typing school and the solicitors' a little down the hallway to his left. Assuming that she did not need to learn a new language, and probably had no reason to learn to type, then the solicitors' and Regent Financial Services seemed much more likely. Even though he wasn't a betting man, his money would have been on the latter, but in the cause of thoroughness he opened the door to the solicitors' office and glanced around the tiny reception area. On the desk was a bell and instructions to ring for the receptionist, who had apparently stepped away from her post. Behind the reception area were two offices, each with part-glazed doors. In one, a lone man worked, puzzling over some papers, and in the other a man was speaking to an older lady, definitely not Mrs Green. There was definitely nowhere else she could have gone within this particular operation.

Down the hall to the right was Regent Financial Services. The door to these offices was also partly glazed. The business name was painted on the glass, but Mickey could see traces of the previous name not completely scrubbed away. He made out the name of Dr Shaw and wondered what Dr Shaw's business had been. Mrs Green wasn't in the reception area, but there *was* a receptionist who asked politely if she could help him.

'This may sound faintly ridiculous, my dear, but I'm sure I saw an acquaintance of mine coming here. A lady, a Mrs Green?'

He had made the request sound faintly absurd and himself slightly dotty, and the girl behind the desk smiled at him in a fondly patronizing kind of way. 'No, I'm sorry, no one of that name has come in here. You might have mistaken Mrs Connacht for your friend, a lady dressed in a dark grey coat. Does your friend have a dark grey coat? It's easy to make a mistake.'

Mickey looked suitably embarrassed. 'Oh dear, oh dear, you must think me such a fool.' He retreated quickly, leaving her smiling at his silliness.

Interesting, he thought. So she was Mrs Green at home and Mrs Connacht when she visited Regent Financial Services. Did they know that she was misleading them, or was whoever she was visiting in on the deception? Unless Mrs Connacht was her real identity?

He left and strolled slowly back to meet Henry. They compared notes, standing outside the apartment block.

'Connacht,' Henry said. 'Connacht.'

Mickey noted his expression, the slight frown as though he was trying to recall something. 'You recognize the name?'

'There's something familiar, but I can't recall from where.' He shrugged impatiently.

'So another visit will be necessary. This time to Mrs Connacht rather than Mrs Green. I'll try to arrange some surveillance on this block, see who comes and goes, if the men can be spared. I think we'll come back tomorrow, early, very early. Early enough that any evening visitors might still be present.'

THIRTEEN

The surroundings of their next visit could not have differed more. Diamond Annie might be the queen of the Forty Elephants but her domain, though within spitting distance of the West End, was one of back-to-back houses, terraced courts, corner shops and people struggling to make ends meet, no matter how hard they worked, be that legal or otherwise. Annie was head of the biggest shoplifting gang in London and probably outside of London too, and the Elephants were women, in the main, led by a woman.

There was one similarity between Annie and Mrs 'Green': Annie also kept them waiting twenty or so minutes, but Henry didn't think it was so that she could attend to her hair and cosmetics. More likely she was ensuring that nothing identifiable as stolen was visible at the house where they were meeting. Though, on reflection, Henry thought this was unlikely too; anything Diamond Annie's girls stole was in a taxicab on the way to the station, packed in a trunk and off on the next train almost before those who had been fleeced realized it was missing. Annie's organization wasn't restricted to London but was countrywide. Anything else her gang might be responsible for was more likely to be left bleeding on the pavement than brought back to Annie's home.

A child opened to the door to them, then ran back inside to check with someone else – they heard a man's voice – as to the advisability of allowing two police officers into the front parlour. The child, a boy of about nine or ten, returned only moments later and ushered them inside and then stood guard in the doorway, looking both nervous and self-important until Annie herself arrived.

The room was clean and neat, containing a single fireside chair and two wooden seats either side of a table beside the window. When Annie arrived, she took the fireside chair but did not look too pleased to see them.

'You read what I gave you. You've no need to come here – all you needed to know was in those papers.'

'And very entertaining reading they were too,' Mickey commended her, taking the lead. 'But one question they don't answer, Annie, is why you went to all this trouble. Your usual rule is if you don't like the look of someone, then they are urged to leave. If they don't respond to the urging, then you send the boys round to make sure they do. So why the surveillance? If you didn't like the look of the man, why put up with him?'

Annie's eyes narrowed. She had a reputation for violence. It was said that she never removed the diamond-studded rings she wore on her every finger, not even in a fight. Especially not in a fight. Mickey had met grown men, big strong men who had no trouble admitting they would be wary of taking on Annie when she was poised for a bruising.

'So my first question is what didn't you like about him? My second, what was it that you didn't like so much that you wanted him watched? And finally, if you really didn't like him that much, why was he still here six weeks later?'

'Were you collecting this intelligence on behalf of someone else?' Henry asked her. He knew she would not respond to this, but he wanted her to be aware that they knew she was being paid to do this. If he was right about that, of course.

Annie's expression did not change, but he noticed a slight tension in her shoulders; he was on the right track. 'And if that's the case, what do they think of you passing this information on to me, or was that part of the original instruction?'

Mickey, appearing puzzled, glanced at him but said nothing.

Annie remained silent for a while, clearly considering her options, and Henry was quite happy to wait her out. He sat staring out of the window, noticing the passers-by. The broad mix of races and origins was not uncommon in the East End of London. Few people looked towards Annie's house, most keeping their eyes fixed ahead or on the pavement in the opposite direction. He doubted many police officers had been inside Annie's house. She was arrested frequently but most of these had taken place elsewhere. And she usually walked away from those anyway.

'I suspect Mr Peach wasn't all he claimed to be,' Henry said finally. 'He moved here and I wonder why that was. He seemed intent on keeping away from somebody or something, perhaps. He was a man who began to lose, but did not take warning and stop. He continued to gamble and yet his financial records show that he was not a gambling man, not a risk-taker. So after the crash of September, why did he continue to pursue these risks and why did he move here? Did he come here asking for protection, Annie? A strange thing to do perhaps, but I think he was a man afraid.'

'You been doing a right old lot of thinking,' she told him. 'He never made any trouble on my patch, but I wasn't sure what his game was. Sure as hell 'e had one. A man like that, come walking down the street bold as brass one day, knocked on Nellie Hayes's door and said he understood she got a room for rent. Never went nowhere else first, just straight to Nellie Hayes's house. Well, if that ain't an oddity, you tell me what is. But why would he come here? London is not short of flop houses and cheap boarding.'

'And so Mrs Hayes let him have the room?'

'When she told me about him, my boys had already spotted him, of course. She wanted to know what to do, if she were right to let him stay. And I figure there's something up and I want to know what it is and so I 'ave 'im watched. You tell me you wouldn't have been suspicious.'

'I would have been suspicious,' Henry confirmed. 'But that doesn't answer my sergeant's earlier question. Why didn't you simply have him removed if you didn't like him? Why let him stay if you were suspicious of him?'

Annie grinned, revealing a flash of gold. 'Figured he might be up to something, figured there might be a profit in it. He was a toff, didn't pretend to be anything but. So I gets to thinking, what's he doing hiding out here? What might be in it for me and mine?'

'It's still a lot of effort to put in on the off chance,' Mickey argued. 'From what I've seen of the report, there's at least a dozen people involved in keeping surveillance.'

Annie shrugged. 'Kids watch anyone what comes in, whether I asked them to or not. Do it for fun and a few coins, don't they? My girls liked to keep an eye out for trouble, it's what they do, ain't it? My boys are always around in case they spot anything what shouldn't be going on. That's what *they* do. So no, not much effort. Not above what's normal. Anyway, the way I see it, it might be good training for them.'

'The problem is,' Henry said, 'I'm guessing he knew he was being followed. I suspect he even encouraged it. Did you suspect that too, Annie?'

She nodded slowly. 'I come to think he was using my people to protect himself. He knew they were around, knew they would be known, knew not many would be willing to take them on. I figure he were a clever sort; I figure he was shit-scared too.'

'Scared of what? Scared of whom? Did you get a sense of that?'

Again the slow shake of the head. 'He didn't seem to do a whole lot of anything. He walked. He drank tea. He went into a few places of business where my people couldn't follow, but if you've seen the notes, you know they went and spoke to anyone they could after. Find out what he wanted.'

Henry nodded, though the truth was he had not read the notes thoroughly yet. But he would, as soon as he and Mickey returned to Central Office. 'And what did you think when he threw himself off the bridge?' he asked.

'I just figured he must be able to swim,' Annie said.

'You don't think he's dead?' Mickey was genuinely surprised at the thought.

'You know, you lot don't always credit me as being too bright,' Annie said, 'but you think about my organization and you must realize that I am indeed very far from stupid.'

'I've never considered you stupid,' Henry said.

'Dangerous, immoral, so crooked you have to screw your hat on,' Mickey agreed. 'But no, not stupid. Sensible enough that you surround yourself with people ready to take the fall for you. Sensible enough that even though everybody and his dog knows what you're up to, you've not been put away for more than six months or so at a time. I suppose that takes a kind of raw intelligence.'

Annie did not look offended at this judgement. She laughed

harshly. 'I read the papers, I know what's in the news, I know what's been happening with the stock markets, and you'd be surprised at how much of it I understand. Had a flutter myself from time to time. Difference between me and Ansel Peach is I knew when to get out.' She leaned forward. 'And I'd not be so stupid as to borrow from the wrong men.'

'And what men might those be?'

Annie narrowed her eyes. 'You read those notes of mine properly and you'll see. Look like respectable businesses, don't they? But I'm not the only one needs to screw their hat on. Corkscrew tight, that's what they are. Corkscrew tight.'

A young woman came and stood in the doorway, and Annie nodded to her and then got up to leave. 'I gave you all I had; I gave it to you because I believe that bastard Peach might bring trouble to my door. So you go and deal with it.'

'And do you consider yourself unable to deal with that trouble?' Henry asked.

Annie, when she turned to him, was not afraid, but he could see that she was concerned. This was not the kind of trouble she was used to dealing with, not perhaps the kind of trouble that could be flattened with a blackjack or have its face taken off by a clutch of diamond rings wielded by a hefty fist.

'More in your line of trouble than mine,' she said.

'So what do you make of all that?' Mickey asked as they walked back towards Scotland Yard. 'It seems our Mr Peach kept within the bounds of Annie's influence when he went off on his walks.'

'When he did stray further, it was because he was sure of his own safety in those particular locations, which suggests perhaps he had alternative boltholes available to him should he need them. Or was there a legitimate reason? Was he looking for work? The solicitor's records are vague as to what he did before the crash. We know he traded on the stock market and that towards the end he bought too heavily on the margin. We need to look more closely at these businesses he visited, if we can establish which businesses he actually did visit. From what I can make out, from a swift perusal of Annie's notes, most of the buildings he visited are tenanted by a number of offices and occupations. It would be easy enough, if any are involved in something illegal, to claim no knowledge of a Mr Ansel Peach or to say that he was simply among the many now seeking work and it would be the Devil's own job for us to prove otherwise. So exactly what is he doing on these walks of his? I don't know, Mickey, none of it makes sense. Annie clearly doesn't believe that he committed suicide. She clearly doesn't believe that he's dead and yet the witness statements . . .'

'We need to examine the witness statements again,' Mickey agreed. 'No one was close to him when he jumped and no one, from what I remember, recalls hearing him splash down into the river or seeing him sink below the surface. We should go and examine the scene for ourselves.'

'We will attend to that tomorrow,' Henry agreed. 'When we have returned to see Mrs Green and also to speak to this Regent Finance Business, or whatever it's called. We must see if they have come to our attention before. And also look at the solicitors' records, see if they are mentioned by anyone, although I don't recall them and I think I might. And we need to have a proper look at Annie's notes as neither of us has done more than skim them.'

'I'm still not convinced by her story of why she came to you. There's more to this, Henry. Annie is disturbed by something. Something out of her ken and out of the ordinary, and that I find worrying indeed.'

Henry nodded. He still suspected that Otis had a hand in this surveillance of Annie's and he was so tempted to spill his suspicions to Mickey. But he had no wish to put his sergeant, his friend, in as difficult a position as Henry felt himself to be in. Impatiently, Henry dug down into Otis's reasons for wanting such secrecy. Government concerns, Otis had implied, but was it not simply more likely, as Otis had also hinted, because those who had petitioned for Richardson's release were important men whose reputations would be smirched if it came out that their protégé had gone on the rampage once released?

If so, then it was no more than they deserved.

He thought of why they had wanted Richardson released – of how, according to Otis, pressure had been brought to bear. The threat of blackmail or extortion . . . which of course was Richardson's stock-in-trade.

He was aware of his sergeant looking curiously in his direction. Mickey knew him too well – he would be aware that something other than the immediate case was on his boss's mind. Henry hoped that Mickey would be able to forgive what might seem like lack of trust.

FOURTEEN

At ten in the evening, long after Mickey had gone home and most of his colleagues disappeared for the evening, Henry sat at his desk turning over the nagging problem laid out in front of him. He had read Annie's report thoroughly now, as had Mickey, but he still felt that he was missing something. There were four businesses that Ansel Peach visited on more than one occasion and two that warranted only a single visit. Henry had briefly examined records on the businesses that afternoon. Five were well-established and associated with charities; they were friendly societies that acted as banks, and small-scale lenders, and had spotless reputations. Henry was inclined to believe that this was misdirection on the part of Ansel Peach. He would, however, dispatch constables to ask them about Ansel Peach or anyone answering his description.

The other business was known to be dubious. Crench and Associates, insurance brokers, were upstairs from a jewellery shop that had twice been prosecuted for handling stolen goods. The owners of the building in which the businesses were housed were directors of both establishments. That would require further investigation, Henry thought, but he guessed that Otis would already be examining this particular angle.

Some of their visits were only a matter of minutes and at others he had stayed inside for more than an hour. One of the addresses Peach visited was the building occupied by Regent Financial Services. Annie's spy had not ventured inside; from the handwriting, Henry guessed that he was only a child, so he was not surprised that he had not followed Ansel Peach up to the fourth floor – supposing that's where he'd gone, which Henry thought likely. Based on this supposition, there was a link, a direct link, between Mrs Green or whatever she wanted to call herself, Mr Peach and this business. Had he gone to meet Mrs Green there? It would appear that their acquaintance was more than casual. This particular office was also well outside of Annie's ground, and the route that Peach had taken was circuitous, as though he had been avoiding certain areas or ensuring that the boy could easily follow him. Now why

would someone want to be followed? Henry wondered. True, his
and Annie's first theory that this was in some way for protection
might hold good, but not when only a child was involved in
the pursuit.

He also had the list that his brother-in-law had prepared of the
so-called gentleman lenders before him. Four of these names also
cropped up in the solicitors' paperwork that had been sent to them
from Enright and Baines. The context of one Mr Russell Clovis was
a private loan, which fit with what Henry had been told by Albert.
Clovis, it seemed, was a businessman and mill owner, who had both
made money and married money. Henry felt he needed to know a
great deal more about this man.

The second name, Sir Anthony Holmes, as a peer of the realm,
was named the landlord of one of Enright's clients. And the third
and fourth were both brothers and business partners, family owners
of a small private bank with a long history. Henry had been able to
find out very little about this establishment – it looked as though
you had to be a millionaire just to step through the door, so perhaps
it was not so strange that these two gentlemen, Linus and Gideon
Eriksson, were in a position to offer loans. He would have them
investigated, of course, but he decided that Otis was probably in a
better position to do that alongside checking out the jewellery business visited by Peach. He would simply pass the names along.

No, it was this man, Mr Russell Clovis, that most interested him,
Henry decided. He was certain that he had seen the name crop up
in those documents that the solicitor, Enright, had given him, so,
tomorrow, he must go back over those records and see what links
could be made and if any of those links were with Robert Cranston.

Henry turned back to Annie's documents, to the intelligence that
had been gathered over a six-week period. There were gaps here,
he began to realize. There were some days when the report was
simply that Mr Peach had not left home, but there were other days
for which nothing was recorded at all. It might be, of course, that
there was nothing *to* record but if trouble had been taken to mention
when Mr Peach had stayed at his lodgings, then it seems strange
that there were four days completely without entry. Four days in
six weeks was not a major omission, but it did seem like a significant
one. The pages on which Annie's records were made were all loose,
and it was possible that she had passed these on to Otis already, if
Henry's guess was correct. If so, why would Henry be kept in the

dark? Had Ansel Peach visited someone that Otis did not wish him to know about?

Leaving work, he took with him the keys for the Helfords' house. The sense had been growing in his mind that they had missed something there – that *he* had missed something – and that subsequent searches had not turned it up either. There was something nagging at him about the place, but he could not call to conscious mind what it might be, and that feeling left him restless and unable to settle. As Mickey would have said, too many bells ringing in his brain. He would have liked to have his sergeant with him this time, but Mickey had long since left the office and gone home. Henry had promised that he would soon follow, but had become too engrossed in the various records.

It was close to midnight by this time but Henry had been unaware of how late it had become while he worked and was slightly surprised and taken aback to find so few people on the streets when he emerged from the gates of Scotland Yard and walked along the embankment. He had thought of hailing a cab, but in the end he decided that the walk would do him good. He had always liked to walk and think – a trait he shared with his sergeant.

It was after one by the time he got to the Helford house and no lights burned in any of the neighbouring houses, although he guessed there might be some staff still awake. He let himself in as quietly as he could, closed the curtains in the living room and then switched on the light, blinking in the sudden brightness. It was much as he remembered it: a square of ornate carpet on the floor, woven with roses and arabesques and a border of dark varnished wood between that and the wall. Heavy, overstuffed furniture that, as in Mrs Green's apartment, seemed to belong to another age. A dark oak table stood beside the window, on which was set a fruit bowl and a vase, both empty, and a photograph of Sir Ralph Helford and his wife. The frame was wooden – Tunbridge ware if he was not mistaken – with tiny little squares of different colours forming a design of roses and leaves. The fact that the frame was treen, Henry considered, was probably the only reason that it had been left alone. Presumably the silver frames had all been carried away, although it still puzzled him that the photographs should have been removed first. That spoke of slow deliberation and was at odds with the carnage that had been wreaked throughout the house, with drawers pulled open and tipped out on to the floor and furniture overturned. In fact, it now struck him that this room was the least touched of all, this and the kitchen, scullery and other servants' offices.

'No,' Henry said to himself, 'this is not right; it is not as it seems.' He moved through the other rooms, closing curtains and switching on lights as he went. The curtains were thick, velvet, chenille or heavy-lined chintz, and he didn't think the lights would show on to the street, not that he was too concerned about patrolling constables hammering on the door. If they did, then they could help him with this new search.

He knelt on the floor of what had evidently been Sir Ralph's study. Some tidy-minded police constable must have shuffled everything back into place and lifted the chair upright once more because Henry remembered seeing paperwork scattered everywhere before. His quick inspection, kneeling so that he could see under the desk and behind the bookcases, told him that the constable in question had been as efficient in gathering Sir Ralph's possessions together as whoever had ransacked the place had been in scattering. Though he noted again that the bookshelves were relatively untouched, just a few volumes having been knocked out of place, so the attempt was either half-hearted or whoever had done it could not bear to scatter these precious volumes on to the floor and risk damaging them. A quick look at the bookcase told Henry that many of these were old, beautifully bound and expensive and there were a number of first editions, both of medical books but also volumes featuring elaborate illustration such as a Tenniel-illustrated *Alice in Wonderland*. Melissa would love these, he thought, and was possessed of a sudden urge to take a few away with him. He very much doubted that anyone else in the household would be concerned about them.

But whoever had ransacked this room *had*. They had neither stolen them nor thrown them on the floor. Now that, Henry thought, was distinctly strange. Even a common thief would understand that these would fetch money and there were book markets all over London that would give cash for such prizes with no questions asked. Of course, whatever they paid would be pennies on the pounds that they were worth, but a common thief would be happy enough.

The day he'd first come to this house he'd had little time to look around properly, and so he had gained impressions of the carnage but had not taken a thorough look. He was correct – he had missed things. Now he really missed Mickey's presence, wishing his sergeant here to share the conversation and the speculation.

The house was cold – it had not been heated in weeks – and Henry found himself worrying about these volumes in the doctor's study. They would turn to damp if nothing was done about them. He pulled his coat tight around his chest, buttoning it firmly, and then went through to one of the bedrooms, took a quilt from the bed and then sat on the doctor's chair with the quilt around his knees. Slowly and methodically, he examined the paperwork that would have been in the drawers, and then scattered across the floor, and now had been haphazardly placed back in the drawers once more. It was three o'clock before he was satisfied and four by the time he had examined the rest of the house to his satisfaction. By the time he left, with a small stack of papers in a shopping bag he had purloined from the kitchen and two of the more beautiful volumes of children's fiction under his arm, it was almost five in the morning. Henry walked back to work – there was no sense in going home. He routinely kept clean shirts and shaving gear at the office, just in case, so he had tidied himself up before Mickey came in at seven.

His sergeant looked keenly at him. 'You've not been to bed,' he accused. 'When did you last eat?'

On cue, Henry's stomach rumbled.

Mickey shook his head. 'There's a café for the market workers on the way across to Mrs Green's,' he said. 'We'll stop in there and have a bite, and you can tell me what you've been up to.'

'No, Mrs Green's first,' Henry said. 'I want to catch the woman early, then I promise we will go and have breakfast somewhere, a breakfast that will even satisfy you.'

'We better had,' he said, 'or you'll have both Belle and your Cynthia to answer to.'

They arrived at Mrs Green's apartment well before eight o'clock. Simmons opened the door to them and scowled. 'What do you mean by coming here at this hour? My lady isn't up yet. Go away and come back at a civilized time.'

She began to close the door upon them, but Henry pushed her aside and shoved the door open. It hit the wall with a bang. 'Kindly tell Mrs Green that we are here,' he said quietly. 'Or Mrs Connacht, or whatever she wishes to call herself.'

He left a dumbfounded Simmons in the hall and went through into the little parlour where Mrs Green had entertained them the previous day, leaving Mickey in the hallway. They were rewarded a few minutes later when Henry heard a noise from further down the corridor and, peering out, saw that Mickey had intercepted a gentleman creeping from a room down the hall, clearly hoping he could get out of the front door unnoticed. 'You'd have done better to stay in the bedroom,' Mickey told him. 'Now go and join my boss in the parlour, there's a good lad.'

'Lad' was the right word for him, Henry thought as the rather shamefaced gentleman padded through in stockinged feet. He didn't look more than twenty. From the quality of his clothes – those he'd managed to get on in his hurry – he was of a prosperous sort.

'If your liaison with the lady is no more than romantic,' Mickey told him from the doorway, 'then be assured we have no real interest in you and would just be having your name and address. And we will be checking up that they are *your* name and address and not some fabrication, but that apart you'll be free of police involvement. So your family won't have that much to hush up.'

The young man, face bright red, bent down to fasten his shoes and would not meet Henry's eye. He was doing his best to ignore Mickey, who was clearly very amused.

'It seems you were right about her evening or night-time visitors,' Mickey commended his boss. 'And here we have the lady herself,' he added as the mistress of the house walked into the room looking a little worse for wear. 'And what name will you be going by today, my dear? Are you Mrs Green, Mrs Connacht or something else entirely?'

'None of your damned business,' she hissed at him. 'I'll report you to your superiors, so I will. You can't come in here like this.'

'It would appear that we can,' Henry told her. 'Now, please, sit down, and once we establish this young gentleman's credentials, I'm fairly sure that we can let him leave.'

The young man sprang to his feet as though he couldn't wait to head for the door, but Mickey was blocking the doorway and Henry waved him back down.

'You'll go with my sergeant through to the kitchen and if Simmons's mood has improved since she greeted us, I'm sure she shall make you some tea,' Henry told him. 'And you will explain to my sergeant who you are, and how you come to be staying the night here and, as my sergeant has said, if your intentions are purely of a romantic nature then I'm sure you will be free to go in due course.' Turning to Mrs Green, Henry's voice became more serious. 'In the meantime, madam, you will speak to me, and understand I expect honesty and if I doubt that honesty, I will have you arrested.'

'On what charge?'

Mickey grinned wolfishly. 'Oh, you'll find the detective chief inspector has a great deal of imagination on that score,' he said. 'So you'd best be honest with him. Come along, lad, let's get you a cup of tea and you can tell me all about it.'

Mrs Green was wearing a long kimono, silvery grey with a deep-blue border and embroidered with cranes. She tightened the belt with a defiant look at Henry and threw herself into a velvet easy chair. He watched as she threw her legs over one arm of the chair and reached for a cigarette and holder from an alabaster box sat on a small table beside it. She lit the cigarette and exhaled a long stream of smoke, leaning her head back against the wing of the chair. She was trying hard to look relaxed, Henry thought, but not quite managing it.

'So what is it to be? Mrs Green, Mrs Connacht, or do you have a preferred other name?'

'My married name is Green – you can use that.'

'And Connacht?'

She grimaced. 'Connacht was my maiden name. I find it useful sometimes *not* to be Mrs Green.' She glanced across at Henry. 'And that's it. I don't use any other names. I'm not a criminal.'

'If you are living from immoral earnings, then you may well be breaking the law,' Henry told her. 'I imagine young men like that pay for your company, particularly if they are still here for breakfast.'

She opened her mouth as though to object and then closed it again and shrugged. 'If he chooses to give me gifts, who am I to object? My husband left me with enough to get back to England, and enough from his estate that I was eventually able to purchase this place. It took an age for the thing to go through probate because he hadn't died in this country. You can't imagine what I went through that first year. Eventually the money was released to me, of course, and I set myself up here. The address is good, the flat is nice, and Simmons is an excellent companion.'

'And the young men? I don't imagine he's the only one.'

'Young men do what young men have always done. I merely provide a safe place for the outlet of those energies. A woman must survive, Detective Chief Inspector. Women survive as best they can, just as they have always done.'

Henry nodded; he knew the truth of that. 'And Mrs Connacht . . . what does she do?'

'She invests as wisely as she can. And for the record, no, she does not buy on the margin and she does not take risks. If you cared to look up the accounts of Regent Financial Services Company, you will discover that they have offered an excellent and very cautious service for the last thirty years to people like me. People who have a little to invest but can't afford to lose it.'

'I could accept all of that,' Henry told her. 'It was the fact that you left your home so precipitously yesterday. You hadn't even breakfasted, you told us, and yet only a few minutes after my sergeant and I left, so did you. And you were a woman in a hurry.'

'Your arrival distracted me. But I suddenly remembered that I had an appointment and that I must leave immediately. There is nothing wrong with that, Detective Chief Inspector, and my story is easily checked.'

'And *will* be checked.'

Footsteps in the hall attracted their attention as Mickey walked the young man out and then came back into the parlour to join them. 'I think I may have lost you a customer,' he told her.

'No matter,' Henry said. 'I've no doubt there are plenty more where that one came from.'

'Not after word gets around that I've been knocked up by the police in the morning,' she said bitterly.

'The little frisson of danger will get most of them more excited than it will put them off,' Mickey assured her. 'Young men like that, they like to break the rules in safe ways. Don't you know that? Presumably you do.'

She shrugged and it occurred to Henry that she was not in fact that worried, merely annoyed. 'He's a nice boy,' she said. 'Very polite. Very generous.'

Simmons was hovering in the doorway, obviously wondering whether she should make tea, prepare breakfast or sweep the policemen off the premises. Henry made the decision for her by getting up and retrieving his hat from where he'd left it on a side table. This parlour seemed to have an awful lot of side tables, he thought. Many little tables, and many rugs. He was curious about the rugs.

'Did your husband really collect these?' Henry indicated the rug-covered floor.

'What, the carpets? Some of them. Others I picked up at the second-hand market down the Portobello Road. There is a Jewish tailor who sets up his market stall once or twice a week, often sells second-hand clothes and textiles. I like them. He knows that, so he saves them for me. They add a touch of luxury, don't you think? The story is merely a bit of romance.'

'And did your husband really die in Egypt?'

'Sadly, that part is true. But we weren't world travellers, unfortunately.' She took another drag on a cigarette and released another cloud of smoke from between elegant red lips. She'd taken time to retouch her lipstick before storming out of her bedroom, Henry thought wryly.

'He was a clerk attached to the embassy. Nothing special, but I did love him.'

'An embassy clerk,' Henry questioned, 'and yet he left you enough money to buy this place?'

'He left me a little money, true, but you're right, not enough to buy this place. But he *had* saved while we were in Egypt. We had accommodation and food found for us, so we had little to spend it on in reality. I supplemented our income, of course. And continued to do so once I returned here. You can judge me all you like, Inspector – better this than be out on the streets, being a low-paid shop girl, or marrying a man I didn't like just to be kept. This way I keep myself, and Simmons. Two women taken care of.'

If she'd expected Henry to have moral objections and to voice them, then she was to be disappointed. He merely nodded; Mickey smiled.

'And your relationship with Ansel Peach?'

An exaggerated sigh. 'No more or less than a friend. He knew my husband from their schooldays. My husband may only have been a humble clerk but he came from a respectable family. When I returned to London Ansel lent me a little money, just enough to pay my rent and keep the wolf from the door until I was able to release my husband's estate. So, when he fell on hard times, I tried to return the favour.'

'What school did they both attend?'

She shrugged. 'I forget. Does it matter? My husband didn't like to talk about his childhood. It was unhappy, from what I can gather. Ansel was one of the few connections he kept up.'

'Did you meet with Mr Peach at the offices of Regent Financial?'

'I may have done.' She removed the cigarette from its holder and replaced it with another but didn't light it. 'I don't see what all this is about. My husband is dead. I have his death certificate somewhere about, should you wish proof of that. Ansel Peach is now dead, driven to suicide. What more is there to say?'

'And your business with him there?'

'Oh, for goodness' sake. I've explained that they invest what little money I can afford to invest and advise me on my finances. I urged Ansel to take fewer risks with what resources he had remaining. I made the introductions and left him to discuss matters. That, Chief Inspector, is all.'

'Did he actually have any remaining resources?' Mickey sounded sceptical. 'His lodgings were the cheapest, his possessions scant. According to the solicitor handling his affairs, there was nothing left.'

She looked troubled. 'I had no inkling he was in such dire straits. Poor Ansel, no wonder he was driven to despair.' She lit her cigarette and waved the holder impatiently. 'What more can I tell you? What else is there to say? I know nothing more.'

Henry got to his feet. 'Find your husband's death certificate and that of your marriage,' he said. 'I would like to know where he went to school, how he and Mr Peach came to be friends. Any records of your financial transactions with Regent Financial services. Gather all of this together and I will arrange for it to be collected.'

'And why should I do that?'

'Because I have asked you to,' Henry told her coldly. 'Why would you refuse to assist the police?'

'Who was the young man?' Henry asked when they reached the street.

'The Honourable Christopher Morton-Hart,' Mickey told him. 'I'm satisfied it was sex he was after, nothing more. So I imagine we won't be pursuing him any further.'

'I would imagine not. Or Mrs Green, at least not in that score, but we need to look into her investments and Regent Financial Services, see that everything is, in fact, above board. There are tens of thousands of women in London alone making a living this way, and many in far less comfortable circumstances. I would not make their lives more difficult by attempting to pursue them – there are enough people doing that already. Unless they kill someone, they are of very little interest to me. But if she has pertinent information about Mr Peach, then we need to know it.'

Mickey laughed heartily. 'So, breakfast. And then to Regent Financial Services, I assume.'

'And over breakfast I will tell you what I discovered last night at the home of Sir Ralph Helford,' Henry told him. 'I knew that I had missed something, and I was right.'

FIFTEEN

Mickey dipped a slice of sausage into the runny yolk of his egg and regarded his boss expectantly. 'So,' he said, 'what did you find at the Helford house last night? And is it worth the pair of us going back for yet another look?'

'Lady Helford said that the references for the servants would still be in her London house, and I did find those for the cook and the maid but nothing for the valet. However, I discovered letters of agreement between Sir Ralph Helford and Messrs Hodgkin and Burke regarding the repayment of certain loans Sir Ralph had taken out and that they had acted as broker for. I looked closer to see who the lender might be and one of Albert's gentlemen came up. Mr Russell Clovis.'

'The mill owner,' Mickey remembered. 'Made money, married money, sees himself as something of a benefactor. I did some background digging the first time his name appeared. I don't know if it will be relevant, but he funds various charities, seems particularly interested in fallen women and, to be fair to the man, in widows and orphans.'

Henry smiled at his sergeant's cynicism, then remembered something Cynthia had said. 'Was anything mentioned about homes for unwed mothers? Only Cynthia mentioned that a man Albert knew from one of his clubs sat on the committee with Sir Ralph Helford and, if so, Sir Ralph could have known Mr Clovis. Perhaps that might be the connection. It's not beyond the realm of possibility that they also knew each other through their clubs, and that's something we must also look into.'

'And this agreement that was drawn up, how much was it for?'

'Now, that's the interesting thing. The original agreement seems to have been for five thousand pounds and Clovis used Hodgkin and Burke to draw up a loan agreement. This was back in September when things began to go wrong thanks to the crash. So Sir Ralph took quite a major hit on the stock market, from the letters that went back and forth between the solicitors and Clovis, and so it seems that what Sir Ralph needed was cash flow rather than an injection of capital.'

'Five thousand pounds is a lot of cash to flow,' Mickey said.

Henry nodded; it was more than two years' worth of earnings for him and even more than that for Mickey. 'From what I can gather, Sir Ralph had drawn various dividends from savings and investments, had bought properties, had overstretched their finances and was hoping to recoup these through investment in the stock market. It appears from his records that he had done this two or three times previously, and that it had paid off handsomely. Then the London stock market crashed and he was found without the funds to cover the immediate business expenses for these properties. Essentially, if he didn't pay the balance, he was in danger of losing both the property and deposit.'

'So he went to Clovis?'

'And Clovis agreed to bail him out. Of course, we must confirm all of this with the parties concerned, but from my reading it was a fairly ordinary business agreement that they came to. The loan was drawn up, signed by the parties involved and countersigned by Mr Hodgkin of Hodgkin and Burke, and the expectation was that the money would be repaid by New Year, when Sir Ralph disposed of at least one of the properties, possibly two.'

Mickey's eyes narrowed. 'Expensive houses then. Were they houses?'

'A small row of cottages in Charing Cross and a property with eight bedrooms. This property was out of town, close to Ilford, and was apparently listed as a convalescent home but was to be a hostel for unwed mothers – a project, I believe, Cynthia has been involved in raising funds for. She mentioned the committee, as I said, and Sir Ralph Helford in this particular context.'

'So he was raising money for all the right reasons but over-stretching himself in the process.'

'So it would appear. Except, as I've said, he was being forced to sell these properties to solve his straitened financial circumstances.'

'Did he have a buyer arranged?'

'It would seem so, but I can only track the transaction so far. For the rest we must deal with Hodgkin and Burke and probably Mr Russell Clovis. Now this transaction seems to have been above board and sanctioned, but then there is correspondence between the two men, Sir Ralph and Clovis, about further funding.'

'So Sir Ralph needed more money?'

'No, I don't think he did. I think rather that Mr Russell Clovis wished to lend him more money.'

'Ah, now it gets interesting.'

'Indeed, and indeed the letters could be read as being a perfectly innocent offer from one friend to another, but in light of what we have seen so far, I am suspicious of them. Clovis urges him to take out further loans and, more to the point, suggests that they do not need to involve the solicitors in this, that it can be a gentleman's agreement. These letters are recent – they indicate that Sir Ralph has lost more money, and, remember, this is before Wall Street crashed. This is a purely domestic issue. Like Mr Peach, Sir Ralph continued to play the markets and to invest in riskier and riskier strategies. I'm no expert in this, so I've handed these papers over to those who know more. I thought our Mr Enright could earn his keep, seeing as we have taken so much of his paperwork off his hands, so I sent them over this morning with a note explaining what I needed him to discover for me.'

Mickey laughed. 'Oh, that will please him. And how long before Sir Ralph's death did all of this take place?'

'As I say, these letters could be read as simply offers from a friend and it's only my suspicious mind that is seeing them other-wise. Apart from this.' Henry took an envelope from his pocket containing a sheet of carbon paper. It was creased and much over-written. Mickey held it up to the light. It appeared to be a letter, the carbon being placed between sheets to make a copy as Sir Ralph accused his friend of attempting to blackmail him, to force his hand to take money that he did not need at a rate of interest that he would be insane to accept and that he did not take kindly to threats being made towards his family. It took Mickey a little while to work this out because the carbon had evidently been used before and possibly after, some sentences being overwritten by others.

'And a few days after this letter was sent, if you notice the date, Sir Ralph is dead. Now the two things may well be coincidence, but . . .'

'And you did not find that letter? Do you think whoever ransacked the house took it with them?'

Henry hesitated. 'I think it possible, but I'm beginning to think that the ransacking of the house and the theft of possessions was not a criminal act in the sense that we would normally concern ourselves with.'

Mickey wiped the final piece of sausage around the eggy plate and looked curiously at Henry. 'And what leads you to that conclusion?'

'There was too much care taken and there were things which were not taken. What thief pauses to remove photographs from silver frames when they can be burned in any hearth? What thief leaves what are obviously valuable books intact on the shelf, without even touching them, Mickey? It would be clear to even the most amateur eye that these volumes could fetch money.'

'But they would be heavy to carry,' Mickey argued. 'Silver trinkets weigh nothing, jewellery weighs nothing and is easily broken up and disposed of. Many housebreakers do not know the value of literature.'

'Indeed not,' Henry agreed, 'but most can spot quality when they see it and know potential profit. Lady Helford told us that her husband usually took her into his confidence, that she was resentful that he had some troubles of late that he had not related to her, but what if he had, or what if she had found out? Helford, had he not died, would have gone down for a great deal more than the five thousand pounds needed for his cash flow. His own house is likely to have been forfeit – perhaps his other properties also – as he seemed keen on releasing immediate capital through these sales. And we must find out if the sales actually went through or not, or if the buyer is known. I wonder if perhaps the widow sought to hold on to whatever property she could to ensure her own future. If she wished to live quietly for the rest of her life, then I imagine the sale of jewels and silver and whatever else of value was in the house, not to mention whatever cash he kept in his safe, would have seen her through.'

'There was a safe?'

'A small one beneath the floor, in the hall between the kitchen and the dining room. More of a strongbox, locked with a key and concreted into the ground. It had been opened, emptied, closed again but not locked, and a section of parquet flooring had been made to fit so that the location was not immediately obvious. Add to that a rug that went over the top and it's unsurprising that it had been missed when the constables examined the location.'

'My, you did have a busy time last night,' Mickey approved. 'Don't be too hard on the constables. They do not have your eyes.'

'Given the timing, the loan, the death, is it not likely that much of this five thousand pounds remained but even a few hundred would be of value to a woman who, by her own admission, was used to managing on very little in their early days. But if I am correct and Lady Helford had the scene staged, her belongings quietly sold for whatever she could get for them from the many fences there are in this city, then she would have left London with a nice little nest egg to fund her retirement where the creditors would not be able to touch. Had she sold her possessions openly, then her creditors might well have been able to seize whatever she made from those sales so she could not risk that.'

'And the killing of Sir Ralph Helford?'

'May have been connected, may not. I still have my mind open on that score.'

'You are presupposing that this respectable gentlewoman knew how to fence her own belongings.' Mickey was amused at the idea. 'Mind you, I did say she was a tough old bird. But what about the threats to the kiddie?'

'What if they too were staged? And as to needing help in disposing herself of stolen goods, I think the answer may well have been her husband's valet. Fred Parks has no criminal record on his own account, but members of his family are well known to us, including a cousin of his mother's, a Mrs Franny Richmond . . .'

Mickey grinned in recognition. 'Franny Richmond – she must be ninety by now. A big family from what I remember. Now that is interesting. And still no sign of Mr Parks, I suppose?'

'Word is out, but he'll have gone to ground and could be anywhere. But this is progress, Mickey.'

'But unless we find the valet, it's not progress we can prove. And I have to admit I feel sorry for the old woman, Lady Helford. She and her family stood to lose everything because her husband blundered. But Mr Russell Clovis would seem to be a man we must examine closely. You say your Cynthia might know him?'

'Albert certainly does – he was on Albert's list of gentleman lenders. Cynthia almost certainly does if he served on the same committees as she and Sir Ralph did, and that looks very likely. It may be that they can give us some background information that we may not have. But first' – Henry paused to drain the last of his tea – 'we have to visit Regent Financial Services and see what dealings they have had with our Mrs Green, or Mrs Connacht as she prefers to be known to them.'

Mickey pushed his chair beneath the table and shrugged into his coat. 'This matter with the toy rabbit and the little girl being threatened . . . I know you consider that to have been staged as well, and I'm inclined to agree, but my question is where did she get the idea? If Lady Helford did create this fiction, then it seems an extravagant one. It should have been enough to tell us that in light of her husband's death she is going away to the country to stay with relatives for a time. Instead of which she . . .'

'Overplayed her hand and actually ensured that the police would keep her under surveillance if only for the sake of the child. No, I agree, Mickey, it seems an odd thing to do. This is a woman not used to dissembling. She was already extending her boundaries by staging a burglary, or asking someone else to do so, if I'm correct about the valet. She's already desperate, but she has had no experience in affairs such as this – she does not know what story is too elaborate. Either that or the child actually has been threatened, of course.'

'I'd rather she made the whole thing up,' Mickey told him.

'As would I, but either the child has been threatened or Lady Helford has modelled her story on something she knows, has heard about and was horrified by. My guess is that she did not pluck this tale out of thin air or out of her imagination. She did not strike me as a woman particularly endowed with imagination. She struck me as a woman comfortable with her status, her ease of life, and the wealth and status of her husband. Now all of those things have been taken away, she is cast adrift.'

'Either way she needs speaking to,' Mickey said. 'But we may have to leave that up to the local police. I cannot see our superintendent authorizing a trip to the West Country, just to ask the woman if she made up a story about a burglary in her own house. Pity, I've never been to Cornwall, and I'm told it's beautiful.'

'I think we may have to settle for finding the valet,' Henry told him.

The receptionist recognized Mickey when they arrived at the Regent Financial Services offices.

'Hello there, did you find your friend?' she asked, but was a little taken aback when they introduced themselves as police officers. 'Oh, goodness. I'd better tell my boss.'

Minutes later they were ushered through into one of the offices by a rather nervous-looking gentleman with a long face, flighty hands and, Mickey noticed, exceptionally large feet. He introduced himself as Myles Tippett, one of the directors of the company. 'I do hope there's nothing wrong,' he asked, fingers fluttering anxiously. He seemed to notice what he was doing then and clasped his hands in his lap. Mickey wondered if he would be able to speak with them so constrained.

'We have a simple question about a customer of yours, or a client I suppose you would call her, Mrs Connacht. I believe she had an appointment with you yesterday?'

'Yes, yes indeed. Mrs Connacht has been entrusting her funds to us for two or three years now. A very nice lady, widowed, you know.' The hands were in action again. 'There's nothing . . . untoward, is there?'

'Nothing at all, but Mrs Connacht had the misfortune to be caught up in an investigation, not regarding Mrs Connacht, you understand,' Mickey said half-truthfully. 'We are trying to establish a timeline of witnesses, so if you could tell us what time her appointment was, and what time she arrived, then that would help establish the whereabouts of certain people. You understand?'

Henry glanced in amusement at his sergeant. He wasn't sure *he* understood, but Mickey had judged Myles Tippett perfectly and the man relaxed and produced a desk diary. 'But, of course, Mrs Connacht was here just after eleven . . . she was perhaps three or four minutes late. She explained that she had been delayed by an unexpected visit and then had to hurry to get here in time. She was only here perhaps twenty minutes.' He pointed at the entry in his diary.

Mickey nodded. That fitted with his own observations.

'We have prepared a new portfolio for her; she came only to

collect that and check the figures on her investments. She comes in perhaps every two or three months, never invests a great deal, of course, and we ensure that her investments are safe, gilt-edged. Of course, the interest returns on these safe investments is never as high, but we would not advise our clients to risk more than we feel secure in doing. We are not some fly-by-night organization,' he told Mickey sternly. He had cast the occasional glance in Henry's direction but not spoken to him. Mickey, it seemed, he could deal with, but Henry, austere, cold and still, was a little too much.

'How much does an investor typically entrust to you?' Mickey asked. 'I'm hearing so much lately about people playing on the stock market, and the difficulties that they are now encountering, I just wondered . . .'

'Oh no, we invest directly into businesses – businesses that we know and trust, and we look for the best investment in the banking sector, an account that will return a smooth and clear level of interest over a long period. Of course, this is not a high-level investment, but you understand people wish for safety, especially with all the shocks that have beset the stock market. And as to how much they invest, well, most of our investors are small: a few hundred here, a few thousand there. Most invest regularly, on a monthly basis, and, of course, this adds up over time.'

'And did Mrs Connacht introduce a friend of hers to you, a Mr Ansel Peach?'

'Oh . . . Oh, yes, she did. But nothing came of it, I'm afraid. I think he came to see us just to please her.'

'But he didn't invest?'

Mr Tippett looked uncomfortable. 'After Mrs Connacht had left, he confided that he did not in fact have anything to invest. That pride prevented him from acquainting Mrs Connacht with the full extent of his financial depredations.'

'But the fact was that he was about to be declared bankrupt,' Henry said flatly, the first time he had spoken directly to Tippett.

'I believe so, yes. The notices had not yet appeared, but he was expecting them very soon.'

For a moment there was silence as they all considered this and then Tippett turned back to Mickey. 'Would you be interested . . .?' He looked speculatively at Mickey and then cast a very quick glance at Henry before closing his diary and assuming that the interview was at an end.

Henry nodded thanks and Mickey reached across to shake the man's hand.

'I could give you some of our brochures,' Mr Tippett said, reaching into a desk drawer. He handed Mickey some printed material and then his hands were free to flap and flutter once again as he saw them to the door.

'So, she was telling the truth,' Mickey said as they left the offices behind them. He sounded mildly disappointed.

'She's still a person of interest,' Henry said, 'but I think she is on the periphery of things. Mickey, I feel I'm losing sight of what is central to our investigation. We need to pull our attention back to Mr Robert Cranston and his actions in the days before he died. And we need to examine these gentleman lenders, but we also need to keep an open mind. I've been keen to connect events that may not need connecting. What if Mr Cranston's death had nothing to do with his debts?'

'But you feel instinctively that it does,' Mickey stated.

'I feel it, but I cannot grasp the evidence for it as completely as I'd like.'

'So, our next actions. We need to find that valet, Parks – I doubt he'll have gone far. We have a list or at least a partial list of items taken from the house, and this can be distributed through the usual channels so that jewellers and pawnbrokers can keep watch, in case our thief tries to dispose of items through regular channels. And we have put out word that we wish to speak with Parks. Sooner or later someone will see him. Much of this can be left to the constables.'

'Second, we need to focus on the activities of Mr Cranston in the immediate lead-up to his death.'

'Third, we need to track down this flamenco dancer,' Mickey added. 'It's due to her that you had any suspicions at all about Mr Cranston's death. As you have said yourself, it could very easily have been recorded as just another suicide.'

'Yes. And fourth, we must visit these so-called gentleman lenders and any other names that have come up in our investigations, especially those we know are associated with Mr Russell Clovis. When we return to our desks, we must compile a complete list and, I think, divide the task between us.'

'And finally, we need to use all the intelligence that Cynthia and Albert might give us in establishing background information on Mr Clovis, Mr Cranston and anyone else likely to move in their circle.'

Henry nodded agreement, a little more satisfied now that he had a framework for the investigation that was to come. 'But not finally. Finally, we need the constables to visit Lady Helford and at least make known to her what we suspect. It's possible that her facade will crack and we may find out more from that quarter.'

'Not her.' Mickey chuckled. 'Like I said, she's a tough old bird. She'll deny everything. And even if we are correct about the valet and he is persuaded to break silence, what will we be able to prove? It will be his word against hers. Some common or garden servant from a criminal background accusing the lady of the house of robbing herself? That will never fly, Henry, and you know it.'

'True,' Henry agreed, 'but that does not mean the question won't be asked.'

SIXTEEN

News awaited them back at Central Office that afternoon. The results of the tests on the brandy from Mr Geoffrey Cranston's study definitely showed the presence of poison. What was puzzling, though, was that this was not arsenic or strychnine or any of the common or garden poisons but rather one that had been favoured back in the nineteenth century. Literally a garden poison, made from the leaves and berries of laurel, laurel water had at one time been the poison of choice for would-be murderers, the raw materials being freely available and the extract easily manufactured.

'Do you remember laurel bushes at the Cranston house?' Henry asked.

Mickey shrugged. 'There were evergreens in the driveway. I suppose they may have been laurel, but I took little notice of them. You think the poison came from within the household?'

'Perhaps not, but it seems an odd choice. We need to know exactly who had access to the house. We also need to wait for the exhumation to ensure that *this* poison did in fact kill Geoffrey Cranston. We have certain facts, but we must beware of jumping to false conclusions. Mickey, I admit to a certain prejudice here, but I have always associated the manufacture of laurel water with women.'

Mickey laughed. 'I'm not even going to ask you why that might be. It's interesting, though, that the wife and sister-in-law insist that Geoffrey Cranston only drank his brandy on occasion, that it was not a daily event. But he did smoke a cigar every evening and it would surely be easier to infuse a cigar with additional nicotine, again poison readily available, than to contaminate his brandy with laurel, which I believe is quite a bitter alkaloid, so Geoffrey may have noticed. Or is this why you wish to wait for the post-mortem before you draw conclusions?'

Henry nodded. 'Although I admit it would be strange if there were two poisons, one in the body and one in the decanter; that would stretch credibility. Mickey, both exhumations are scheduled for tomorrow morning. I suggest that you go to the Cranston one and I go with Albert. He has promised to ease my path with Ferdy Bright-Cooper's family. The father and the father's solicitor will be present, so I don't imagine it will be an easy morning and I'm grateful for Albert's offer.'

'Sounds like a sensible division,' Mickey said. 'And while I'm out that way, I'll keep my eyes open for laurel bushes.'

More news arrived when they were applying themselves to other paperwork later that day. Henry had organized for constables to make enquiries about the flamenco dancer at costumiers and theatrical outfitters, and it seemed that this investigation had finally borne fruit. A dozen such outfits had been hired by a small theatre for members of the chorus. Half an hour later Mickey and Henry set off hoping to catch the dresser before preparation for the evening performance began.

The theatre was small, and the dresser was a Mrs Danby, responsible for looking after a chorus line of twelve with, as she told them, three costume changes, as well as those performers listed on the bill, which were obviously her priority. When asked if it would be possible for someone to take a costume out of the theatre without her realizing, she bristled somewhat but then admitted that it probably would be as each dancer was supposed to look after their own gear and that she only became closely involved if something was torn or stained or didn't fit.

At Henry's request, the dancers were assembled. Most had just arrived or were warming up or eating a hurried meal before getting ready for the evening show. He assembled them at the side of the stage, in various stages of dress and undress, some with robes loosely tied around their costumes and others still in their street clothes.

Henry came straight to the point. 'On the thirty-first of October, a party was held, a fancy-dress party to which one of you came as an uninvited guest, dressed in flamenco costume. Now, you are not in any trouble, I have no interest in the fact that you gatecrashed a party. What I am interested in, is that you sought me out and, without my knowledge, delivered to me a note. And I do know that it was one of your number, and I can assure you that no trouble will come to your door if you tell the truth.'

The girls eyed each other nervously and Mickey glanced at his boss. Henry was not exactly believable when he said that there would be no trouble from this – his look was too austere, his posture too rigid and his eyes too cold.

Mickey smiled at them all. 'I'm sure it was sold to you as a practical joke,' he said, 'a bit of fun for the gentlemen. And after all, what did you do apart from borrow a costume for an hour or two after your evening performance? I'm sure you wouldn't have been the first young lady to do so.'

Again, the swift exchange of glances and then one stepped forward, white-faced and anxious. 'I didn't do anything wrong,' she insisted.

'Of course she didn't.' Another girl backed her up. 'Some stage-door Johnny asks you to do something simple like that and gives you cash for it, of course you're going to do it. There's not one of us here hasn't done something similar. Borrowed a costume to go out for dinner maybe, I mean not a flamenco costume, but . . .'

There was a murmur of agreement but it was obvious that all were nervous, probably more anxious about the dresser finding out the adventures that her costumes had been going on than the business at the Halloween party, Mickey thought. However, he had no doubt that Mrs Danby knew but chose *not* to know, so it was best not to confront her with facts she was unable to deny. None of these young women could afford to lose their job.

'So what were you asked to do?' Mickey asked gently. 'And the man who asked you to do it, was he known to you?'

The second girl answered. 'He'd been hanging around for a few days, chatting to the girls as they came out. He bought two of us dinner. We don't like to go out on our own with gentlemen, not until we know who they are. You never know these days, do you? So many funny types around. Anyway, he took a liking to Millie, said he had a job for her.'

'And what job would that be? To dress as the flamenco dancer and deliver a note?'

The girl called Millie merely nodded. She was small and dark-haired, rather fragile-looking, Mickey thought. 'He put me in a taxi, told me where to go, told me lots of people would be in fancy dress so I'd fit right in. Gave me money for the taxi fare home and a whole five pounds if I delivered the message. Didn't seem no harm in it. I mean it seemed a bit strange, but not as strange as some things we're asked to do.'

A ripple of giggles and agreement.

'And do you know his name, this "stage-door Johnny"?'

'When do we ever know their names?' the second girl said. 'Sometimes they give their actual names, but mostly, you know.' She shrugged eloquently.

'And what name did he give?'

'Called himself Joe Brown, said he was a solicitor or something. I mean, he was nicely dressed and all that, but I don't figure he was a solicitor. But it weren't him that gave me the note. That was an old woman.'

'An old woman?' Mickey exchanged a quick glance with Henry. 'What did she look like?'

'Didn't get a good look. She was in a taxicab and he was with her. He got out of the taxi, inspected me to make sure I looked the part, I suppose, said I would do, and the old woman leaned past him and gave me the letter. She was dressed in black, had grey hair, but I didn't take much notice to be honest. They'd got another taxi waiting for me. He got back in the first one and I got in the second, did my job, went home.'

'And he's not been back since?'

A general shaking of heads. These girls would have seen him if he had been. The dresser arrived just then and told Henry and Mickey in no uncertain terms that she needed her girls to get ready. They had two performances that day – one at five and one at eight – and now the policeman were definitely in the way. So if they'd found out that all they needed to know . . .

Mickey took the details of the girls he had spoken to and they went on their way.

'You think our young Millie Stevens knows any more than she told us?' he asked.

'Not a great deal more. There might be some facts she remembers,

some detail when she thinks about it more, but it's intriguing about
the old lady.'

'You're thinking she was Sir Ralph's widow?' Mickey said.

Henry nodded. 'And I'm wondering if her male companion
was the valet. Her husband had been killed in what everyone was
treating as a hit-and-run . . . so why would she be so worried about
Robert Cranston? How does she even know him, for that matter?
What was she telling me? "Don't look for the obvious," the note
said. So she suspected that something would happen. She suspected
that Cranston was in danger, just as her husband had been.'

'If it was her, this shines a different light on things,' Mickey
agreed. 'Well, I will go along with your theory about the house being
ransacked by the valet, or some other person in her employ, but this
other matter, it makes me think her story about the child being
threatened might be true.'

Henry nodded. 'I think we should treat it as though the threat
was definitely real. The local constabulary have been informed, both
in Cornwall and in Aberdeen, and a welfare check should definitely
be made. Mickey, I would hate to think that anything should happen
to that little mite because we have not taken appropriate action.'

'To threaten to hurt a child . . . that is going too far,' Mickey
agreed.

SEVENTEEN

Henry shivered. There was frost on the ground that morning
and a thick fog; it seemed appropriate weather for an
exhumation. He had arrived in Albert's car and the two of
them had taken refuge there, it being the warmest place, while
everyone else assembled. Now common decency demanded that
they should go and join the mourners, the coroner and the gravediggers, and watch as the body was dug out of its sadly simple and
turf-covered grave, just outside the family graveyard. Ferdy had
committed suicide and could not be buried on consecrated ground,
not even privately consecrated ground, and so the family had planted
him just beyond the hedge as close to his ancestors as they could.
Henry supposed that given a little time they would either have had

the grave moved or have the hedge replanted to surround it too and bring it symbolically back into the fold.

There were about a dozen people present – a lot for an exhumation. Henry had attended three or four previously and usually it was just the coroner, the gravedigger and himself as representative of the police force. But this was an important family – a consciously self-important family. The coroner stood a little apart, his assistant supervising the action of the gravediggers. Beside him was the family solicitor, and the father and the brother of the dead man. There were three gravediggers and on the opposite side of the plot, himself and Albert. Two servants hovered, refilling the stirrup cups members of the family and their entourage were holding. Albert stood miserably beside Henry; it had been made very clear to him from the moment they had arrived that he was no longer privileged to be part of their wider social group. Refreshments had been offered but the offer had been grudging. Mere politeness, nothing more.

'I've known them all my life, Henry,' Albert said quietly. 'Stayed over at their houses, and Ferdy has stayed at mine. We served together in the bloody army, fought side by side as fellow officers. Both decorated, both wounded, we made it through all of that. Our families welcomed us both back like we were brothers and now, now I'm just a nothing to them.'

'It's their loss, old man,' Henry said quietly, but he knew his words were no compensation. These last months had been full of pain for Albert and this reopened wounds. 'I must, however, speak to the father and the solicitor – ensure they understand the process.'

'I think I might just go and wait in the car, if you don't mind,' Albert said.

Henry watched him go, knowing there was nothing he could say to make things better. He had been deeply sympathetic with the family – after all, this must be a traumatic process for them; not only had they lost a son in tragic circumstances but there was now the possibility that he had been murdered. However, their treatment of Albert had eroded some of Henry's sympathy, and he was under no illusions as to how they might view him. Frankly he cared nothing for that, but Albert deserved better. Albert was a good man and a good friend.

The coroner stepped forward as Henry approached. 'Detective Chief Inspector, I've been explaining to the family that the . . . that the body will be taken from here for examination but that this is merely a formality, a matter of being perhaps overcautious, and that no one wishes to cause the family more distress. The body will be reinterred later today, or perhaps tomorrow. At the very latest tomorrow.'

Henry turned his chilliest gaze upon the coroner and saw the man quail. 'I can give no such assurance,' he said firmly. Out of the corner of his eye he saw Ferdy's father flinch. 'A post-mortem will be carried out, a formal investigation – the body cannot be reinterred until we are fully satisfied that we know everything there is to know. The body must be examined for signs of violence. If Mr Ferdinand Bright-Cooper met with a violent end, other than by his own hand, then it is a police matter and will be fully investigated.'

Perhaps fortunately, the gravediggers had at that moment reached the level of the coffin and were now beginning the preparation for raising it to the surface. Trestles had been placed beside the grave and an undertaker was waiting, some little distance away, to transport the body to the mortuary. Henry stood back and watched; he had nothing more to say to the family and they certainly had nothing more to say to him. He could hear muttering and Albert's name and then Cynthia's, and he made to move away before they said something that might offend him more deeply. He fancied he could hear Mickey's silent applause at this tiny bit of wisdom, but, in truth, he wanted to turn around and tell the Bright-Coopers exactly what he thought of them.

He stiffened as he heard Bright-Cooper senior say something about a man marrying his father's secretary said a lot about a man's character, and that he had only allowed Ferdy to continue with the friendship because he knew in time Ferdy would grow out of such frivolity, such an unequal association.

Henry turned sharply. 'It is thanks to my sister, her good sense and her acumen, that their family will come through this mess somewhat better than yours is doing,' he announced, and then walked away before he could say more. He knew he should have left well alone.

Albert took one look at his face when Henry got into the car and asked, 'What did they say?'

'Nothing that bears repeating.'

'And what did you say?'

'Nothing but the simple truth.'

'Ah,' Albert said. 'Well, never mind, old chap. My father thinks very highly of you – there will always be a position in his company or in mine when I get back on my feet.'

Henry laughed. 'Albert, there may come a time when I need to call you on that,' he said.

'You shouldn't be let out without Mickey Hitchens,' Albert told him. But Henry could tell that he was cheered by the thought that someone had stood up for him, even though he could only guess at what had been said.

Mickey's experience that morning was somewhat different. Neither Mrs Geoffrey Cranston nor her sister attended, and Mickey couldn't blame them; it was a bitterly cold morning, and why would anyone want to stand around in a churchyard watching their loved one being brought back into this world when he had passed through to the next? He oversaw the formalities, the handing over to the coroner and the transportation to the local hospital, and then his driver took him to the Cranston house.

This time Mickey had him pause in the driveway while he examined the evergreen hedges. They were mostly holly, but there was also laurel.

Mrs Cranston and her sister received Mickey in the same room as before. They looked even older and more worn out, and Mickey felt deeply sorry for them as he spoke.

Nora was absolutely horrified. 'But why would anyone poison Geoffrey? Detective Sergeant, what is going on here?'

'We are endeavouring to find out,' Mickey assured her. 'Might I ask, ladies, if Sir Ralph Helford was known to you? Or Mr Russell Clovis?'

'Clovis.' Nora did not trouble to hide her distaste. 'An execrable man. Robert brought him here once. He was loud, Detective Sergeant, loud and uncouth.'

'We have heard of Sir Ralph Helford, of course,' Mrs Cranston said. 'Such a tragic accident, but why do you ask?'

'They are names that have cropped up in the course of our investigation. There may be no connection, but we have to look at everything. Could you tell me why your son brought Mr Clovis to your home?'

'Business, I suppose. He came to speak to Geoffrey and remained for dinner. We did feel obliged to offer him the chance to remain for the night, but fortunately he went on his way. He was staying with some other local family, but I forget who. Is it important?'

'Possibly not,' Mickey said. 'Mrs Cranston, I'm sorry to ask this, but might I be allowed to examine your husband's study once again? Last time we were uncertain what we might be looking for, but if your husband perhaps did business with Mr Clovis, there would be some record of it?'

'You may look, of course, but I know for a fact that Geoffrey did no business with Mr Clovis. He told Robert that this man was a snake, that he would lead to trouble. Geoffrey was a good judge of character, but I'm afraid Robert often was not. He would take too much at face value. He could be . . . swayed by the success of others, by the glamour of it, I suppose. Sergeant, I don't want to speak ill of my son – I loved my son deeply and dearly – but while his father was a good businessman, within what he knew, of course, Robert was ambitious. Sometimes that ambition got the better of him.'

'Did you get the sense that Mr Clovis wanted your husband to invest in something?'

She thought about it and then shook her head. 'I had the sense that he wanted Geoffrey to buy something, but I may be wrong or' – she looked to her sister – 'perhaps stand security on Robert's behalf. But I can't be certain of that.'

'But you did have the sense that your husband sent Mr Clovis away with a flea in his ear?' Mickey said bluntly. This raised a smile from both ladies.

'That was the sense I had,' Mrs Cranston agreed.

He hoped to hell they were right. The thought that these two ladies might lose what little they had left frankly horrified him.

Geoffrey Cranston's study felt as cold and damp as before, perhaps even colder and damper, Mickey thought, and he was momentarily glad that Henry was not here with him. And then he was sorry that his boss wasn't present; he and Henry worked well, they complemented each other and, having worked with many other chief inspectors in the past, Mickey valued the fact that he himself was valued.

He had already gone through this study once, but he began again, systematically now, removing books from shelves, opening them, examining the shelf behind. He found nothing new. He moved to the desk, knowing that Henry would have made a thorough examination, but it never hurts to have a second pair of eyes on something.

Again, nothing new. He sat in the chair and looked around the room, wondering aloud where he would hide something had he been Geoffrey Cranston.

'Not on the bookshelves, and there doesn't appear to be a safe or a strongbox, not even one buried in the floor. And there is evidence of a fire sometimes being lit, though not often enough in my book, so it's unlikely he'd have stuffed anything of value up the chimney.'

Mickey's gaze fell upon a stack of maps and local history documents on the desk that he had previously looked at but dismissed as unimportant. He picked them up now and re-examined them, this time fully unfolding the maps, and out fell two documents. Mickey pounced on them.

Mickey's smile was wolfish. 'Well, the devil dug from the bottom of the barrel when he made you,' Mickey told the signatory to one of the pieces of paper. Clovis's signature, florid and confident. But why hide them, these two letters? Why not just burn the damn things?

Presumably, Mickey thought, straightening up and stretching his tired back, Geoffrey had kept them so that he had evidence both of his son's foolishness and Mr Russell Clovis's perfidy, but that still didn't answer the question of why they were hidden and not simply filed among his other papers. Did Geoffrey fear that someone would have access to his files? Someone whose presence he did not welcome?

Robert Cranston had been scared, Mickey already knew that; he had written to his father begging him to go away and take his mother and aunt with him. Geoffrey Cranston had obviously also been uneasy in his mind. Had he taken any legal advice? Mickey wondered. He remembered having seen on the desk a solicitor's letter relating to a tenancy agreement, or some such. Mickey found the letter and discovered that it was an application from a tenant farmer to be allowed to buy his rented land. It seemed this had been agreed to and the solicitor had drawn up the documentation, the letter informing both parties that it now needed signing. This had been around a year ago, and another letter confirmed signature, and that the deeds had been passed to the new owner. So if Geoffrey Cranston was seeking legal advice, had he applied to this solicitor, Mr Thomas, for assistance?

The address on the letterhead was local, no more than a few miles away, and so Mickey decided that Mr Thomas would be his next port of call. Taking his latest finds into his pockets, he went to bid goodbye to his hostesses and find his driver.

Bridget was waiting for him in the little sitting room, her sister-in-law, she told him, had gone to lie down. 'She's not been well. I am worried for her. And now, tell me frankly, what else *should* I be worried about?'

Mickey took a seat opposite her. 'It depends on what Geoffrey finally agreed to do. As far as I can see he stood his ground, but I've just found evidence that Mr Clovis had threatened to expose Robert's misfortunes to the world, and to drag the family name through the mud if your brother-in-law did not borrow money from him to pay Robert's debt, and did not secure those loans on this house and land.'

Bridget's face lost all colour. Mickey wondered if she was going to faint, but she rallied. 'And did he sign those papers?'

'As I say, I can find no evidence of him having done so, and it seems this intention was to tell Clovis to publish and be damned. I found a letter from Robert to his father telling him that he understood the decision that his father had made, and that somebody had to stand up to Clovis. Of course, in and of themselves, these letters mean nothing, not in legal terms.'

'So what do you suggest we do?'

'Nothing. If you should receive communications that you find difficult or threatening, then contact me and I will do what I can. I'm on my way now to see Mr Thomas, the solicitor that your brother-in-law used. Is it possible that your brother-in-law sought advice from him?'

She nodded. 'They are old friends. Although most of his business is conveyancing, the drawing up of wills that sort of thing. He would be no match for someone like Clovis. I knew that man brought trouble the moment he came through the door.'

'He's a very confident man,' Mickey stated. 'Most people in his . . . I hesitate to call it "business" but no doubt that's what he would describe it as . . . would not undertake these dealings themselves. They would employ an agent and keep at a distance, put themselves in a position to deny sanctioning any heavy-handedness. That confidence tells me that he considers himself well protected. If anything worries you, you can contact me at Scotland Yard. And please don't hesitate – this is a bad business all round.'

'And do you believe my brother-in-law was poisoned?'

'I think it's possible. But I'm keeping an open mind. The post-mortem will tell us more, but it will take some time before the toxicology results are available to us. If there is obvious evidence of poisoning, then we may have the results within a few days, but if they must look further, then it will take longer.'

She nodded. 'Poor Geoffrey – we knew he was desperately worried about something but he would not confide. He was old fashioned, I suppose. He believed it was a man's duty to care for the finances of house and home. But he was an honest man – what hope do honest men have?'

EIGHTEEN

B
ack at Central Office there was no sign of his boss and Mickey was told that he had been summoned to the assistant commissioner's office. The rumour was that he was in trouble.

It was another hour before Henry returned, and he was bristling with rage. It took a cup of tea and a bit of persuasion before he calmed down enough to explain to Mickey that the Bright-Coopers had complained about his behaviour at the exhumation. They had demanded Henry's suspension and certainly insisted that he be taken off any investigation that had anything to do with their son. The assistant commissioner had declined to do either, but Henry had been reprimanded for his behaviour and put on notice that a further complaint from such influential a family would lead to an official black mark on his record.

'What did you say to them?' Mickey wanted to know.

Henry shrugged. 'They were speaking ill of Cynthia and Albert – I couldn't have that.'

'Well, what's done is done. Now, I had an interesting time at the Cranston house, and then at their solicitors. Geoffrey Cranston seems to have been possessed of more sense and more gumption than his son, that's for sure.'

He spread the documents he'd found on the table in front of Henry. 'Geoffrey took pains to make sure these were not discovered accidentally by either his wife or sister-in-law or anyone else happening to enter his study. I found them folded into a map, quite well hidden.'

Henry picked up the first letter. This was from Geoffrey Cranston to his son and was clearly in response to a letter Robert had sent to him. Henry read aloud:

'"You will understand, Robert, that I will not be blackmailed. You brought that man to our home, in seeming expectation that we would crumble under the weight of scandal that he proposed to bring down on us and I do pity you for the straits you find yourself in. But know this, my boy, that the Cranston family will stand against this, and that we will survive. I will not risk, or have risked, our home and land and I will not stand surety for your debts. I have already agreed to deposit money in your account, for your use, on the understanding that at length it will be repaid. But understand this, I will not stand surety for any loan that you may wish to take out, as this man wishes you to do, and I will not listen to his threats."'

'Strong stuff, and the second document . . .?'

'Is a letter of agreement that it seems Mr Russell Clovis brought to the house on the night he came there with Robert. Obviously Robert needed his father's signature. Clovis anticipated no problem in getting it. They were both disappointed.'

'And now both father and son are dead.'

'And only circumstance ties Russell Clovis to them. Circumstance is a tenuous string at best. But there's more. It seems the day after Clovis's visit, Geoffrey Cranston went to see his friend and local solicitor, Mr Thomas, and had this drawn up.'

'A will. And a codicil.' Henry scanned the document and smiled grimly. 'So he did suspect that Clovis would be underhand in his dealings – if he couldn't get what he wanted legitimately, he would try other ways.'

'And so he had his will re-drawn, signed it there with a solicitor's clerk and another client who happened to be visiting as his witnesses. Mr Thomas said Geoffrey Cranston was in a hurry, determined to get things done immediately. He'd been in ill health for some time, as you know, so his haste was understandable, but, as you can see, he wanted to make sure that his wife and sister-in-law were in sole possession of the house and land. Effectively, he wrote his son out of the will.'

'Effectively he dispossessed his son completely. Ensured that he had absolutely no claim on anything.'

'And then there is the codicil. Which states that if anything untoward should happen after Geoffrey's death, should any documents emerge that seems to suggest that he signed any agreements either with his son or with Mr Russell Clovis, that these documents must be forgeries.'

'And would this codicil stand up in a court of law?' Henry wanted to know.

'Mr Thomas was fairly sure that it would, but it seems he took further, and immediate, advice, from a senior partner and re-drew the codicil according to that advice and had it witnessed appropriately. Geoffrey Cranston seems to have returned that same day, if you see the date, and signed this amended document. It seems to me that Geoffrey Cranston was a very frightened man in the days before his death.'

'And his son survived him only by two or three weeks,' Henry observed. 'Was there any evidence that Clovis contacted Geoffrey in the interim?'

'Not that I could find. My guess is that Clovis realized he could not intimidate the father but now father and son are gone, and the two women left alone, I'm expecting a renewal of his attack – no doubt he will see the woman as a much weaker barrier to what he wants. He most probably didn't know of the legal protections that Geoffrey Cranston put in place and no doubt took him for some country bumpkin who would not have the wherewithal to ask for help.'

Henry nodded. 'Unless Robert told him, of course. A visit to Mr Russell Clovis seems to be well overdue. I have tried to arrange this but unfortunately he is out of town for at least another week. So that will have to wait.'

'And do we know where he is?' Mickey asked.

'Visiting family somewhere near Dublin, but that's all I have been able to discover. We'll have to wait it out. He'll make his move, and we've plenty to be getting on with in the meantime. There is still a great deal we don't understand.'

NINETEEN

The following day brought news that caused both Henry and Mickey to pause. The post-mortem on Geoffrey Cranston seemed to support a natural death. He had suffered for some time with both stomach and duodenal ulcers that his doctor knew eventually would be the end of him, and he had died of a massive internal haemorrhage. The surgeon conducting the post-mortem could find no obvious evidence of poison, but samples of the stomach, the lungs, the intestines, hair and nails had all been taken for testing. Henry knew it could be quite some time before they had any information regarding possible poisoning, and the tone of the post-mortem report seemed to suggest they should not hold their breath.

The post-mortem report on Ferdy Bright-Cooper also arrived and there was no evidence at all to suggest that he had not taken his own life. The family had paid for a post-mortem to be carried out very swiftly on discovery of the body, and this second tallied with the first: a shot at very close quarters, evidence of alcohol in the stomach. But there was a small surprise – there had been a comment at the first post-mortem regarding bruising to the torso, which had been put down to a fall from a horse earlier that day. The second post-mortem suggested that the bruising was more extensive, and that there were broken ribs, bruising to the kidneys and to the liver, and when Henry telephoned the pathologist requesting any thoughts the man might have on this that he had not chosen to put in his report, he was told, 'I don't think this was a fall from a horse. I think someone, or more than one, set about him with boots and fists. The man was beaten black and blue, he's not been in the ground so long that the evidence of that is gone. In fact, some bruising undoubtedly developed post-mortem. And no, it's not post-mortem lividity I'm talking about – sections under the microscope show distinct differences.'

'Where are you going?' Mickey asked as Henry set the phone back on its cradle and grabbed his hat and coat.

'To see the Bright-Coopers and find out who might have beaten seven shades out of their son, and why they were so keen that this wasn't reported at the first post-mortem. What do they want to hide?'

'Henry, that's not a good idea. Let me go and ask the questions. You're in enough trouble with the Bright-Coopers as it is. You do not need a second reprimand and the likes of the Bright-Coopers can cause trouble all the way to the top – you know that.'

'You're telling me I shouldn't be doing my job just because these people happen to have money?'

'I'd never tell you that, and you know it. But money buys influence and there are other ways to skin a cat, Henry. You don't need to charge in now, all guns blazing. In fact, you don't need to charge in there *at all*. At least let me come with you.'

Henry looked as though he might agree, but then a message arrived for Mickey. Nora Cranston had telephoned. A solicitor's letter had arrived that morning, and Mickey had said that she should contact him if anything frightened her. This frightened her very much indeed.

'You can go see the Cranston ladies. I'll see to the Bright-Coopers,' Henry told him.

'No.' Mickey was firm. 'Henry, you will come with me to see the Cranston ladies and then we will go and speak to the Bright-Coopers. By that time your mood will have cooled a little. Henry, you know that I am right.'

Detective Chief Inspector Henry Johnstone frowned, and for a moment Mickey thought he was going to argue and pull rank, but then he shook his head. 'Very well, Mickey, I'll play your way, but it rankles, and you know that. They have name and money, but it seems to me they are severely lacking in common decency.'

'You'll find no argument from me,' Mickey said. 'But, Henry, that doesn't matter right now. We have a job to do, and you'll do it better with a cool head. So put them from your mind for the moment, their snide comments and the hurt they cause people you love – they are hurting too. Their son is dead, and dead by his own hand, which is a deeper pain than thankfully either of us will ever know about and, from the look of it, he was beaten badly before he shot himself dead. Be the bigger man and show a little compassion. Your Cynthia is capable of looking after herself, remember, looking after Albert and the children too. She does not need you riding to her rescue.'

Reluctantly, Henry nodded and Mickey breathed a sigh of relief.

* * *

It had begun to snow by the time they reached the Cranston house, a white blanket spreading softly across the land. The driver was of the opinion that they should not hang around for too long. The sky was full of it and the road already treacherous.

Bridget met them in the sitting room, a merry fire burning in the hearth, though the rest of the house, with its flagstone floors and inadequate heating, was chill and dreary.

'This came this morning. What should I do about it? I have spoken to Mr Thomas and he assures me that they can take nothing from us, but it is still so terrifying.'

Henry took the letter and read it through. It was from the solicitors Hodgkin and Burke, and it gave notice that Mr Russell Clovis intended to foreclose on the debts owed to him by Mr Robert Cranston and underwritten by Mr Geoffrey Cranston. That the house and farm and other ancillary properties had been entered as surety against certain loans and that legal proceedings would follow.

'And so he makes his move,' Henry observed. 'It is as well that Mr Geoffrey Cranston took the steps he did.' Though, he thought, it would be the scribbles of a country solicitor against the type of legal counsel that Russell Clovis could afford, should Clovis actually produce a document he claimed had been signed by Geoffrey Cranston. The outcome could not be certain.

'Be assured,' Mickey told her, 'your brother-in-law took steps against this possibility, and Mr Thomas can give you the details. But I suggest that you and your sister-in-law perhaps go away for a while and let the solicitors fight it out between them.'

'And how much will that cost? Can we afford for this to go to court, Detective Sergeant Hitchens?'

'Hopefully it won't come to that,' Mickey said. 'Speak again to Mr Thomas, be sure you know what your rights are and what your brother-in-law put in place. And then if you have family to visit, or friends that you could go and see for a while, get away from here. This has been a time of great distress for both of you – perhaps a change of scene might help.'

She looked at him shrewdly. 'You're afraid that he'll send bailiffs knocking at our door, even if they have no right to do so?'

Mickey nodded. 'Robert was afraid of that when he wrote to his father. It might be better for your peace of mind if you did leave for a while, close up the house. Is there someone who can manage the business of the farm?'

'Mr Thomas has that in hand,' she said with some relief. 'We have decided that we are going to put this place on the market. We are going to sell and begin again somewhere else.'

Mickey nodded. 'A sound idea.'

'It won't be possible for them to sell until this matter is settled one way or another,' Henry commented as they got back into their car. 'While Russell Clovis makes his claims on this property, they can do nothing.'

'We just have to hope that this is not a big enough fish for Mr Russell Clovis to be too troubled about catching,' Mickey said. 'After all, the farm and the land can't be worth that much, not compared to the other fish he almost certainly has frying. And it would take a fight to get it. My betting is he will make a lot of noise for a while, hope to frighten them into action, and then turn his attention elsewhere.'

'I hope you're right,' Henry said. 'But men like Clovis don't like to lose, even the smaller battles.'

The snow was falling more thickly now; it was bitterly cold even inside the vehicle. Mickey hoped that the cold would dissuade Henry from today's course of action. He suggested that they turn back towards town but Henry would have none of it. 'We are going to see the Bright-Coopers,' he said.

'We could telephone the Bright-Coopers?'

'I want to see their faces when I ask my questions. I *need* to see their faces. The telephone will provide me only with their voices, and that isn't enough.'

'You want to see them squirm,' Mickey said, but for once he didn't sound amused.

Henry, looking out of the window at the heavily falling snow, did not trouble himself to disagree.

TWENTY

The worsening weather meant that it took them almost two hours to reach the family seat of the Bright-Coopers, and by the time they did so, Mickey, Henry and the driver were chilled to the bone. The roads had not yet been cleared of snow, which was still falling very heavily, and several times on the journey the car had skidded. Mickey sensed that Henry was regretting his decision but was too stubborn to say so.

At the end of the tree-lined drive, the view opened out and the house rose up before them like a self-satisfied, many-windowed monolith. The driver, hopeful of a better welcome in the kitchen than the chilly welcome his superiors were likely to get front of house, drove the car around to the rear of the house, and Mickey silently wished that he could go with him.

The door opened and a butler asked their business. Mickey introduced himself and Henry. The look on the butler's face suggested Henry's fame had preceded him. It behoved the staff to take their master's side, Mickey thought, and he was not surprised, when they were let in with great reluctance, that they were kept waiting in the fine but very cold hall. Marble floor, high ceiling, no fire.

Mickey stamped his feet impatiently, spreading snow from his boots and leaving grimy puddles on the white marble. Henry, in contrast, stood stock-still, his hands thrust into his pockets. After ten minutes or so, the butler came back and suggested that the housekeeper might have a word with them if they returned to the back of the house and went through the tradesman's entrance. He implied that this was the only proper way for two police officers to enter a house such as this.

Mickey felt like thumping the bastard but also knew that he was just carrying messages.

'I'm here to see the master of the house, not the housekeeper,' Henry said, and the chill in the hall seemed to deepen.

'My master has no wish to see you,' the butler told him. He sounded calm and in control, but Mickey could see that he was uneasy. Come to that, Mickey was uneasy. He rarely saw Henry in this kind of mood, and when he did, it usually meant trouble.

'Very well,' Henry said, but then, instead of turning back towards the front door, he set out across the hall and opened one of the doors that led off to the side – the door through which the butler had earlier disappeared. Mickey followed cautiously, the butler in more rapid pursuit.

'All right,' Mickey muttered to himself, 'so that's the way we play it, is it?' To be truthful, had this been a more modest abode, Mickey would have behaved in exactly the same way as his boss was now doing, but social habits and the desire to keep out of the mire meant he was usually more circumspect when it came to dealing with the rich and well connected. Mickey's father had driven a coal delivery wagon and his mother had taken in washing and cleaned floors in houses not nearly as posh as this one. Mickey really had dragged himself up by the bootstraps. In contrast, Henry's father had been a doctor, living in the sort of house that Mickey's mother might have cleaned, but the doctor would have been no less of a servant to those who resided in places like this. The difference in social standing was something Mickey ignored most of the time, his role as detective (and his friendship with Cynthia) gaining him entry to places his father would have merely dreamed of. Occasionally, though, Mickey's caution in dealing with what were supposed to be his social betters reasserted itself in the cause of self-preservation. If Henry was going on the rampage, Mickey was going to stand back and hopefully stay clear of the flak. Or come to the rescue, depending on which was more appropriate.

Henry threw open the door and stood on the threshold, seeming to take pleasure in letting the chill air into the warm room. From where he stood, Mickey could see the fire burning in the hearth and two men sitting, one behind a desk and one in a comfortable chair off to the side. They seemed to be going through some paperwork but looked up in astonishment as Henry stormed in.

'I have questions to ask you,' Henry said.

The man behind the desk stood up and Mickey guessed that this was Mr Bright-Cooper senior, Ferdy's father. There was a superficial family resemblance, but this man was heavier and more jowly than his son had been.

'And I had you reported to your seniors. I have no wish to have dealings with you. I asked that you be removed.'

'No notice was taken of your request,' Henry told him. 'No, I have travelled here to bring you news of your son and to ask you questions about the condition of his body. I will not be ignored.'

Bright-Cooper's eyes flicked uneasily but he stood his ground. Mickey wondered who the other man might be. He guessed something to do with business, possibly the family solicitor, or a land agent or something of that sort. He, too, was now standing but had moved off to the side as though taking care not to cut between these two adversaries. He had, in fact, Mickey realized, adopted a similar position to the one Mickey had taken.

'Why did you not report that your son had been attacked and

badly beaten, in all likelihood by at least two assailants? He had been kicked and stamped upon, his ribs broken. His liver could easily have been ruptured, his kidneys were bruised, his legs so black and blue that even walking would have been painful for him. Even sitting or lying, he would have found no rest.'

'He had fallen from his horse,' Bright-Cooper said coldly.

'Horses do not have booted feet. The marks they leave are quite different. So who attacked him, and what message did they intend to send to you?'

Henry took a step into the room and Mickey turned his attention to the second man, watching his reaction. This was news to him, Mickey could see that, so not somebody in Bright-Cooper's confidence then.

Mr Bright-Cooper seemed to remember that he had someone in attendance on him. 'That will be all, Briggs,' he told the butler. And then to the other man, 'Michael, if we may continue this another time?'

The man nodded, gathered his possessions together and went into the hallway where Briggs hastened to fetch his coat and ring the bell to tell the maid to have his driver bring the car. The man came up quite close to Mickey, the two of them looking back into the room, equally curious, equally wary, if for rather different reasons.

'He was attacked?' the man asked Mickey, speaking very quietly.

'Brutally so.'

'Was it because . . .?' He shut up before he finished the question, suddenly aware that he might be overheard.

Mickey looked squarely at him. 'Who might you be?' he asked.

The man was slightly taken aback. 'Michael Farrant,' he said. 'I deal with some of Mr Bright-Cooper's business affairs.'

Mickey filed that piece of information away; his attention now once more on his boss.

'You must have known about the beating. Did he come to you, did he ask for your help? Or were you the cause of it – something you have done? Were your son's problems not of his own making after all?' Henry snapped at the older gentleman.

'How dare you come here insinuating—'

'Something you have done then,' Henry said. 'The guilt must be painful. You have done something and your son was punished for it, whatever it was. The burden was so great that your son went on to take his life.'

'My son had debts. He could not bear the shame of them.'

'Debts that, I believe, could have been cleared with no difficulty. Your family has sufficient money. The sale of Ferdy's wife's jewellery alone would have covered his losses, or so I'm led to believe.'

'And who told you that? That brother-in-law of yours? A man in trade, who knows the value of nothing.'

'And the price of everything. Yes, I know. He is beneath you. But he was Ferdy's friend, as was I. I knew them both during the Great War. I came to respect your son and I am happy to say that I believe that respect was returned.'

'Respect? You don't know the meaning of the word. If you did, you would not come bursting in here, into a house that is grieving, with your accusations.'

Mickey had not been aware until this moment that Henry had known Ferdy Bright-Cooper for so long, or under those particular circumstances. But then Henry rarely talked about the war, and when he did, he only touched upon those happenings that Mickey had been witness to. Mickey also noted that the two men were standing closer now. They were of equal height, but Henry was slimmer, muscled and athletic. His unconscious boxer's stance provocative.

'I'll see you ruined,' Bright-Cooper told him. 'And that sister of yours too.'

'Big mistake,' Mickey breathed.

Henry's fist connected with Bright-Cooper's jaw.

Moments later they were standing out in the cold, waiting for the driver to be summoned, and Michael Farrant was laughing heartily as he got into his own vehicle. 'You have an almighty right hook,' he said. 'It gave me great pleasure to see that, but I fear you have let yourself into a whole world of trouble.'

'You made a comment as we stood together in the hall,' Mickey said. 'You began, "Was it because". Because of what, Mr Farrant?'

Michael frowned. 'I meant nothing.'

'Then I will make an appointment to see you at a later time,' Mickey said. 'Your address, please, Mr Farrant, and a convenient time to come and visit.'

Michael Farrant got into his car, but Mickey was in the way, and he could not close his door.

'Mr Farrant?'

'They argued, that's all I know. They argued because Bright-
Cooper senior was putting pressure on his son to make further
investments on his behalf. Ferdy told him it was useless, that it was
a stupid decision. Of course, his father then lost his temper.'

Mickey was puzzled.

'You mean it was Bright-Cooper senior who beat seven shades
out of his son?' Henry questioned. 'The father and the brother
perhaps. Is he another man who dislikes being crossed?

Mr Farrant looked very uncomfortable but nodded. 'I don't know
for certain. But I do know that the brother is a brute of a man . . .
You could not have found a nicer fellow than Ferdy but his younger
brother, well, he's a real chip off the old block. I do know that
Ferdy was distraught that his father blamed him for the family
losses, even though it had been his father who had insisted the
investments be made. Ferdy warned him against them. But people
don't usually say no to Bright-Cooper senior.'

Mickey stood aside and Farrant drove away. 'You guessed as
much, didn't you?' Mickey asked.

'I grew up with a brute of a father, you know that. You recognize
the signs. And I knew Ferdy back in the Great War. There were
times, Mickey, when I almost thought he would do anything not to
go back to his family, even getting himself killed. He loved his time
in the army, he loved the fight. He did not lack courage, Mickey,
not ever. But he could not upset his father or his brother because
he knew if he did, then his mother and his sister would suffer for
it. It was a relief to him when his sister married and their mother
took to spending a great deal of time in her daughter's home. But
even when Ferdy married, he could not fully escape because he was
the eldest son, the inheritor. And now he's dead.'

'But what the hell were you thinking just now?' Mickey asked
as they got into the car. He understood now why Henry would hate
this man, but even so, this was strange behaviour even for Henry.
'If you get away with just a suspension, you'll be lucky. I don't
know what the hell has been getting into you lately.'

Henry turned to look at his sergeant, massaging his knuckles. 'I
can't tell you,' Henry said. It was almost a breath of sound. 'Not
yet. Just keep the faith, whatever happens.'

Mickey's eyes narrowed. 'You know I will,' he told his friend.

TWENTY-ONE

I t was almost eight o'clock in the evening by the time they got back to Scotland Yard and all three, the driver included, were frozen through. Snow had given way to a sticky rain that froze on contact with the ground, their clothes and their skin, and Henry stamped impatiently as they crossed the reception area, attempting to free the ice from his boots.

'Detective Sergeant Hitchens.' An urgent call came from the officer stationed at the front desk. 'It's your wife, sir. She's been trying to contact you.'

His tone also caused Henry to pause.

'My wife?' Mickey asked. 'What's wrong?'

The constable raised his hands, placating. 'Now, she's all right, sir, and Detective Inspector Prothero has gone because she knows him, and it was felt that it would be better for her to speak to someone she knew. There was an attack, sir. She's not hurt, I don't think. It was at the theatre, sir. They're still there.'

Mickey raced down the steps and into the yard, waving at the driver who had been hoping to have packed up for the day. A moment later and they were on their way to the theatre, Mickey a bundle of anxiety in the seat beside Henry who, not knowing what to say, kept his mouth shut. The journey seemed to take a long time but it was, in fact, only about ten minutes or so before Mickey was running inside through the stage door and Henry following in his wake.

Belle was holding court, settled in a comfortable chair, her leg upon a cushion set on a stool. Prothero, dapper as always, was seated beside her, the sleeves of his dark jacket exposing a good length of shirt cuff and some rather elegant cufflinks. 'She's all right, old man. No major harm done. Just a sprain, and we got constables out interviewing all and sundry in the area. Fortunately, there were witnesses.'

'I'm all right.' Belle extended a hand towards her husband. 'I was almost at the theatre when someone knocked me to the floor. As I fell, I twisted my leg. The doctor says I have a badly sprained ankle. Sally's gone on in my place tonight and will probably have to do so for a few days.'

Sally, Henry remembered, was Belle's understudy. 'Was it an accident?' he asked. 'Belle, what happened?'

She shook her head. 'Definitely not an accident, I'm afraid. Fortunately, I yelled so loudly that Jim, our doormen, and his boy, came running out. And there was a man across the street out with his wife – he came running over too. There were two of them, you see – one knocked me down, but you see, Henry, the other had a knife.'

'A knife! A robbery then.' Mickey, holding Belle's hand, was examining his wife closely, checking for other injuries.

'It's possible,' Prothero said, 'but I think not. The fact is your lady's handbag was not snatched, despite the fact that she dropped it in her fall. And, according to witnesses, the man with the knife was ready to strike, even though she was already helpless on the floor.'

'Helpless' was not a word normally associated with Belle, Henry thought, but that did nothing to ease his mind. 'Do you think that Belle was deliberately targeted?' He voiced the question that they were all skirting around.

'According to the number of public, Mr John Keane, who was out with his wife, two other women had passed by – lone women, well-dressed – and the two men who attacked Mrs Hitchens were standing on the corner of the road and ignored them. It was only when Mrs Hitchens turned the corner and therefore came into their view that they ran towards her.'

'Despite the witnesses?'

'It would seem so. Mr Keane, to his credit, came running over straightaway and was then joined by the doorman and his young assistant, but the man with the knife turned on them all, seemingly prepared to fight it out until his friend called him away and then they both ran. I think Mr Keane would have given chase, but he had his wife to think about.'

'We've shaken somebody up, that's a certainty,' Henry said.

There was a sudden commotion by the stage door and a young woman, clearly distressed and angry, marched through into the dressing room. Henry recognized her at once. 'Malina? What's wrong? What are you doing here?'

'I went to your flat, but you weren't there. I went to Scotland Yard and they said you were here. Henry, we've been trying to reach you for the past hour and a half. It's Melissa. Someone's taken Melissa!'

'My God,' Belle exclaimed. 'Mickey, get my coat.'

She struggled to her feet and grasped Malina by the arm. 'Cynthia must be frantic. How did you get here? Is there room in your car?'

She looked at Henry, who seemed to be momentarily stunned. 'Well, move yourselves,' she demanded.

'They're coming for our families,' Henry said quietly. 'Mickey, what the hell do they think we know?'

Cynthia's household was in uproar. Uniformed officers were already there, as well as Detective Inspector Prothero, who had arrived just ahead of them. He patted Henry on the shoulder and said that he would find out what they knew, and that he should go and be with his sister. Mickey settled Belle into a hall chair. Albert, hearing their voices, emerged from his study. He looked wretched. Cynthia flew down the stairs, the elderly lady who was nanny to all three of her children following more slowly and unable to control the tears.

Cynthia threw herself at Henry. Never in his life had he seen her more distraught.

'My baby, my baby. They've taken my baby girl.' She was striking Henry with her fists. Henry tried to catch her hands and in the end just wrapped his arms around his sister and held her as close as he could, but he was at a loss to know what to say. He looked longingly through the door of the green salon in the direction of his colleagues, Prothero and the others in conference in the corner of the room. *That*, he knew how to do. How to set up an investigation, how to follow evidence, but this . . .

He held his sister tighter still and then finally surrendered her to Albert, who stood quietly, stroking his wife's back and hair while making those small, soothing noises that a parent makes to calm their distressed child. And it occurred to Henry that suddenly their roles were reversed, Cynthia and Albert. Usually she was the one that held everything together; now it was Albert's turn to be the stalwart.

'Take us up to Melissa's room, please,' Mickey said to Malina. On the way over, she'd explained what had happened. Melissa and her nanny had come back from a walk, the child had gone upstairs to put her coat away and not come back down. On investigation, she was nowhere to be found.

Malina began to lead the way, but Henry was ahead of her. He knew where Melissa's room was, and he pushed past the constable who was standing guard there. Malina had told them what had been left on the bed, but he was unprepared nevertheless. An old rag doll that Melissa had kept from early childhood lay on the bed, a knife piercing through the body and pinning it to the mattress. A long strand of bright red hair, Melissa's hair, was wound tightly around the doll's neck. Henry felt his knees weaken and put out a hand to clutch the door frame.

'Steady now,' Mickey said. He took Henry's arm and led him out on to the landing, setting him down on the top step. 'Now, you stop there till you get your senses back. Let me take a look, and when you are ready, join me, and we'll examine the room together like we always do.'

Henry looked up at his sergeant and nodded. 'I just need a minute.'

'Of course you do.' He turned to Malina. 'Are you the one that came up and found this?'

She nodded. 'I saw it as soon as I stepped over the threshold. I didn't go in. I suppose I just panicked. I called nanny. Actually, I screamed for nanny and she came running in and the both of us went to look to what was on the bed. Nanny couldn't bear it. She reached out as though to take the knife out, but I stopped her.'

'Good,' Mickey praised. 'You know you shouldn't disturb the crime scene. So how did they take her out?'

'Down the back stairs,' Henry said. 'At least, I imagine that's what they did, and most likely they came in the same way, through the yard and in by the rear door. But the question is why didn't she cry out?'

'There was a strange smell in the room when I entered,' Malina said. 'A chemical smell, like you get at the dentist or the doctor's sometimes.'

'Chloroform, in all likelihood,' Mickey said. He glanced around the bedroom. 'Did she put her coat away?'

Malina crossed to the wardrobe and then paused. 'What if there are fingerprints? What if I smudge them when I open the door?'

'Reach out for the top edge of the door, lever it from there, then you won't be touching the knob.'

Malina did as she was told and swung the door wide. 'The coat's not there,' she said. 'Oh my Lord, that means they were waiting for her when she came in. Someone was hiding out in her room. Someone was here already and we didn't know about it!'

Mickey took a deep breath. 'So she came in, they grabbed her, probably held a rag with chloroform over her mouth and nose and, when she was unconscious, they took her down the back stairs. They probably prepared the doll beforehand and just took the time to cut a bit of her hair before they left. I'm going to need my kit. I need to return to the office and get it.'

A hand rested on Mickey's shoulder. 'No need for that, old lad, I'll be taking over from here,' Prothero said quietly. 'Mickey, you and Henry can't possibly work this case, you know that, but I promise you, I will do everything you would have done. You know I'm no slouch.'

Mickey felt as though the world was crashing down on him. Looking at Henry, he knew that his boss was feeling the same. If they could work on this case, be useful, go in search of Melissa then they could cope with this latest horrific turn of events. But he knew in his heart of hearts that they would never get permission to do so and, remembering the events of the afternoon, that Henry would, likely as not facing suspension, be out of the game anyway.

'Who should I choose to work with me?' Prothero asked him.

Mickey thought about it and suggested a couple of names, men he knew would be as thorough as Mickey himself. 'So what am I supposed to do? What's Henry supposed to do? Sit around twiddling our thumbs?'

For the first time, Prothero looked awkward. 'Henry's been called to see the assistant commissioner in the morning,' he said quietly. 'Henry, I don't know what you did, but you're in a heap of trouble.'

'And Mickey?' Henry asked.

'As far as I know, no one is interested in seeing him. And there's enough other crime to go around to keep him out of mischief.'

Henry nodded. Unsteadily, he got to his feet and staggered back down the stairs to find his sister.

'What did he do?' Prothero asked very quietly.

'Thumped some bugger that insulted his sister,' Mickey told him.

'So what's he planning on doing to whoever has taken his niece?' Prothero asked, raising a sardonic eyebrow. 'Mickey, neither of you can work on this case, but that doesn't mean I can't keep you informed.'

Mickey breathed a sigh of relief and then followed his boss back into the hallway. Belle was still sitting on the hall chair, looking lost. Albert and Cynthia were being interviewed by officers, and Mickey could see them through the door of the salon. Malina stood guard in the doorway, her arms folded, staring daggers at the policemen. Henry and Mickey aside, it was well known that she was no lover of the constabulary. Having grown up in Gypsy camps and traveller communities, she had no reason to regard any of them with favour. But there was desperation in her eyes too, Mickey could see; she'd be willing to accept anybody who could help get Melissa back. Malina loved Cynthia and her family.

She turned to Mickey. 'I can't bear it, not being able to act.'

'If I can borrow a car, are you happy to come with me and do something?'

'Anything, you know that.'

Mickey glanced at his wife, who was looking at him expectantly. 'You think Malina's people might be able to help?' she said.

'They can keep an eye out, they can listen to the whispers, get into places that the police can't.'

'Why the hell didn't I think of that?' Malina was suddenly furious with herself.

'Has Cynthia got that little Ford of hers here? And you know where the key is kept?'

'Yes to both.'

'Before you go,' Belle said, 'Malina, maybe you can find me a walking stick so I can at least get around, and direct me to a telephone. I have friends all across London, you know that. The theatrical community is spread almost as wide as the Gypsy one, and the more eyes we have on this the better. Melissa is distinctive with that red hair of hers. Whoever's got her, they've got to keep her somewhere.'

'Good.' Mickey approved.

Henry had been listening to all of this. 'What can I do?'

In that moment, Mickey pitied his boss. Henry was used to being in control, to directing operations, not standing on the sidelines. 'For tonight, your sister needs you here. Go and sit beside her, hold her hand, just be with her, Henry. Who knows what tomorrow will bring.'

'A difficult interview with the assistant commissioner, apparently.' Henry smiled wryly. 'I know I have brought the situation upon myself, Mickey. I need no telling.'

He turned away and walked slowly into the salon, taking his place on the sofa beside Cynthia and grasped her hand as Mickey had instructed. Cynthia looked up in surprise and then laid her head on Henry's shoulder. Mickey realized he was breathing a sigh of relief. He had been desperately afraid that Cynthia would see this as Henry's fault in some way, or Mickey's fault, or both. That their investigation had brought this to her door. But the bond between brother and sister was too strong. She might blame him, but she could not hate him. She knew how much he loved Melissa, how much his heart, too, must be breaking at the thought of where she might be, and what those who had taken her might have done to her.

Mickey pushed those thoughts aside. Going down that road, he told himself, would lead nowhere good. This is an investigation; he would work the case, follow the normal procedure and, even if he was not directly involved, there was still a lot he could do. He had to go on believing that.

Henry's words came back to him. *What the hell do they think we know?* he had asked. Mickey could think of nothing in their investigation so far that would have presaged this level of aggression – for Belle to be attacked and then Melissa to be taken, even if no instructions had been left. Nothing that said to not call the police, nothing that could be constituted as a ransom demand, just this strange threat: the stabbed doll, the hair twisted around its neck. It reminded Mickey of the toy rabbit, disembowelled and slashed and wrapped in butcher paper that Lady Helford had shown to them. So regarding the threat to Lady Helford's great grandchild, did Melissa's kidnapping make it more likely to be true? What was the woman not telling them? What did she know that she wouldn't say? Again there had been no sense that threats had been made about police involvement, just that oblique warning of the toy rabbit. What *had* the note said that she had burned in the fire?

Mickey decided that the local constabulary should question Lady Helford again. And if she wouldn't answer them, then other means needed to be employed.

Malina had taken Belle through to Albert's study and provided her with one of his walking sticks. It had all the scars of a life lived slashing at brambles and nettles rather than one of giving support, but Belle announced that it would do very well. 'Be careful,' she told Mickey as Malina left to gather up her coat and bag. Belle would explain to Cynthia where they had gone. In her bag, Belle had a little book that Mickey knew contained the addresses and telephone numbers of a great many boarding houses, and small hotels where travelling theatricals and those who needed cheap lodgings in the city tended to stay. The landladies of these places knew everything, Belle assured him.

Mickey was a little dubious that this could be of help, but his wife was probably correct – the more eyes on this the better, though he knew theatrical landladies were also inveterate gossips and news of the kidnapping would be all over London before dawn.

Did that matter? Would it cause the kidnappers to act precipitously and harm Melissa? Mickey understood that he had no way of knowing one way or another but there was something odd about a kidnapping when a ransom demand had not been made, with no warning to keep the police out of things. Sufficiently odd that Mickey felt that the normal rules did not apply.

Mickey drove in silence as Malina gave him directions, allowing his thoughts full rein.

Nothing made sense lately. It felt like they were being led along the garden path. First there was the death, made up to look like suicide, of Robert Cranston. That had brought them to the Cranston family, and to the solicitor who told them of other suspicious deaths, or deaths that might be viewed as unusual, such as that of Ansel Peach. On the face of it, this was another unfortunate but common-place suicide of a man despairing of his financial situation and yet, and yet, the behaviour of the man was not what you'd expect. Something bothered Mickey about all of that. Diamond Annie certainly didn't think that this man was in any way commonplace or that his suicide was in any way ordinary, in fact Annie was doubtful the man was even dead.

Then there was Mrs Green, alias Mrs Connacht. Henry had dismissed her as being relatively unimportant in all of this, and Mickey had agreed, but now he was not so sure. And what about Sir Ralph Helford? Had the hit-and-run really been an accident, or was it much more than that? Was his family really being threatened? Had Lady Helford really staged the ransacking and thefts at her family home?

'There's something exaggerated about all of this. Something almost theatrical,' Mickey said.

Malina glanced at him. 'About all what?'

Mickey hesitated for a moment and then he decided that he had nothing to lose. 'You want to listen while we drive? Then I have a story to tell. Maybe you can make more sense of it than I can.'

'I like a good story,' Malina said. 'And frankly anything to take my mind off this.'

'I can't promise that,' Mickey told her. 'But this is how the land lies.'

For the next hour he told her about their investigation, about the strange paths it had led them down, and about Henry's assault of Ferdy's father – because assault it certainly was, however provoked.

Wide-eyed, Malina asked, 'Will he lose his job? I mean, it's one thing to say something and get that complained about, but to strike a member of the public, even an obnoxious one, that's common assault, isn't it?'

Mickey nodded grimly. 'I don't know what's got into him lately, I really don't. He's not been right, even for Henry.'

'No one's been right lately,' Malina asserted. 'With all that's happened, everyone's unsettled. People are scared, frightened that the depression will come over here, like it's started in America. You should see the crowds around the street-corner preachers – you know, the ones that talk about the end of days, Revelations and all that stuff. There was one at the end of our road a couple of days ago. Gathered quite a crowd, he did, until the police moved him on. Wearing one of those sandwich boards over his shoulders, with some quotes on it, claiming that the Wall Street Crash was a sign of God's displeasure or some such. You know what they're like – everything is a sign of God's displeasure.'

Mickey laughed and then frowned. 'Yes, but I wouldn't have thought you got those sorts at the end of *your* street. Cynthia's house is in a pretty exclusive area, isn't it?'

'It's the first time, now I think about it. One of the maids came back with some tract he'd shoved into her hand. Reckoned he was quite insistent, even followed her down the street for a bit before she said she'd take it just to get him off her back. Apparently he'd done it to a few of the maids. Someone reported him and the police came after that and sent him on his way.'

She looked at Mickey, who had grown suddenly tense. 'I've just said something, haven't I?'

Mickey nodded, trying to cast his mind back. Street-corner preachers were so commonplace that he usually ignored them. He regarded them as a little crazy but mostly harmless. He knew the better ones made a decent wage from their oratory, preaching a little sermon, passing the hat or leaving a cap laid down for

donations from passers-by. Preachers, political reactionaries, revo-
lutionaries were all part of the background cacophony of London,
setting up their soapbox wherever they could, and as long as they
didn't do it in a forbidden area, such as outside a labour exchange,
nobody official took much notice of them. If necessary, the local
constables usually moved them on in a friendly sort of manner, but
something else was, as Henry would say, ringing bells.

'There was a preacher like that outside a café where we had
breakfast the other day, shouting the odds,' Mickey remembered.
'Little man in a flat cap, his sandwich board was almost too big for
him. It dragged on the ground when he walked.'

'No, this guy was big. Tall, wore a trilby, I think, and a heavy
overcoat. But they are ten-a-penny, Mickey.'

'True,' Mickey agreed. But there had been another one, hadn't
there? A tall man, in the streets when they walked back from seeing
Diamond Annie. On the edges of her territory, Annie not being one
for religious types, or for anyone she could not profit from, come
to that. And he had been tall and wearing a trilby or a fedora, Mickey
couldn't call to mind which. He, too, had been loud, and distributing
small booklets full of biblical verses.

Probably nothing, Mickey thought, but the bell would not stop
ringing. It occurred to him that this would be the perfect disguise
for anyone observing the police officers in their duties, or for
watching Cynthia's house and seeing which maidservants went what
way, by which door they entered. Whether the door was left locked
or not – and Cynthia's doors were rarely locked in daytime, he
knew that. It was only last thing at night, when the butler went
around checking security before he retired. Beyond that, Cynthia's
home was a relaxed one, not like some houses where the servant's
comings and goings were closely observed, monitored and often
written down.

Could it be that someone had been watching them, himself and
Henry? The more Mickey thought about it, the more he felt that
Henry was probably the target of their observation and perhaps their
malice. True, somebody had attacked Mickey's wife, but even that
seemed staged. He had no doubt that Belle had been in danger, but
there were many other places on her route where she could have
been felled and stabbed and left for dead or indeed left dead, and
no one would have known; there would have been no one to inter-
vene. The route from Mickey's house to the theatre was a good

half-hour walk, and Belle was in the habit of cutting through alley-
ways and narrow streets on this route that was so familiar to her
she never thought of looking for danger. No, whoever it was who
attacked Belle wanted it to be known that she had been attacked.
Wanted to divert Mickey and Henry, wanted to clear the way for
the snatching of Melissa. Or perhaps simply wanted them to
understand that both of their families were under threat and
that their attackers had the resources to directly threaten them
simultaneously.

'I think this is bigger than a few gentleman lenders charging
high interest,' Mickey said. 'Something tells me that this is more
personal. Something tells me that there is hatred behind this, not
just money.'

Malina glanced at him. 'Those out for personal revenge are far
more dangerous than those who just want the cash,' she agreed.
'They'll go much further, won't they, Mickey?'

'I'm afraid they will.' But that got him no further in knowing
who or what or how they could resolve this.

TWENTY-TWO

They reconvened for a late breakfast the next morning – Malina
and Mickey had returned, and Belle had slept the night at
Cynthia's house. There were police officers on the door and
others in the street, and the newspaper seller on the corner carried
news of the kidnapping. As Mickey had predicted, everyone knew
that Melissa had been taken and was speculating about a ransom
demand and talking about Albert's recent business troubles.

The mood was sombre. Cynthia picked at her food and Albert
drank coffee and smoked as though it was going out of fashion.
Initially, they had not been aware that Mickey had even borrowed
the car the previous day. It had been some time before Cynthia even
realized that Mickey or Malina had departed, and then Belle had
explained their errand.

Cynthia brightened a little when Malina told her that the word
was now out among the traveller community, both within London
and outside, and that word would spread. If anyone sought to take

Melissa out of the city, or even to hide her close to any of the markets or trading places or the stopping places for the traveller folk, in or about the boundaries of London itself, they would be seen.

Belle reiterated that the theatrical community were equally well spread, that so many eyes were now looking for Melissa, observing anything strange or untoward that they would outnumber the police by perhaps three or four to one.

Cynthia tried hard to smile, but Mickey could see the effort. Henry, across the table, nodded approval. The siblings had aged, Mickey thought, as had Albert.

'Does Cyril know?' Malina asked. He was away at boarding school. He and Melissa were very close, but it had been decided to wait until morning before Cynthia contacted her son. The local police had been informed, however, and the headmaster forewarned in case of any strangers or suspicious activity in the area.

Cynthia nodded. 'I spoke to him an hour ago. He wants to come home, but I think perhaps he should stay where he is. We'll decide later on today what to do. The truth is I would like him back here, but I don't know what to do for the best. What could he do if he did come home? What can any of us do?'

'I thought they were supposed to send a ransom note or something.' Albert sounded almost petulant. He did not understand the script that was playing out; it didn't match with anything that was familiar to him from fiction or from what he might read in the newspapers.

'That still might happen,' Henry said quietly. 'I suspect whoever has taken Melissa wants us as frightened as we possibly can be before they act. That way we are more likely to give them whatever they want.'

'We would have given them anything from the outset,' Cynthia said. 'You know that.'

'*I* know that, but do they?'

There was silence for a moment, and then Mickey got up and said that he must leave. He still had work to go to.

'But you had no sleep,' Cynthia objected.

'I will be fine, my dear. And I'm already late. Henry, are you ready?'

Henry nodded. His appointment with the assistant commissioner was at eleven. He'd done his best to tidy himself up and had borrowed a clean shirt from Albert, but he knew his clothes were crumpled and his eyes dark-shadowed and bleary. 'I will go and see the assistant commissioner, receive my reprimand, and then come back here,' he said.

Mickey kissed his wife and asked what her plans were for the day.

'Belle will remain here, within my house,' Cynthia said firmly. 'With the doors locked and if necessary the windows barred. I will keep her safe, Mickey. I will not fail in my duty of care again.'

'You failed at nothing,' Mickey told her. 'Melissa will be found. The fault is not yours.'

Cynthia was suddenly in floods of tears and the other women gathered around, offering comfort. Albert stood up, rocking back and forth on his heels, and then followed Mickey and Henry out into the hallway. 'The morning newspapers are full of our business,' he said. 'Oh, it's not that I care for any of that – nothing matters now apart from the safety of our little girl, but do you think it will force their hand?'

'I think not,' Mickey said with more confidence than he felt. 'There was no message warning you not to call the police, no sign that they were bothered about this. They must know, because of your relationship with Henry, that this could not be kept quiet. The publicity will be difficult, I know, but perhaps it may help.'

Albert nodded. Mickey could guess that he was also worried about the financial implications of all of this, that his creditors would now be apprised of the full extent of his losses, or worse, might believe the exaggerations in the press. The business deals he had been trying to set up to revive his professional standing might well suffer. He could also see that Albert felt guilty about worrying about this, but he understood. Business was a part of his life that Albert could control. It was something he could manage – do something about. Albert could negotiate his way into and out of most situations and had confidence in his ability to do so – the recent misjudgements notwithstanding. About his missing daughter, he could do nothing. It would be equally hard on Henry, Mickey thought. Henry understood all too well how difficult it was to be forced to stand by and do nothing when every fibre within him told him that he should be out there investigating. Doing what *he* was good at. Managing those things that *he* could manage well. Henry would be chafing with the frustration of that.

'Do you think you'll be dismissed from the force?' Mickey asked as they walked away from the house.

'I don't know,' Henry said flatly. 'And, somehow, I can't bring myself to worry about that. Mickey, in my wildest nightmares, I never believed that anything like this could happen.'

Mickey paused. 'I think we may need to summon a taxi,' he said. 'Or borrow your sister's car again.' He indicated a gathering of people at the end of the road. They were being held back by the two constables, but they had spotted Henry now and were pushing forward. Journalists and photographers.

Henry stared blankly in their direction and Mickey cut back into the house and retrieved the car key for the little Ford he had driven the night before. It was still parked at the kerb where he had left it.

'Come on, Henry.' He tugged on his boss's arm. 'I have warned Albert. The constables will keep the pack at bay. There is nothing to be done about it.'

'There's nothing to be done about most things,' Henry said bleakly as they drove away.

TWENTY-THREE

Melissa woke. Her head was hurting, and her eyes felt as though someone was prising them from their sockets with a teaspoon. And she felt horribly sick.

'There's a bucket by the bed,' a quiet voice said, 'if you feel nauseous.'

Melissa managed to roll sideways and put her head over the side of the bed before retching painfully. It was hours since she'd eaten, so not much came up and she only spat bile into the tin bucket.

A cloth was pressed into her hand. 'Wipe your mouth and then drink this. It will make you feel better. It is the chloroform that has upset your stomach, and I have some cream for your lips – your mouth will be sore. Chloroform can burn the skin a little, if it's not administered carefully. And I don't think he was too careful.'

The woman did not sound particularly bothered about that, Melissa thought. It was as though she was simply explaining, not excusing, and now she'd mentioned it, Melissa realized that her mouth and indeed the skin around her mouth did indeed feel very dry and very sore, and that her lips were cracked. She sat up properly, wiping her mouth with the cloth and then glaring at the woman who stood a few feet away from her. The woman held a cup in her hand and held it out to Melissa.

'It's orange juice with a little warm water,' she said. 'It will make you feel better, and look, there's more in the jug over there. I sweetened it – the sugar will help.'

Melissa made no move to take the cup from her. The woman shrugged, then drained it herself and set it down beside the jug. 'Well, when you're ready. But look, I'm still standing upright, aren't I? It isn't poisoned. So be a good girl and don't make a fuss. The orange juice is there, and there's some salve next to it in that little pot. I'll leave the bucket just in case you need to be sick again.'

'Who are you? Where am I? What am I doing here?' Melissa could hear her voice was croaky. Her throat felt dry and terribly sore. The woman, who was tall and whose dark hair was fashionably cut, did not reply. She ignored Melissa's question, merely opening the door on the opposite side of the room and preparing to step through. Melissa took a leap from the bed towards her and was brought up short by a length of rope and a chain that encircled her waist and fastened to an iron ring set in the wall. Melissa sprawled on the floor. The woman watched dispassionately as she scrambled back to her feet.

'Now then, no need for all that. You can reach the orange juice, there's a chamber pot beneath the bed, and you already know about the bucket. Later, I'll bring you some food. Now be a good girl.'

And with that she closed the door behind her and Melissa was left alone.

For a moment or two, Melissa stood beside the bed, taking in her surroundings. The room was very quiet. There was a barred window quite high up on the wall and the door itself was small – the woman had to duck her head as she went through. An attic room then, Melissa thought. The floor was boarded – she could see exposed wood closer to the door, but the rest was draped thickly with colourful rugs. It was this oddity that caused Melissa to pause. It was evident that she'd been kidnapped, but what a strange room to keep a prisoner in. Her head was still pounding and her throat felt as though it was as cracked and dry inside as her lips were. Reluctantly, she crossed the room to where the orange juice sat in a jug on a little table. Her hands shook and she was forced to use both of them to hold the jug steady, feeling the warmth of the liquid, so that she could pour the orange juice, diluted with the sugar syrup, into the cup. Begrudgingly, she was forced to admit that it was the best thing she had ever tasted and, as the woman had promised, it soothed her throat and began to ease her headache.

How long had she been unconscious? Melissa wondered. The last thing she remembered was running upstairs to put her coat away, opening her bedroom door and then being grabbed from behind by a man, much taller and more powerful than she was, who had thrust a cloth across her nose and mouth. She remembered that she tried not to breathe, that she'd kicked out, that she tried to stamp her feet on the floor and hope that someone heard, but everything must've happened so quickly. Melissa had a final, vivid memory of consciousness deserting her, a strange smell filling her nose and a sharpness catching the back of her throat, but that was all.

She drank some more of the orange juice. The warmth was going from it now, and so she decided to finish it. The warmth was soothing. She'd have to take it on trust that this woman would bring her food and drink, though she wasn't sure she could swallow much at the moment – even the orange juice struggled to go down.

She was still feeling vaguely nauseous, but the headache was clearing a little and her eyes were less blurry.

'Uncle Henry will come for me,' Melissa told herself. And then more loudly, 'Uncle Henry will come for me,' but the heavy curtain hanging by the barred window and soft rugs on the floor seemed to absorb her voice and deaden the sound. She had the feeling that, had she been capable of it, she could scream at the top of her voice and no one would hear. Not that she could scream, even after drinking – all she could manage was a hoarse, raven-like croak and the pain in her throat grew worse when she said anything out loud. Her lips were cracked and, when she moved them, she could taste blood. The juice, wonderful as it was, stung when it touched her mouth.

Frustrated, but deciding that if she was going to get out of this, she had to be pragmatic, Melissa opened the little pot of salve and sniffed it suspiciously. It was greasy and had a herbal scent – lavender and something else that she could not identify. She rubbed a little on her hand, just to make sure before attempting to touch it to her lips. It felt all right, just greasy. Cautiously, Melissa greased her lips with it, keeping the cloth she had been given to hand just in case she had to wipe it away, but after the initial slight stinging it did indeed soothe the pain.

So, Melissa thought, what would Uncle Henry do? She could feel her own panic begin to rise as the chloroform-induced nausea began to wear off, the terror as the full impact of the kidnap dawned on her. She had been violently ripped from her home and family and brought here for who knows what purpose. Angrily, Melissa stamped her feet, the noise of that too being absorbed by the thick rugs. She wasn't going to panic; she was going to try to stay calm. Uncle Henry would tell her to think this through, to take stock. To analyse it.

Analyse it, Melissa told herself again. Be scientific, just like Mickey Hitchens would be.

Fighting back the tears, and the terror, and a rising sense of despair, Melissa forced herself to think clearly. They had kidnapped her and probably wanted money. She had been given orange juice and cream for her mouth, so the woman at least perhaps didn't want her to suffer too much. Melissa wasn't sure about the man; when he had gripped her it felt as though iron bands had wrapped around her body. No, the man was something else again.

Cautiously, Melissa set about examining her surroundings. The room was small, probably servants' quarters at the top of a big house. She couldn't reach the door – the rope wasn't long enough and it was fastened to a chain around her waist and tied with a complicated knot that Melissa could tell immediately that her fingers were not strong enough to loosen. Another equally complex knot attached the rope to the ring in the wall. Malina had a brother who worked on the Thames barges. Melissa had met him and he'd shown her some of the knots he used in his work. She was reminded of these now. She tugged and pulled for a few moments, but the rope was coarse and the knot was very tight and already her fingers were sore.

She would need something to wedge between the twists of the knot, or something to cut through the rope.

She climbed up on to the bed and managed to grasp the window bars, pulling herself up just enough to look out. Rooftops and sky and a few pigeons. Where was she? she wondered. Still in London? The skyline did look familiar, but perhaps that was wishful thinking.

Reluctantly, Melissa lowered herself back on to the bed. She still felt sick and weak, although the sugar in the orange juice had helped revive her a little. She sat on the bed and looked around at the small room, at the high-barred window, the locked door, the bucket and it all got too much. Although it hurt her throat, lips and eyes, Melissa began to weep. Eventually, it was only exhaustion that made her stop and, pulling the blankets tight around her body, she drifted into an uneasy sleep.

TWENTY-FOUR

Mickey looked into Central Office and dropped down into his desk chair, feeling bone-weary. He had escorted Henry to the assistant commissioner's office then come back here, but now he'd arrived, he wasn't sure what to do next. It was true what Prothero had said last night – there was plenty of crime going on and he would be better off keeping busy. He shuffled through the folders on his desk and then crossed to Henry's to see what might need redistributing while Henry was on 'gardening leave'. It was now inevitable that Henry would be suspended. Lying separate from the rest was an older file, and Mickey remembered that Henry had ordered something from the archives a few days before. Curious, he picked it up, carried it back to his own desk and began to flick through. It was quite a hefty piece of work and contained a lot of technical and financial information that Mickey could not even begin to decipher. This, it seemed, was a case of extortion and fraud against a number of parties and which had resulted in a twelve-year prison sentence for one of the perpetrators and an eight-year sentence for another, two of which were to be hard labour. It was known that there were others involved who had been arrested and imprisoned.

The investigating officer had been Detective Chief Inspector Hayden Paul, a memory that caused Mickey to grimace. His bag man was Detective Sergeant Walter Cole but other officers were named in the investigation, including Detective Inspector Henry Johnstone.

'I remember this,' Mickey muttered to himself. 'Not well, but I do recall something of it.' The date was September 1919, just under a year after the end of the war and around the time when promotion had brought Mickey to Central Office for the first time.

Mickey began to read with more care, recollecting that there had been something in this case that Henry had recognized or remembered and which he had felt impacted on their current investigations. On reading the paperwork, Mickey realized that there were strong similarities. It seemed that a group of men had been lending money at high rates of interest but, not satisfied with that, they had blackmailed their debtors into taking on yet more debt, becoming expert in digging up often minor scandals from their past. The case had finally been broken after the suicide of a young woman. She had written a long letter to her family, explaining why she couldn't go on any longer. The letter was enclosed within the folder and in it she said that she could not face a life of continued penury and scandal, not now that those extorting money from her planned to reveal that she had once become pregnant by a married man and that this married man had obtained an abortion for her. She was frightened that not only her own family would be drawn into this scandal, but that the wife and innocent children of this married man be impacted.

Mama, I fell in love. And for a long time I still had feelings for him, though I know that to him I was a mere dalliance. His wife was away, he was bored and the truth is I think there was little more to it than that on his side. And I feel so foolish that I was taken in by his concern, his blandishments and, yes, his gifts. And now that time has passed, I understand that I'm in love with someone else, and I wish to marry him, but they are threatening to expose me, to tell my fiancé what I have done. And they're threatening to tell this man's wife what we did. They have photographs and letters, Mama. I don't know where they got them from, but I cannot have all of this on my conscience, and so it is better that I'm no longer here. I hope you will forgive me.

Looking at the record, Mickey could see that she had been only twenty-two years old when she had died. The family had taken the very brave step, Mickey thought, of allowing all of this to be made public. They had contacted the police but also approached the family of the man in question. The wife had been horrified, of course, furious and disbelieving at first, but she had become an unexpected ally and, being a woman of independent means, had helped the family through what was a very difficult time. And it was this woman's name that shocked Mickey to the core. 'Mrs Connacht,' Mickey read. 'Well, bugger me. Surely that can't be a coincidence?'

The dates and ages were wrong for this woman to be the Mrs Connacht, or Mrs Green or whatever the devil her name was. But there could well be a familial connection.

Mickey grabbed his hat and coat and was out of the door.

Henry walked away from his meeting with the assistant commissioner just after noon, not sure what to do with himself next. All his certainties were gone, and he had no idea whether this issue could be resolved in his favour. As he came through the gates at New Scotland Yard, he saw a familiar figure standing on the embankment. Otis Freeland.

Otis turned and walked away, and Henry followed him to a Lyons' Corner House and joined him at the table well away from the window.

'I don't have to ask how your meeting went,' Otis said. 'Henry, I am deeply sorry.'

'Are you? Otis, I am entirely cast adrift.'

'I told you that you should isolate yourself, make yourself a better target, but did you have to do so in such dramatic fashion?'

'It seemed like a good idea,' Henry began. 'No, that's wrong. It was not an idea, it was merely a moment. I was angry. I was more than angry.'

Otis had ordered tea and toasted teacakes. Henry watched as Otis inspected the teapot, giving it a stir. 'I promise you, Henry, your life will all be restored to you. I will make sure it is.'

'You can't promise that. They've taken Melissa. Otis, if anything happens to that child, I will personally hunt down anyone who could have prevented it and I include you in that.'

'No one expected that to happen,' Otis told him. 'And should you be in a position where you need to hunt me down, then I will deserve whatever you decide to do to me. But I have men looking for her and she will be found. Between us, we have eyes and ears all over the city, do we not? Police officers will do all they can to protect their own and I expect, from reports I have of your sergeant and your sister's secretary departing in Cynthia's car late last evening, that Malina Cooper will be playing her part as well. Richardson has nothing to gain by killing Melissa and everything to gain by holding her in reserve. It's you he is after, Henry—'

'And he could have me and be welcome, you know that. And how do we know that Richardson is not observing our meetings?'

'We don't,' Otis said simply. 'I have men watching, but whether he is or not will alter nothing. The man is arrogant, Henry, you know that. He believes that he is above us all, cleverer than any of us, and prison has not changed that. In fact, it seems to have reinforced this notion, and I would guess that his unexpected release has further ensured his belief in his own self-worth and the stupidity and fearfulness of others.'

'And so now what do I do?'

'You do the hardest thing of all,' Otis told him. 'You go home and you wait.'

Mickey had left Henry in charge of Cynthia's car but, rather than drive, Henry decided to walk. His initial intention had been to go back to his flat and change clothes, but he found that his steps had taken him in the opposite direction and after a time he realized that he was heading for Diamond Annie's territory.

She met him at the door, took one look at his face and stepped aside, directing him into the same small front parlour where he and Mickey had waited previously. This time he took the fireside chair and, leaning towards the grate, rubbed his hands, only now realizing how chilled he was.

'It ain't right,' Annie told him. 'Not taking a kiddie. I'll beat a man to a pulp without thinking twice, but in a fair fight. You may not like me, Henry Johnstone, but you know what I will and will not do. What most *decent* people will or will not do.'

Henry looked at her. 'Are you decent people, Annie?'

'You got your reasons for coming here, so you best tell me what they are. I figure you're coming for help. I figure you're that desperate.'

He was that desperate, Henry realized. Malina and Belle were using their connections, Mickey was doing whatever it was that Mickey was doing – his sergeant would not allow himself to be distracted by official prohibitions on him working on the case. He was somewhat comforted by the idea that Mickey was still positioned close to the investigative team. Henry no longer had that privilege. He told Annie what he needed to know, then closed his eyes.

When Henry woke, he found a rough blanket had been cast over him, another scuttle of coal had been put on the fire and there were voices outside the door. A moment later the door opened and Annie came in with two men. They looked nervously at Henry, who felt that he was the one at a disadvantage, slumped in Annie's chair with one of Annie's blankets over his lap. One of the men held a newspaper in his hand with Melissa's picture blazoned on the front page. In the picture she looked a little younger and Henry remembered that it been taken at the Henley Regatta the previous year alongside Cynthia and Albert, Ferdy and a few others that he did not recognize, in a group photograph. There was an enlargement of Melissa inset into the main picture.

'Word's out, in the press. Word's out on my side of the law too,' Annie told him. 'You owe me – don't you forget that.'

'I owe you,' Henry agreed. He'd just sold his soul to Diamond Annie, Henry reflected, but at that moment he didn't give a damn.

Mickey climbed the stairs to Mrs Green's flat, hammered on the door but received no reply, and could hear no sound from within. The front door was unglazed and there were no windows on to the landing. He hammered on the door again and then stepped back. Mickey always reckoned he could sense when a place was empty, and not just in the way that there was no one home. He went back downstairs, looked around for a constable and, having obtained one, took him back upstairs and told him to break down the door. Mickey had broken down enough doors in his time not to want to do it again.

The constable, a little hesitant until Mickey told him that he would bear all responsibility, did as he was bid and a moment later Mickey was inside. The apartment was indeed empty. No sign of Mrs Green or Simmons. No sign of the little side tables, or the oddly placed Victorian antiques, or the mountain of soft rugs. A few pots and pans had been left in the kitchen, as had the small table at which Mickey had sat and drank tea. The bed had merely been stripped and left where it was, along with the bedroom furniture.

'Done a flit, have they?' the constable asked.

'Looks that way,' Mickey agreed. 'Now you stop here – I've somewhere else to go and then I'll be back. Anyone tries to get in, you arrest them, you got that?'

Leaving a very puzzled constable behind, Mickey stormed back down the stairs and along the street to the building that housed the offices of Regent Financial Services. He was unsurprised to find that this too had packed up and gone. He didn't have to break the door down here; it had been left ajar, only a scatter of empty folders on the floor and headed notepaper on the desk to testify that the company had ever been there.

Mickey knocked on the door of the language centre, the solicitors' and the other businesses on that landing, and the ones above and below, and was told that the staff of the Regent had come in two mornings before, packed and gone. No one knew anything more.

Much to Mickey's chagrin, when he asked how long Regent had actually been in the building, he was told that it only been about six months. It seemed that while the inhabitants of the office had been friendly enough, no one really knew much about them.

They had taken too much at face value, Mickey told himself, but now his dander was up and Detective Sergeant Mickey Hitchens was on the hunt. He did not like being taken for a fool.

Mickey used the telephone at the language school to phone Scotland Yard and soon had reinforcements and an associate bringing his murder bag to him. He would examine the scene, both in the Regent offices and at Mrs Green's apartment. This at least was something he could be getting on with, and no one could interrupt him on the grounds that it was directly implicated in Melissa's kidnapping, though Mickey was absolutely convinced these things were linked.

Feeling a little better than he had for some hours, Mickey returned to Mrs Green's flat and began the slow and careful examination of what was now a crime scene.

TWENTY-FIVE

Henry, not sure what to do with the rest of his day, had returned to the Helford house and let himself in by the rear door.

The Helford house was cold and beginning to feel damp, and Henry lit a fire in the main living room, deciding that he would bring back down anything he found of interest to the small room and study it there. Then he began his third search of the premises, beginning this time in the attic rooms and working his way down. The three servants had all been quartered at the top of the house.

Henry thought it unusual that the female servants had been on the same floor as the valet, but he supposed that as there was no room on the kitchen level, it was either that or give the valet a room on one of the floors used by the family. Not that it was much of a family, Henry thought. An elderly couple, rattling around in what was really quite a large house. In the servants' quarters, the beds were neatly made, and nothing appeared to have been touched, but the three of them had evidently left, taking all their worldly goods with them.

Henry examined the floorboards but found nothing loose. He searched beneath the newspapers that lined the drawers and beneath the drawers themselves, but there was nothing untoward. He examined the stairs as he went down – no hiding places. He began to question himself: what was he actually looking for? Was he just occupying his mind? Was he just putting off returning to Cynthia's house, that place of despair? Henry sat down on the stairs, put his head in his hands and almost gave in to his own sorrow. Almost.

He took a deep breath and got to his feet and went down to the first floor of the house where there were four bedrooms, one of which was used as Sir Helford's study. The couple evidently did not share a room, although there were connecting doors through to a small dressing room that seemed to belong to Sir Helford. Those items that were left were masculine in nature: ties, collars, bone collar studs. A few dresses still hung in the wardrobe in Lady Helford's room, and, this time, Henry took more care over the examination of the furniture, the floor, the bed. The bedclothes had been dragged off, the rug beside the bed thrown to one side, drawers tipped out on to the floor, but the more Henry looked at it, the more he realized that the damage was trivial. It was beginning to look much more likely that Lady Helford herself had either staged the scene or had it set up for her.

Sir Helford's bedroom was similarly disrupted and similarly uninformative. Henry passed the study, glancing at the bookshelves and checking that the precious volumes he had spotted were still there. He was tempted to arrange for the books to be taken away and stored somewhere until Lady Helford should return. He would have room for them at his flat, he supposed. He didn't rate his chances of getting them entered into the storeroom at Scotland Yard – especially not at the moment when Henry himself was *persona non grata.*

Henry paused. What would he do if he was no longer a detective?

He pushed the thought aside and instead of going into the study he went to the bedroom at the end of the hall, which was evidently set out for guests. He had noticed before that this room was untouched. The bed had been made up, and he thought that strange, but perhaps the Helfords had been expecting guests. He slid a hand inside the bed; the sheets were chill. It didn't take long for an old house to forget the warmth of fire and family and to draw into itself the dampness and neglect that characterized abandonment. Henry sympathized; there were times when he felt he had absorbed that cold sorrow. He remembered his war years as ones of perpetual chill, even in the heat of summer, that sense that even the sun had no heat in it.

Slowly, carefully, but not convinced he would find anything, Henry systematically examined the room, looking beneath the rug, stripping back the bed and tilting the mattress on to its side, exposing the bedsprings beneath. He studied the drawers and the wardrobe, moving the furniture out so that he could see behind and examined the drawer linings – old newspaper again. The base of the wardrobe had been decked out with a piece of wallpaper that Henry recognized from Lady Helford's bedroom. It was decorated with large blue cabbage roses and small sprigs of daisies. He lifted it out. There were panels beneath and he found that one was loose and Henry worked at it for a time, trying to pull it free. Eventually, when he bashed it with his fist in frustration, the panel tilted. Henry laughed at his own ineptness and then reached into the small gap revealed by the lifting of the panel. It was not possible to put your hand beneath the wardrobe itself; it stood on a solid plinth, but once the panel was removed from the inside of the wardrobe floor, in the space beneath the plinth, Henry could see a box. Just a cardboard box that might once have held chocolates or sweetmeats of some sort. He reached inside and retrieved it, before examining the space to see if there was anything more. No, just the box.

He took it downstairs and was satisfied to find that the small front room was now warmer, the fire burning happily in the hearth. However, the coal would not last long, and he hadn't seen any additional fuel elsewhere. It would not take long for the room to grow cold again. He opened the box and then took time to examine the contents. There were two bundles of letters, what looked like a will and a few other papers. Henry realized that he would be better off taking this away and examining it in the comfort of Cynthia's house.

It was only mid-afternoon, but it was growing dark outside, rain clouds gathering. Henry, checking first there was nothing of interest about the box, crammed the contents into the pockets of his coat, let himself out of the house and then went to return the key to the neighbour. He was asked about Lady Helford and told them that she had gone to visit relatives in the West Country. Then he went to find Cynthia's car and headed back to his sister's house, hoping there would be news but suspecting there would be none.

TWENTY-SIX

Melissa didn't know how long she'd been asleep, but she woke when the door opened and the woman returned. A man was with her this time, but not the man who had grabbed Melissa in her bedroom because this man was smaller and more slightly built. He picked up the empty jug and the cup and made room for the woman to put the tray down.

'Sensible girl,' the woman said, noting the empty jug. 'I hope the little pot of salve helped too. There's no need for anybody to be uncomfortable, you know.'

The man laughed at this and the woman glared in his direction. 'Comfortable for now, anyway,' he said.

'Now eat up – I can promise you it isn't poisoned.'

Again, the man seemed to find this incredibly funny.

When they had both left, Melissa sat staring at the door, trying to hear their footsteps on the stairs. From the sound, she guessed that the stairs were carpeted and even the near-silent sound of shoes on carpeted wood disappeared quite quickly. Perhaps a few steps and then a landing and then a turning in the stairs? She was desperate to find out anything about her place of imprisonment, anything that might conceivably help her.

From her observations, she had deduced something about the relationship between the man and the woman: the woman was sympathetic, if cool, but the man didn't give a damn about Melissa. Using the mild expletive felt rather nice. 'Damn, damn, damn,' she repeated. 'Well, damn both of you. Damn all three of you.'

So yes, there were three of them. Something told Melissa that there was nobody else in the house. Perhaps these three, but that was all. And her, of course. Had there been anyone lower in the pecking order than the woman, then that person would have brought the food, they would have presented her with the bucket. That man had only come up because the woman had her hands full with the tray, so there was a small possibility that Melissa might have caused her problems. But the woman was not important to him and so was probably not important to the big man either. She was useful, but Melissa didn't think that she was their equal. The man thought the situation was funny and the other man, the one that had actually kidnapped Melissa, well, he was obviously the most important one of all.

Feeling that she had actually learned something – even if there was nothing she could do with that knowledge – Melissa went to investigate the contents of the tray. More orange juice, warm like before. Sandwiches – cheese and ham – which looked as though they'd been cut with a very blunt knife. So, fresh oranges, fresh bread – were they close to a market? No cutlery, of course, so nothing that she could use to help her untie or cut the rope. Could she break a plate, use a shard of the crockery?

Melissa thought very hard about this. It sounded like a possible plan, but as soon as they collected the tray they would, of course, see the plate was missing and then she might be in real trouble. Melissa had no doubt that she was *already* in real trouble, but for now they were at least being decent to her and she had absolutely no wish to make her situation more difficult. Uncle Henry would advise her to keep calm, and to keep her kidnappers calm. Not to make trouble for herself. She had no doubt at all that her uncle, her parents and Mickey Hitchens would be out looking for her, and Malina too, and probably Nanny and Cook.

She took the tray back to the bed, pulling the blanket around herself and tucking her feet beneath the quilt. Her coat had been left hanging on the bed post and Melissa was glad about this because she suspected she would need it later. The room was not warm. It wasn't particularly chilly, so she guessed the rest of the house must be heated. The fire grate was close to the bed, but it was blocked off. She put a hand on the chimney and it did not strike especially cold to the touch so yes, somewhere there was a fire lit. And this house had electricity, she noticed for the first time. Although there was no longer daylight coming through the window, there was a bulb hanging from the ceiling and although it was dim, it meant she would not be left in the dark at least. She hoped.

She chewed her sandwiches slowly, swallowed with difficulty, helping them down with mouthfuls of orange juice and was suddenly glad that there was a chamber pot beneath the bed.

Having finished her meal and returned the tray to its place, she fished around beneath the bed and found the pot. It was set right at the back, close to the wall and on bare board, the rugs not extending that far. As she pulled it out her hand caught something sharp, and she realized it was a floorboard nail. And that although it was still fast in the wood, she could get her fingers around it.

Might this be something she could use?

Watching the door just in case they came back, Melissa relieved herself and then tucked the pot back under the bed. She took the cloth that she'd been given earlier so that she could wipe her mouth and she wrapped it around the nail. She had to lie flat on the floor, her arm at full stretch, but by tugging the cloth this way and that she discovered that the nail was, in fact, slightly loose. It would take time to work it out of the board, but perhaps she would be able to get it free. It at least gave her something to do, Melissa thought.

She was so involved with her task that she almost did not hear the footsteps coming back upstairs and when she leapt back on to the bed, she was glad of the dimness in the room, so they would not be able to see how flushed she was. Her heart raced and she tried hard to control her breathing.

The woman came back, but this time it was the big man who was with her. He stood in the doorway, silhouetted against the light from the landing. He had to bend as he came in as his head and shoulders were above the door frame. He almost filled the gap.

He said nothing, and neither did the woman. She picked up the tray and walked back towards the door. Melissa wanted to tell her that she'd used the chamber pot and that it would need emptying, but something about the way the man was standing and the woman was behaving warned her that she should keep silent.

The man stood watching her until the woman had gathered the tray and come back to the doorway, and then he stood aside and let her through. For a moment, Melissa was terrified that he would remain and that she would be alone with him.

She held her breath and, what was more, she knew that he was aware of her holding her breath. He was aware of how much he frightened her. He was aware of it because he was used to frightening people. Finally, he followed the woman through the door and closed it behind himself. Melissa listened to them go back down the stairs and something occurred to her all of a sudden. No one had locked the door, not this time or before. The handle had turned, the door had opened and when they had left, there was simply the sound of the sneck locating in the door frame, the ordinary sound of a door closing.

They knew she was tied up tight, so it presumably didn't matter to them if there was no lock on the door. But it mattered to Melissa. It mattered very much indeed.

She forced herself to wait until she was certain no one was coming back and then she emptied the chamber pot into the bucket and put the bucket in the furthest corner of the room and then she crawled back beneath the bed and resumed her work with the floorboard nail.

TWENTY-SEVEN

It was well after seven before Mickey arrived at Cynthia's house, hungry as a horse but quite excited. He had discovered a number of fingerprints at Mrs Green's flat and had dropped them off in the department to be looked at the following day. And he had brought with him the folder that Henry had requested from the archives. He set it before Henry like a trophy.

'You were right,' he said. 'Our current investigation did have a precedent. The old files you had requested had been left on your desk, so I took a look. You remembered correctly, extortion and blackmail and of a very similar pattern to our present problems. And Mrs Connacht is the key to it all.'

'The Connacht woman? In what way?' Henry looked warily at Mickey.

Mickey quickly explained what he had been doing with his day and then glanced across at the bundles of letters and documents that Henry had laid out on a side table in the dining room.

'So is this to be our office then?' he asked. 'What about the servants? What about mealtimes?'

'Cynthia and Albert always use the small dining room unless they have guests and, although we might be guests, we are not sufficient in numbers to need the extra space. Not that anyone's been eating anything much anyway,' he added. 'Cynthia has had a tray taken up to her room and Albert has kept to his study. Cook, of course, has continued to cook as though she was feeding an army. Everyone must do what they must do, I suppose. There is comfort in that.'

'And I'm glad to hear it,' Mickey told him. 'I need sustenance as do you, as will Belle and Malina, I'm sure, and perhaps, when we have eaten, we can distract Cynthia and Albert with some of our findings. The poor loves will be so desperate for any information. I suppose there's been no word?'

'Not a thing. I've been gone most of the day, truth be told. It must have been harder for Albert and Cynthia to be just waiting and waiting and nothing happening.'

'Indeed, it must,' Mickey agreed.

They adjourned – Henry and Mickey, Belle and Malina – to the small dining room, and Henry went down to the kitchen to tell Cook that four people at least would be very grateful of some food. Over dinner they told one another what they had been doing. Mickey's news about Mrs Green and the Regent Financial Services angered Henry a great deal.

'Fools,' he said. 'We've all been fools.'

'Well, now you know that, you can do something about it,' Malina told him sharply. 'This other business, the old investigation, was it your investigation?'

Henry shook his head. 'This was just after I became an inspector. I worked on the investigation, I prepared many of the files and much of the evidence ready for the court, which is how I knew about it, but the chief inspector in charge was Hayden Paul, and he is now dead.'

'Murdered,' Mickey said to Henry's surprise. 'But I will return to that in a moment. 'And you did much more than just prepare papers. It's a decade ago, so you've probably forgotten the detail, but you were responsible for discovering the name of the chief suspect. You cross-referenced these files with others in our archives and that helped the fingerprint department identify Mr Finn McCready as the chief perpetrator – a man with known associations to the Fenians. He was suspected of being a bomb maker, but the authorities could never find proof of that, but he was undoubtedly engaged in fundraising for his cause, and extorting money seem to be quite an acceptable way of fundraising in his eyes.'

'McCready?' Richardson's alias. Henry had almost forgotten that he went by that other name. 'You're right, Mickey, but it's impossible to call everything to mind at once. I knew the bells were ringing in my head, but I could not think what tune they were playing. *McCready*.'

'He was released six months ago. The eventual charge was extortion. There were menaces and threats involved. Blackmail. Suspected abduction – though the child was returned and the family refused to testify, even after the man was caught. It seems they were too afraid of reprisals. The only one other associate that was fully identified was a man called Donnetz. He served his time and went on his way – he was a registered alien and once out of prison was sent back to his home country. It might be hard to trace his movements after that.'

'So how does the Connacht woman figure in this?' Belle asked, and Mickey told her about the suicide and how Mrs Connacht helped the family bring her case to court.

'And now this name has come up again?' Mickey said.

'You said this Mrs Connacht sided with the family of the girl that died,' Belle objected, 'so if she was on the side of the angels then, what's happened now? Can it be the same woman? From what you said, she was younger than a wife with children might have been ten years ago.'

Henry frowned. 'She was a woman then in her forties, from what I remember. Her daughters were grown, sixteen or seventeen I believe, or around that age anyway.'

'But you are forgetting that Mrs Green told us that Connacht was her maiden name,' Mickey reminded them. 'So I'm thinking the right age for a daughter . . .'

'Her mother was a brave woman, undoubtedly,' Malina said, 'but the family would not have escaped scandal, would it? If the daughters were of an age to be courting, it would have affected them both badly. Who would want to marry the daughter of the family embroiled in this kind of scandal? The husband charged with infidelity and with obtaining an abortion, and, what, sent to prison?'

'He was, yes. In fact, he died in prison. Some men are not strong enough to withstand incarceration, and he was one of them.'

'So the poor family suffered so many losses.' Belle was sympathetic too. 'If this woman is indeed the daughter, or one of the daughters, she might well feel bitter about the experience.'

'None of which explains why she has left with such haste or why Regent Financial Services has also departed. Did she owe money?' Henry asked.

'No, we tracked down the landlord. She may have given us the impression that she owned her flat but in fact she rented. Her rent was always paid on time and there were no complaints about her from anyone else in the building. She has lived there for some fifteen months. Regent occupied its office space for just over six. The landlord in the office block says they had excellent references and those are being traced, so we'll have to wait and see what this turns up. However, you are all forgetting something, and Malina has touched on it. The husband was exposed as a fraud and a liar. It was not just the young girl who died – he regularly exploited women and was a known associate of this McCready.'

Richardson, Henry corrected silently.

'When everything came to court, and the scandal truly broke, the family found themselves cast out. Mrs Connacht indeed helped the family of Elsa Bryant, the young suicide. Her family had stood against the extortionists much as Geoffrey Cranston had attempted to do, allowing their good name to be dragged through the mire in the hope that it would help others. It seems the Bryants then managed to live out the rest of their days quietly. They were not rich, they were not important, they disappeared once more into obscurity but for the Connacht family, making a stand spelled ruin.

'I was able to pursue this line of enquiry further through court cases and a trip to the newspaper archive. Within two years the Connacht side lost everything. The husband was imprisoned, the wife had squandered what she had from her family money on lawyers in fighting a libel case that in the end she could not win. Her husband was accused of not just having the affair and procuring an abortion, itself an imprisonable offence, but to have also been part of this gang of men who targeted mainly older women, coercing or persuading them into investing in companies that did not exist, bankrupting them, and, if they sought to withstand this coercion, then threatening their families or exposing them to scandal. In light of the present investigation, it's a very similar scenario. In court, McCready declared that Mr Connacht was no innocent, that he knew exactly what they were doing and the infidelity and the ending of pregnancy were not his only sins. He testified against Connacht.'

'McCready had also been accused of murder.' Henry took up the story, uncomfortable at how much Mickey had discovered and how much Henry now realized he would have to reveal. 'You had perhaps just come to the Central Office – these events might have taken place just a little before. The case was sprawling and involved and I was attached to the investigation, under the auspices of Detective Chief Inspector Hayden Paul. Detective Sergeant Cole was in effect his second in command, despite his lower rank. He had once reached the rank of inspector, did you know that? He was demoted by a disciplinary board though I don't recall the exact details.

'Anyway, there was an elderly lady who had refused to give McCready any more money. Her name was Jessica Wills and it was Connacht who had made the introductions – I believe she'd been a family friend. There is quite an amount of evidence to suggest that it was Connacht who was, in fact, the mastermind behind the organization, and not McCready, but this was something we could never prove and the family could never accept, which is why Mrs Connacht kept spending money on his defence against the extortion claims. Nor could we prove that McCready had killed Jessica Wills, though most of those involved in the case became convinced of that. Anyway, in the end the Connacht family was ruined and I lost track of what became of them.'

'And when you heard the name Connacht the other day, did you make the connection?' Mickey wanted to know.

Henry had felt momentarily something of his old self, but now that excitement faded. He ignored the question and said, 'None of this brings us closer to Melissa. Mickey, I cannot bear—'

Mickey reached out and grasped his friend's shoulder. 'None of us can bear it if we think about it, especially not her poor parents, but until the kidnappers contact us and let us know what it is they desire, all we can do is track down other leads. We can only hope that eventually all the paths converge.' He paused and looked closely at Henry. 'Did you eventually make the connection?' Mickey pressed again. He wanted to know. 'When Mrs Green said that her maiden name had been Connacht?'

'Not immediately. I knew that I recalled the name from somewhere, but this was so long ago.' He looked away awkwardly.

'What are you not telling us?' Mickey asked him. 'Henry, do not lie to me.'

Malina and Belle looked horrified at Mickey's directness.

'A sin of omission,' Henry admitted quietly. 'Not one of commission. Mickey, I—'

'I don't care for excuses, Henry. We have stood together against everything the world has thrown at us since I met you in 1916. We fought side by side, and after the war, when I came to Central Office, we investigated side by side. We've looked down the barrel of a gun more times than I care to remember, so do not lie to me now.'

Henry paused, but only for a moment. 'Otis Freeland,' he said. 'He came to see me not more than a few days before Robert Cranston was killed. He told me that Richardson, the man you refer to as "McCready", had been released from prison and that both Detective Sergeant Walter Cole and Detective Chief Inspector Hayden Paul, both long retired, had been murdered in their homes.'

'I had wondered if either Cole or Paul could be reached to tell me more about this case. Yes, I know your opinion of them was low, to say the least, but it was in my mind that they might be of use. It didn't take me long to discover that they were dead, and that both their deaths were violent. And it seems to be relevant that the deaths of Cole and Paul were disguised as suicide. Someone is playing games, Henry. And you are in the line of fire, it seems to me. Now tell us all you know. And tell me to begin with why you refer to this man as "Richardson". He was imprisoned as McCready.'

'A suspected Fenian bomb maker, and extortionist, a blackmailer. Mickey, would it surprise you to know that he was also working for the British government?'

'And you knew this back then?'

'I uncovered it by accident. Whatever department he was working for did their best to protect him. By rights, Mickey, he should have hanged for what he did. Jessica Wills was only one of his casualties. I wanted to pursue the matter, but both Detective Chief Inspector Paul and Detective Sergeant Cole were resistant. They talked about matters of internal security, and how I, of all people, who had lived through the war, should understand that the British government was only protecting our interests. Perhaps it was, but I began to think that there was more to matters. And in time I began to realize that both Detective Chief Inspector Paul and Detective Sergeant Walter Cole were as corrupt as hell and that I couldn't prove a damn thing.'

Both Malina and Belle were looking askance at him. 'Briefly, Richardson was undercover. He was a man who should have been imprisoned or even shot for actions he took during the war, but he was offered a deal. He would risk his life and get a chance to save his neck. Then by 1919, he was in London, fundraising for his cause. Of course, we knew nothing of this when we began the investigation. The investigation started because a young woman committed suicide and her family accused the man she'd been having an affair with of procuring an abortion. It was a very sordid affair but once we looked into the background – no, when *I* looked into his background, I realized that there was far more to this. His connection to Richardson, McCready, began to emerge. Complaints had been made against McCready and then withdrawn, and I began to be curious about all of this, about what the truth was. It was evident that people were suffering and—'

'And you had to be the one to put it right,' Belle said. 'Oh, Henry, what can of worms did you open?'

'One in which I discovered that certain officers were accepting bribes in order to persuade complainants not to pursue their cases.'

'Cole and Paul,' Mickey said.

'They laughed about it. They were proud of the fact. They invited me to be part of their little scheme, and when the government offered them payment in order to keep quiet about McCready, to go easy on the gathering of evidence when it came to the death of Jessica Wills, this was too much.'

'And so you pushed the case?'

'And so I was transferred to another investigation. By that time, I had put together most of the reports for the court. It was easy for them to say that I was no longer required and could be better used elsewhere. But I know that Richardson was responsible for the death of Jessica Wills. He was seen leaving her house on the night she died and was found in possession of silver and jewellery. Neighbours reported hearing an argument and one saw a man who met his description leaving. They had become concerned about the violence of the argument – it could be heard through the walls – and shortly after McCready left they knocked on Miss Wills' door and subsequently discovered her body. She had been beaten about the head with a poker.

'I know that both Paul and Cole took bribes, and from any side that was offering a bribe. Connacht went to prison, and I am deeply sorry for what happened to his family – that was never the intent. I have reason to suspect that it was Detective Chief Inspector Paul who persuaded the wife in her pursuit of the libel trial for his own gain. She had endangered their investigation, you see, and he was not a man who liked to be crossed, so in the guise of friendly advice, he recommended a lawyer. I could not prove it, but I believe that he took payment from this lawyer. In the end, of course, she lost everything. Her husband had been convicted and died in prison. She could not prove that he had not been the chief agent in what had gone on. In the end she was reacting to any small suggestion in the press, to any implication of further guilt and threatening to sue.'

'So what happened? Were they ever brought to justice, these men, these police officers?' Malina sounded as though she were unsurprised by corruption within the police force. Given her history, Henry understood.

'Both took early retirement within six months of the case ending,' Henry told her. 'They didn't get their full pensions, but they seem to have thrived, nonetheless. They should both have been dismissed, disgraced, stripped of rank and pension. But I managed to get McCready put inside for longer than he would have been. I made a deal, Mickey. I had evidence against Cole and Paul and I took it to the highest authority I could find. No one wanted the scandal, but strings were pulled and McCready, Richardson, or whatever you want to call him, was imprisoned. Not for long enough, and not for a capital offence, but I had to be satisfied.'

'And Detective Sergeant Cole and Detective Chief Inspector Paul retired,' Mickey said.

'I did what I could,' Henry said. 'It was not enough, but I did what I could.'

They fell silent for a moment, then Malina asked, 'And you believe that it is this man, this Richardson, who has taken Melissa?'

'I do.'

'And this Otis Freeland, what is he?'

Mickey laughed harshly. 'That is a very good question. He's a government man, though exactly what department, he's never revealed to us. And is he helping in the search for Melissa?'

'I met with him today. He is doing all he can, Mickey, I believe that. Otis told me that according to their intelligence, Richardson wanted my suffering to be greater and longer than anything a simple knife in the back might bring, but it never occurred to me or to Otis that he might attack my family It should have done, of course – Richardson made threats against me when he was imprisoned – but he has been out of my mind for so many years.

'Otis had a man inside the prison, befriending Richardson once it became obvious that there were those high up who wanted his release. Otis and his people wanted to find evidence to keep him there, but there was none forthcoming. However, he bore me no goodwill and certainly no forgiveness, and he was almost certainly wise to the fact that he was in a cell with an informant and didn't care. He swore revenge and he said that he would not be the only one in search of it. He blamed me most of all for his imprisonment and he knew that I did my best to try to make the murder charge stick. I failed in that and sadly that failure has led to this.'

'Then why hasn't he been in touch? Why not ransom Melissa? What does he want?' Malina wanted to know.

'Ultimately, he wants me,' Henry said. 'And I would willingly trade my life for Melissa's, you all know that.'

'It's not going to come to that,' Mickey told him. 'We have eyes and ears everywhere; she will be found, and she will be found safe.'

'And this Connacht woman, how does she fit in with what is happening now?' Belle asked.

'She was known to us as Mrs Green,' Mickey said. 'And, lo and behold, Mrs Green visited this Richardson, McCready on three occasions in the past year and seems to have been communicating with him for some time.'

'But McCready had done her family so much harm, why would she involve herself with him?' Belle wanted to know.

'That is something we need to discover,' Henry admitted. 'Richardson came out of prison and resumed his old business of extortion and blackmail. And we know this Connacht woman, this Mrs Green, specialized in entertaining wealthy young men in her bed. Who knows what they told her? Who knows what pressures could be brought to bear on them afterwards?'

'Is there any suggestion that—'

'That Ferdy was one of her clients? It's possible, I suppose. What I would like to do now is find a way to tie Richardson – McCready – to this business with Robert Cranston and Mr Russell Clovis. It is too much of a coincidence to think that there are two separate organizations following the same path. I see Richardson's hand in all of this, but most likely Clovis's money. So why is Clovis financing him? How did our Mr Clovis actually come by his wealth? And I wonder how many more Cranston families there are, being put under pressure to pay debts they did not wish to have on loans they did not wish to take. How many more family members are being threatened?'

A little later, as though belatedly remembering that he was host in his own house, Albert came through and slumped down at the table. He looked as though he'd been drinking heavily. Mickey told him a little of what had happened during the day, but Albert was barely listening. It was going to destroy him, Mickey thought, more thoroughly than any financial losses had done. He'd been through a great deal already, but compared to this . . . nothing could be compared to this.

'Will you be staying tonight?' Albert asked. 'I know Cynthia wants Belle to remain, and you, of course, are just as welcome.' He got up, not waiting for an answer, and wandered back out again. A moment later he heard the study door open and then close. Mickey followed him and tapped gently on the door, slipping in before Albert gave a response. Albert was seated at the small table on which his microscope was sitting. He was looking at the slides, one after another, and then setting them aside.

'Did Melissa make those for you?' Mickey asked.

Albert hesitated, then he nodded. 'Mickey, tell me, what are the chances? Should we be preparing for the worst?'

Mickey came over and sat close by, picking up the slides and examining them. 'She has a fine working method – these are beautifully prepared,' he said. 'I don't know, no one can know, because this is not a usual kind of case. Although I have dealt with kidnappings only rarely, and it is usual for the ransom demand to be made almost immediately.'

'And when the ransom was paid, the child was returned?'

'Yes,' Mickey said quietly. 'The child was returned.'

He left Albert to his microscope slides, hating himself for having lied. In Mickey's career he had twice been involved in kidnap cases. In one of those, the child had indeed been returned, but it turned out to have been a relative who had stolen him away in the first place. An uncle who believed himself cheated out of his inheritance. The second time, a ransom demand had been made and the ransom paid, but the child had been killed within the hour of the event taking place. The parents had lost both money and their infant.

He had managed to get through the day keeping busy, but now the depression settled around Mickey shoulders, weighing upon him heavily. In fact, the entire house seemed to be heavy, dragged down by grief. He knew how much Henry loved his niece; he loved his nephews too, but his relationship with Melissa was special. It was Mickey who got on better with the boys, having more in common with their interests in cricket and fishing, but for Melissa it was all about books and pictures and more recently, science. Melissa was most like her mother, the boys were very much like Albert, good, solid sorts.

If anything happened to Melissa, Mickey didn't know how any of them would survive it.

The woman had come in once more that evening. Melissa was tired and guessed it was very late. Through the high windows, she could just glimpse stars and she could hear trains close by. She must be near a railway track. The woman brought water but no more food, and she came and went very quickly. Melissa guessed that because the big man was in the house, the woman dare not stay and even try to be nice. Melissa waited for a long time after she'd gone before she moved and then she slid back under the bed. The nail was almost free and in a few more minutes, Melissa emerged triumphant with a long, sharp tack between her fingers that might have been made of pure gold for the way she felt about it.

Now to see if it could be at all useful. She set about wedging the nail between the coils of rope that made up the elaborate knot, wriggling it backward and forward and trying to work even a few strands free. Her hands were cold and her fingertips very sore by the time she'd been trying this for about half an hour. But Melissa was determined.

Earlier something had happened that had made her even more determined, even more afraid. She had thought she heard raised voices and she listened very hard. The big man – she was sure it was him – was shouting at someone and then there was silence. But when the woman came up and brought the water, her face was bruised and Melissa had seen the marks of fingers on her wrist, black and blue.

Slowly, patiently, fingers sore and soon bleeding, Melissa worked on the rope. The woman had been nice to her, but the small man was enthralled to the big one, Melissa was absolutely certain of that. In time, it was possible that the woman might be persuaded to help, or at least Melissa had thought so at one point. Then when the woman had returned later in the evening she had seen the woman's face, the black eye, the blood, the marks on the arm, and she knew that she was meant to see them, meant to notice. The bruises had not been there when the woman had come up with the big man but Melissa was certain that he was now sending her a message, as much as he was to the woman he had hurt. Don't cross me, don't even look like you disagree. Don't ever think of making me angry.

She was only thirteen, but she knew a lot about the world, a surprising amount because her mother talked to her and explained things to her, because Malina came from such a different place, and because her uncle was a detective chief inspector, and because his friend was Mickey Hitchens. Melissa, born into wealth and raised by parents who adored her, was under no illusions about how lucky she was or how other people lived and died.

TWENTY-EIGHT

Henry had mentioned that he had visited Diamond Annie, had hinted that she might be putting the word out, but he had said little, and news and other revelations had over-ridden any small detail that Henry could tell, and so he'd been spared the necessity to fudge the issue. The following morning, a little after Mickey had left for the day, a telegram arrived at the house informing Henry that Annie had an address at which Sir Ralph's valet could be found. Henry spared no time and left a few minutes later.

Annie had guessed that Fred Parks would not be far away from his relatives so used her connections with Franny Richmond, the valet's great-grandmother who was a fence that she occasionally employed, to find out more. It turned out he was lodging in a house only a few streets away from Franny Richmond and was reported to be rather nervous, constantly looking out for trouble.

Henry almost called Mickey, wishing to bring his sergeant into this action, but his fear was that Annie's enquiries would get back to Parks and he would run, so he could not risk the delay. Henry was convinced that the valet held a clue to part of the puzzle. Henry had never felt more alone or more outcast. He knew that all he had to do was to summon Mickey, but he would not jeopardize his friend's career, and so instead two of Annie's men accompanied him.

The house was at the end of the terraced street. It looked more rundown than most, the net curtains at the window yellowing and worn. Henry was very familiar with streets like this. Those houses inhabited by families were largely clean and neat, curtains washed and, in more prosperous houses, a bowl of fruit or occasionally a vase of flowers was placed in the window as the sign of that prosperity. It was a simple act, but an important one when establishing status. The front steps were usually clean and scrubbed, the door furniture polished, even if the door itself was not always well painted. But always in such a street, there were also two or three houses usually occupied by single working men, sometimes with a live-in owner but often not. These houses were frequently the worst in the street, cramped and overcrowded and dirty, the front step unwashed and the curtains grimed and discoloured. Henry knocked on the door and heard movement inside. Then one of Annie's men shouted, 'He's making a run for it,' and Henry saw a man leap out of an upstairs window, on to the flat roof of the outhouse and then on to the next. Henry set off at a pace down the street that ran parallel to the outbuildings. He knew the man would have to come down here before he reached the next house and so it was that Fred Parks jumped down into the street and took to his heels, the three men in pursuit and Henry in the lead.

A moment later and Henry brought him down with a rugby tackle that Albert would have been proud of. Fred Parks hit the cobbled street hard and lay sprawled out with Henry sitting on his back, grunting in pain. Henry twisted Parks's arm behind his back and lifted him to his feet. A moment later the shrill blast of a police whistle was heard and Henry swore. Annie's men disappeared as one constable rapidly followed by another rounded the corner.

'Detective Chief Inspector Henry Johnstone,' he announced himself, momentarily forgetting that he had no longer had papers to back this up, that he was on suspension. He continued regardless, 'And I want this man arrested.'

The constables were not known to Henry, and he hoped that habitual deference to rank might overcome any reservations they had. Henry knew how he looked, dishevelled and dusty, his clothes streaked with mud from the street and the man he was holding protesting his innocence.

'And what would the charges be?' the older of the two constables asked.

'Theft, housebreaking, petty larceny and possibly kidnap,' Henry said, realizing as he spoke that he was probably going a little too far. Fred Parks certainly thought so. He was shrieking, shouting that he had nothing to do with any of those things, that he was an innocent man and ask anybody around here.

Residents were coming out of their houses, the noise in the street telling them that something too good to miss was going on, and the constables were now looking wary.

'I suggest we take him to the police station and you can ask questions later,' Henry said coldly. 'I don't think you gentlemen want a riot on your hands, and the natives do not look friendly.'

The constables decided that he was probably right in this instance, and together they walked their prisoner to the police station. A knot of local people followed, a knot which rapidly grew into a crowd. Fred Parks was known to them – he was a local, he was due their protection. Henry was a stranger, and what's more he had been observed with two others who were certainly not from round there, and who had been seen to disappear right sharpish when the police had arrived. Henry could hear the whispers, their murmurs and their shouts and was quite profoundly relieved once they were inside the divisional station, even though he was aware that his problems were only just beginning.

Now he decided it really was time to call Mickey, and possibly one of the other inspectors; he needed backup, even if that meant more trouble. With a little difficulty he managed to convince the station officer not only to detain Fred Parks but also to summon assistance in the shape of Detective Sergeant Mickey Hitchens and hope that no one enquired too closely about Henry himself in the meantime.

Inspector Prothero arrived with Mickey about an hour later and the sergeant had evidently brought him up to speed, at least to the extent that Fred Parks was a person of interest in the ransacking of the Helford house. The arresting constables had made their statements by then and were back on the streets dispersing the crowd. Prothero glanced in Henry's direction with a frown and even Mickey kept his distance, though he cast a concerned look at Henry. After a while, Fred Parks was brought up from the cells and handed over to the police officers who had come from Scotland Yard. Mickey finally came over to where Henry sat. 'What the hell do you think you were doing?'

'Following where my investigation led me.'

'Not *your* investigation. Henry, you are on suspension. You're not doing the case any good, not doing any of us any good. If you knew where Parks was, why didn't you let me know? I could have brought in men to arrest him, Henry. Why did you not trust me with this? I thought we agreed last night? No more secrets, no more lies.'

Henry blinked. He had not thought of it from that perspective, that Mickey should think he was not trusted. That Mickey should think that Henry would not take him into his confidence. The truth was, of course, that Henry had taken Mickey into his confidence on several matters and he could see the hurt in his friend's eyes, and at once he felt sick with it all. The secrets he had been forced to keep. The mire in which he was drowning.

Prothero was waiting impatiently.

'They promised I can do the questioning,' Mickey said. 'So if there's anything I don't know about that you want me to ask him you'd better say now.'

Henry shook his head.

'Then go home, Henry. Go and be with your sister. We'll talk later when you can tell me if there's anything else you're keeping from me.'

The black Mariah had been brought round and Parks was bundled inside, Prothero and Mickey crowding into the front seat beside the driver. Henry was left to walk alone through streets he did not know and was only thankful that the crowds had dispersed.

TWENTY-NINE

Mickey sat across the table from Fred Parks. The man's face was bruised, and he had a cracked rib, but the police surgeon had passed him fit to question and Mickey was not inclined to cut him any slack.

'Lady Helford paid you to ransack the house,' Mickey said flatly, 'to steal her goods and fence them for her. We both know you have the contacts. Now I know Lady Helford was a desperate woman and I'm prepared to believe that you . . . cared about her welfare.'

'Lady Helford is a fine woman, and her husband was a good man. And I was a good valet. Did my job well.'

'So you were loyal to them? Loyalty is an admirable thing. And I am prepared to accept that you did what you did from the best motives, but I need to know more. We spoke to Lady Helford a few days ago, and she told us that her great-granddaughter had been threatened. A little mite, only a few years old. I don't take kindly to kiddies being threatened—'

'No more do I.' Parks pounded angrily on the table. 'Bad enough they killed her man, but to threaten that little girl – no, that is beyond everything.'

'And who did the threatening? And were the threats made before they left London?'

'The master had got himself into a sticky mess. Of course, he never told me about it, but I picked up things here and there – you know, you hear things. I know he was scared. I know he made some bad dealings and that Mr Russell Clovis was at the back of it. There was a bad sort if ever I saw one. He was no gentleman. Then when the master got himself killed, I made sure the mistress got away.'

'*You* made sure?'

'I knew where the master kept his money. I knew where he kept the key to the safe. But I didn't steal nothing. I know you take me for a thief – you and your kind always do – but I earn an honest living. Always have. Just because certain members of my family have been less than honest, don't mean we all are. You tar us all with the same brush, you lot. Not a chance you'd believe anything else.'

'My heart bleeds,' Mickey said. 'So tell me what happened. Everything you know. We believe the Helford child is safe, she's up in Scotland with her mother and has the local constabulary keeping an eye, but another child is at risk, taken from her family and if you have any feelings at all, then you can only imagine what her parents are going through.'

Parks lit a cigarette, inhaled deeply and then inspected the glowing end. 'I seen it in the papers. She's his niece, ain't she? The man what broke my rib.'

'So, start talking,' Mickey said, 'if you wish to keep the remaining ribs intact. If you want me to believe that you are, if not innocent, at least not culpable and that you acted in the best interests of the Helford family, then you'll tell me it all now, everything you know.'

Henry had returned to his flat. He needed a change of clothes and he needed time to think and to get his thoughts under control before he saw his sister again. He felt overwhelmingly that he was just making matters worse; whatever he did at the moment seemed to be the wrong thing, and if he couldn't trust his own judgement then what could he trust? He had also arranged that any intelligence that Annie's or Malina's people managed to gather should be dropped off at his flat, this being neutral ground, not police, not the grieving parents, so when he opened his door, the rustle of paper informed him that something had been pushed through his letterbox.

Henry bent to scoop up his mail, discarding what he quickly identified as bills and reminders that a subscription to a magazine was due. These he dropped on the hall table, but three other slips of paper, and a fourth in an envelope he took through to his living room and, after switching on his electric fire, slumped down in his favourite leather chair and began to look them over.

The first, written in an appalling scrawl, suggested that a young girl answering Melissa's description had been seen in a street near Newgate and there was an approximate address. The second spoke of gossip that had been overheard in a pub and related to Henry himself, that he had disgraced himself by hitting someone important. Henry guessed that the men involved in the gossip were police officers – news was no doubt spreading all over London by now and his name would be in the newspapers by morning. The pub was named, and Henry satisfied himself that it was close to Scotland

Yard and therefore of little interest where finding Melissa was concerned. The third piece of intelligence, tucked into the envelope, was more interesting. A boatman, one of Malina's contacts, reported a sighting of two men and a woman. One was a counterfeiter by the name of Christopher Masefield and the other well known for blackmail and had served time for threatening to abduct the child of one of those he had victimized. Several aliases were listed and Henry wished fervently that he could simply go into the archive and examine the official records. He would have to be content with passing this intelligence on to Mickey.

The informant, of course, had decided to remain anonymous, and Henry only knew that this person must be one of Malina's contacts because they had opened their missal with *Malina asked that I sent you this.*

The fourth slip of paper was simply an accusation that the Jews were bound to be involved in some way. Henry cast that aside; there wasn't a serious investigation in London that didn't receive such accusations from some member of the public are other. It was usually the Jews, sometimes the Armenians and more recently the Russians, whatever social and cultural group happened to be most visible at any given time and therefore managed to have offended somebody or other.

Henry tucked these notes into his coat pocket and then went and found the clothes brush to give the fabric a good beating, trying to eradicate some of the marks from the cobbles and the mud that now streaked the front of it. The coat had been a gift from his sister; it was long and warm and Henry felt suddenly embarrassed that he must have walked across London covered in street dirt, dishevelled and unkempt.

Satisfied that the coat looked a little less uncared-for, Henry changed and packed more clothes in his bag and then prepared to leave. He felt suddenly uncomfortable with the idea that other people knew where he lived – though actually, as a police officer, it was hard to keep that sort of thing secret. He would be loath to leave this place with its view of the river.

He remembered also that he'd had little time to look over the paperwork that he had taken from the Helford house, and that was at Cynthia's, so he should attend to it next and hope that Mickey had new information from Fred Parks. He would drop the missals that had been pushed through his door into Scotland Yard on his way to Cynthia's house and see if Mickey could make progress where he could not. Most of all, Henry hated the helplessness he felt, the helplessness that must be increased manyfold for his sister, for Albert and for Melissa's siblings.

'Pull yourself together, man. This is no time to wallow,' Henry told himself. 'Use your brain, use your skills – no one has taken those away. You can find her.'

But could he? Was she even still alive? The silence from her abductors was the most disturbing thing of all.

THIRTY

'**M**r Ansel Peach, he's our link.' Mickey looked pleased with himself. They were all gathered in Cynthia's little sitting room, bright-yellow silk on the walls, cosy chairs. In truth, the room was somewhat crowded having been built as a small bedroom or a study and was usually just Cynthia's private space with the occasional guest.

'Ansel Peach is dead,' Henry stated.

'Perhaps not. The valet, Parks, he said that he remembered Mr Ansel Peach coming to the house and that his master was always worried when this man appeared. He spoke of him as an arrogant man, obsequiously polite. He believed that his master felt great distaste for him, but whenever this Mr Peach called, Sir Ralph would drop anything else he happened to be doing and attend to him. He also denied going with Lady Helford to give the letter to our flamenco dancer, so I had pictures taken over to the theatre, one of Parks and one of our so-called Mr Peach. The girl picked Peach out immediately as the stage-door Johnny who had asked her to deliver the message to you.'

'Have your colleagues made any progress in tracing my child?' Cynthia asked wearily. She didn't see how this Mr Peach fitted with what had become her only concern.

Mickey reached over and patted her hand. 'Good men are working on it, but I've not strayed from the subject, my dear. All these things are interconnected, and this Mr Peach seems to be at the heart of it. I suspect he is a courier, a messenger between the different individuals involved. He seems to have been at pains to be both visible and unseen—'

'Mickey, you're making no sense,' Cynthia told him, 'especially if this man is dead. Now you and Henry should be going and looking at these addresses that he's been given, asking questions at the public house. Mickey, I would be out pacing the streets if I was allowed.'

'And all you'd do is waste shoe leather,' Mickey told her gently. 'As soon as Henry gave me the address, we had men round to the house. There is a little redhead girl living there, but she is not Melissa. She is the niece of the man who lives there, come for a visit. You cannot blame those who watched – she is very like your daughter to look at but somewhat younger.'

Cynthia slumped back in her chair. Reason told her that had there been any real news about Melissa, someone would have informed her instantly, but she still held on to that little tiny bit of hope.

Albert was pacing. He seemed to find it impossible to be still. 'So this Ansel Peach fella – what's he got to do with anything?'

'When I had some of my colleagues checking through the records, matching his face to what we already had, it appears that, as we suspected, "Ansel Peach" is an alias. His name is Christopher Masefield – or should I say *one* of his names is Christopher Masefield.'

Henry jerked to alertness. 'Christopher Masefield was named in that letter pushed through my door today.'

'Indeed he was, and, in fact, it was checking Christopher Masefield and his known associates that brought me back to Ansel Peach,' Mickey told him. 'Seeing Masefield's face in our records, I recalled the description of Peach. So I sent a messenger to Annie, who had it confirmed that this was indeed the man lodging on her patch, the man she had followed so assiduously. Annie has an instinct for wrongdoers. Having spent so much of her life on the wrong side of the law, I suppose she recognized a fellow player.'

'Annie?' Cynthia asked. 'Never mind. This woman has given you a lead?'

'Possibly so.' Henry nodded. 'Malina, is it possible to find out who sent this note to me? How did they recognize this man?'

'I can ask, but I can make no promises, and if he's a boatman, then it's possible he isn't even in London anymore. Remember, Henry, they are doing this as a favour to me and because there is a child involved. My people are still very suspicious of the police and will do nothing to attract official attention to themselves.'

'And the other man Masefield was with? Have we identified him?'

'Not definitively, but it's possible he is Richardson. One of the aliases listed in the information you received, Manny Stevens, seems to be one that he used before he was imprisoned.' He glanced at Malina. 'Your informant would seem to have a long memory.'

'Those who work the Thames all have long memories,' Malina said. 'It pays to know what to remember and what to forget.'

'Mickey, I cannot bear this.' Cynthia's tone was shrill. 'A ransom demand I could deal with but this silence. I don't know if she's alive or dead or harmed.' She took a deep breath, trying to control her emotions, and Albert came over and put his hands on his wife's shoulders.

'We'll get her back – you can be sure we will. We are all going to move heaven and earth to make sure of that.'

Cynthia took a very deep breath and then said with effort, 'So you think this Ansel Peach person might not be dead after all?'

'Not judging by the fact that he was sighted so recently. The intelligence we have received from Malina's friend is new. No more than a couple of days old at most. There is now a general alert across the entire city for this man as there is for Mrs Green, and for Manny Stevens or Richardson or whatever other name he is going by. Their images have been circulated. If they break cover someone will see and the report will come back to me.'

Cynthia nodded, but she did not look totally convinced. 'And so why did you think he was dead?'

'Because he was reported to be among those who lost money and chose to commit suicide rather than face his debtors,' Henry said. A little too late, he remembered, given the current company, that this may not have been the most tactful way to put things.

Albert let it pass. 'And now that is in doubt? Well, obviously it is, as the man has been seen, but I'm not quite sure I understand.'

'Mr Peach was supposedly seen jumping from a bridge, but it seems the witnesses who saw him have since disappeared. Only one remains and he admits he did not see anything clearly. He saw a man standing on the parapet and he heard others shouting but from his angle he could not be certain what was going on. Then a bus passed him and obscured his view. When he reached the scene, there were three people looking down at the water apparently trying to see where the suicide might have plunged into the river. The police were summoned, of course, and an alert went out for a body. As the supposed suicide had left his coat on the bridge with personal items in the pocket, assumptions were made . . . I spoke to the witness today – he admits that he did not see the man jump from the bridge, that when the bus went past him he could, in fact, see nothing. He could just hear the shouts from other observers and so he believed a man must have jumped.'

'A clever play,' Henry said. Something else elaborately staged.

THIRTY-ONE

T he day had passed slowly and now it was night-time again. The tiny window was Melissa's only clue as to what was going on in the outside world. She had used the little table, perched shakily on the bed and climbed up so she could see further out of the window at the skyline that she had thought was familiar but now seemed less so. She could not guess where she might be.

She had been fed twice, sandwiches again and a jug of water left with her. The woman had come up to bring her food and each time one or other of the men had been with her and she had said nothing. The first time Melissa had encountered this pretty, dark-haired woman she had seemed quite confident, quite at ease, but that had all changed. She was frightened, Melissa thought. Really frightened, and that frightened Melissa too.

She had worked hard on the rope and had succeeded in cutting through some of the fibres – she'd given up with the knot; it was too complex and too tight for her to make any headway with – but it was such slow progress and her fingers were so sore. Every time she thought of giving up, the knowledge that people would be looking for her kept her going but she had cried a lot that day and she knew that her face was blotchy and her eyes were puffy and in reality Melissa was getting desperate.

The woman had emptied the bucket that Melissa had been using to empty the chamber pot into, and Melissa was very grateful for that because the room had begun to stink. Each time she frayed a little more of the rope, she pulled hard, to see if it would break but it was tough hemp, well twisted and coated with tar of the sort that Melissa had seen on boats, so it was taking her a long time to get anywhere with it. She was careful when anyone came into the room to keep the blanket round her shoulders so nobody could see the rope and to keep her fingers tucked in beneath the blanket so nobody could see that they were now bloody.

It was fully dark and Melissa had fallen into a light doze when the door opened again and the big man and the woman both came into the room. She had changed her clothes, Melissa noticed, wearing a tweed suit as though she was preparing to go out. She had a coat draped over her shoulders.

Melissa sat up and eyed them both warily. The man approached the bed. He had a knife in his hand and Melissa yelped fearfully. The woman had picked up Melissa's coat. The man held a knife close to her face. He was laughing at her, though he made no proper sound, his lips pulled back in a rictus smile. He made Melissa think of a cruel clown. She retreated from him as far as she could get, and he made a grab at her and she yelped again.

'She's just a kid, you don't have to frighten her,' the woman said, and then she too backed off as the man turned.

'Don't you tell me what to do.' He backhanded her with his left fist, knocking her sideways. The move was effortless and Melissa's eyes widened. She held her breath and tried not to make a sound as the man came forward again, this time picking up the rope and cutting it through with the sharp knife. This too was effortless and Melissa, who had worked on the fibres of the rope for hours and knew just how tough it was, was shocked and even more afraid when he once again waved the knife in front of her face. She was so thankful that he hadn't cut close to the knot and seen the work she'd done but had simply picked up a loop of the rope and cut through. Melissa didn't want to think how he might have reacted if he'd seen how hard she'd worked to fray the fibres.

'My uncle will come for you.' It was the only thing she could think to say, but she felt she had to say something. 'He'll kill you.'

This time the man really did laugh out loud. 'Little girl, he already tried that once and he failed.'

He grabbed her hair and pulled her to her feet. Then he entwined his fingers into a handful of her red waves and pulled hard. Melissa screamed aloud as he wrenched a thick strand of hair from her scalp and dropped it on to the bed.

It hurt. Melissa was sobbing now, pained and humiliated. The woman was urging her to put her arms into her coat and Melissa managed it somehow, managing also to keep hold of her precious floorboard nail. She shoved it into her pocket and when the woman wrapped the blanket around her shoulders after helping her with her coat, she held on to that tight.

The man, sufficient terror inflicted, walked towards the door ahead of them.

'What's going on?' Melissa managed to breathe.

'Hush,' the woman told her. 'We're leaving here.'

'Where are we going?'

'Hush,' the woman told her again, and would say nothing more.

It was two in the morning when a telegram arrived. It was brought up to Henry's room. He read it, not quite comprehending what it meant, and then banged hard on Mickey's door. Mickey came out on to the landing, tying his dressing gown. 'What the devil?'

The house was roused now, doors opening all along the corridor; those that hadn't been woken by the strange sound of the doorbell in the early hours were awake now and police constables on guard downstairs were rushing up concerned by the sudden furore.

'I know this place,' Mickey said, looking at the address in the telegram. 'It's a little alleyway that cuts through from Royal Mint Street to Chambers Street. It goes beneath the railway line. Henry, you cannot go alone.'

'I must, it's me he wants. It is only me he wants. If there is a chance of getting Melissa back, then I must go.'

'Of course you must, and we will be out of sight. But we will go with you, the constables and I.'

Henry did not reply. He went to his room and pulled on his clothes, and minutes later he was out of the house, Mickey and the constable in pursuit. It was fortunate, Mickey thought, that he knew where Henry was going because his boss had given them no time to prepare and no time to organize transport. Mickey left one of the constables manning the phone, calling for backup while he and the second took another of the family cars, Albert's Bentley, and set off in pursuit. They left the house in turmoil, Mickey with a sinking feeling in his belly. He could understand that Henry would do anything to save Melissa, but this was not the way, Mickey felt it instinctively. This was not the way.

The street door was open, and Henry rushed into the house, but it was immediately obvious that there was no one there. The silence closed in around him, told him that the house was empty. He ran from room to room and up the stairs and then again from room to room until when Mickey found him he was seated in the attic bedroom, shoulders bowed and a look of utter defeat on his face. He held between his hands a long strand of red hair. The ends were bloodied and it was clear that it had been wrenched from Melissa's head.

Gently, Mickey took it from his hands and dropped it into a manila envelope. Then he took his boss by the arm, led him out into the hall and told the constable to take him downstairs and wait for reinforcements to arrive.

'She was here,' Henry said.

'Yes, she was. She was here and she was alive and Richardson is just piling on the pain. You can see that, can't you?'

'What do I do, Mickey? What the hell do I do? Can't go back to Cynthia and tell her . . .'

'And tell her that her daughter is still alive,' Mickey told him sternly. 'That's what you can do, Henry, that's all any of us can do right now.'

Melissa had been bundled into the back of the van, the woman with her. She was thrown left and right as the van drove across cobbled streets and then on to a metalled road and then on to another road that sounded different beneath the wheels. She guessed they were heading out of the city.

'Where are we going?'

The woman put a finger to her lips. She looked defeated, Melissa thought.

'My uncle will come for me.'

'Shut up back there, or I'll come back and make you be quiet.'

Melissa fell silent and pulled the blanket more tightly around herself. It was cold in the van. It smelt earthy, like potatoes and mud, and the windowless compartment was very dark. She tried to wedge herself into a corner so as not to be thrown about quite as much, but it didn't really work. She was bruised and battered when it eventually came to a stop and the rear doors opened.

Melissa was taken into a house. She couldn't see it properly but it seemed very large and echoey. She was taken down to the basement and pushed down three steps so that she fell hard on to the flagstones. Unlike the attic room, there was nothing covering the floor, no light filtering in through the window, and no bulb keeping the darkness at bay once the cellar door had closed. Melissa groped her way around the walls until she found a corner and then she curled up with the blanket tight around her shoulders, knees drawn up to her chest, and she wept bitterly.

It was worse than it had been before. Henry had gone back to Cynthia's house and explained what had happened, but their hopes had been raised and now it seemed they had fallen further than before. The despair that overtook them was even deeper and darker. Cynthia could hardly bear to even look at him, Henry could see that. He felt that he had failed her utterly and completely.

It seemed as though they could not even comfort one another any more. Henry sat alone in a small dining room, everyone else having drifted away. Mickey had not returned, nor sent word about what he was doing and Henry felt, once again, as he had told Otis, utterly cast adrift.

The door opened and Belle and Malina came through. Belle was still leaning heavily on the stick. Henry wanted to tell them that he did not need company, that their sympathy would only make things worse, but they went across to the table that he was using as his unofficial desk, each picked up a bundle of notes and brought it back to the dining table.

'We may not be detectives,' Belle told him, 'but we both have decent brains and, let's face it, nothing else to do just now. It might be that between us we can spot something. Three heads being better than one and all that.'

'So,' Malina said, 'what are we looking for?'

Henry just stared at both women; he didn't seem to be able to make words articulate. His throat closed and nothing would come out. In the end, Malina picked up the piece of paper from the top of the pile she had brought from the table and looked at it. 'This looks like a letter from Sir Helford, is that right?' They had brought with them notepads and pens and Henry wanted to say that they wouldn't even know what was helpful, never mind how to record it. But Malina was not going to be dissuaded, and neither was Belle. She set the letter down on the table between them so both women could read the contents. When they had done, Belle commented, 'I think this man had gambling debts. Anything else in that pile to tell us what he owed and who he owed it to?'

Malina began to rummage through the paperwork and Henry blinked. They had picked up the stack of papers that he had brought from the Helford house on his last foray there, the letters and deeds and the will that had been hidden beneath the wardrobe.

'Here, there's something else. A letter talking about an extension of credit, look.'

'Gambling debts?' Henry managed to croak. 'No one said Sir Ralph was a gambler.'

'Oh, but he was,' Belle contradicted. She had been examining her own pile of correspondence. 'He was a member of at least two clubs, look. Private members clubs, and I know that in at least one of these gambling takes place.'

Henry did not trouble to ask her how she knew that. Belle's career in the theatre had taken her to all sorts of places that Henry did not question – neither did Mickey. They passed the paperwork they had been examining across to Henry, who scrutinized it eagerly. Belle was right. One was an acknowledgement for the receipt of a membership fee. Another an extension of credit.

Henry took a deep breath. 'I'd not yet had a chance to take a look at these,' he said.

'Then we will split the task between us. You tell us what you need us to look for.'

'And I will get us coffee,' Malina said. She got up and rang the bell, and it was clear to Henry that she must have requested refreshments earlier because they arrived within minutes. The young maid who brought the tray looked with interest at the three of them gathered around the table and Henry could see faint hopefulness in her gaze. She would go back to the kitchen and report that Mr Henry and the two ladies were working on the investigation together. Henry could guess how odd that might sound, but also that the staff would be taking comfort from the fact that Henry at least had not found himself buried under the weight of despair. He wished that was true.

Through the morning they worked, drinking coffee, eating biscuits and the little cakes the cook sent up fresh from the oven.

Once, Malina went out into the hall to gather the morning papers from the side table. 'I want to know what they are saying about all this,' she said. 'We have to hope that the kidnappers don't have an inside man and are as reliant on the daily news as we are?'

'An inside man?' Belle questioned.

'She means whether we have a leak within the police service. Do we have a Hayden Paul or a Walter Cole?'

'Ah,' Belle said. She cast an anxious look in Henry's direction and then joined the other two in examining the newspapers.

The local newspapers were full of the kidnapping and picked over the bones of Albert's losses and even Cynthia's humble origins. Henry had taken his own share of the headlines. Assaulting a man of Bright-Cooper's standing was, according to some, practically a hanging offence. One editor called for his resignation, another for a public apology. A third took a more sympathetic tone: *Detective Chief Inspector Johnstone must have been under strain with the vicissitudes his family is suffering. That so many families up and down our proud land must be suffering.* It somewhat spoiled the tone, Henry thought, by predicting a rise in crime among the common classes, the implication being that Henry was, himself, from the common classes, so what more could you expect in terms of behaviour?

'They know about the house where . . . where Melissa was kept,' Belle said, handing a newspaper paper across the table to Henry. She frowned. 'Henry, when did you get to that house? What time?'

The telegram arrived just after two. 'Not later than half past, maybe a quarter to three. Oh, no, but you are right. That would have been far too late for the morning edition.'

'So they must have had this news earlier. What, before midnight, perhaps? They would just have had time to change the presses. The article is short, little more than a headline and some slight exposition.'

'Little more than might be included in a telegram.' Henry leapt to his feet and hurried through to Albert's study. It was, Henry thought, a measure of the family's collective grief that Albert was with Cynthia in her little sitting room, that he could no longer even take refuge in his study. He called the operator, asked for the number, waited impatiently for the call to be put through and, when connected to the editor, did not even try to dissemble about who he was and what he wanted to know.

He would no doubt be the subject of another headline, Henry thought, but what did that matter now?

Back in the small dining room, he flopped down into his chair. 'A telegram, received some four hours before our own telegram arrived. No address but the information that the house where Melissa had been held had been discovered. That she was no longer there, but that there was evidence of life. And that I had been first on scene.'

'As they knew you would be,' Belle said gently. 'This Richardson knows you well, has studied you, it seems.'

'I feel that I'm being played,' Henry said. 'Manipulated.'

'You are,' Malina agreed, 'but, Henry, that might be to our advantage. He wants you to know he is pulling your strings – it might well be possible to return the play.'

Lunch brought sandwiches and more cakes and Henry found that he was hungry for the first time in days because he was finally beginning to make connections.

Sir Ralph Helford had extensive gambling debts. These had been paid for him – and Henry gathered that Lady Helford did not know – and so he now owed more money to Mr Russell Clovis. Sir Ralph was up to his neck in debt and was not only keeping that fact from his wife, but Clovis was blackmailing him about quite another matter. It took a while for Henry to piece it together; it seemed to be about a case that Sir Ralph had given evidence in some years before, in which he had been an expert witness. And then it dawned on him.

Henry got up and crossed to the table, selecting the folder that Mickey had brought to him, the one he had requested from the archives, the one covering the McCready-Richardson trial and all the ancillary documents relating to that. He found the letter from Elsa Bryant, the young woman who had committed suicide. 'Her married lover, Mr Connacht, obtained an abortion for her,' Henry reminded them.

'Mr Connacht was brought to trial because, of course, obtaining an abortion is an illegal act. The girl could not be prosecuted as she was already deceased, but Mr Connacht was brought to trial and Sir Ralph Helford gave evidence, I'm sure of it. The thing I didn't realize is that Mr Connacht always denied the charge. He was adamant that Miss Bryant suffered a spontaneous miscarriage and that he had her see a doctor afterwards.'

'And did the doctor support his claims?'

'There's no record of that. So far as I can see.'

He rummaged through the paperwork for a few minutes while everybody held their breath. This seemed important though it was, in fact, only one small detail in Sir Ralph Helford's life; he had been a practising physician and surgeon for many years and an expert witness on numerous occasions. Of course, he had not been knighted back then; that honour had been bestowed much more recently. A decade ago Ralph Helford was a distinguished surgeon but an unusual choice as expert witness in a case like this.

Henry found the information he was looking for. It was brief, a mere sentence, which is why he had missed it. The surgeon who had carried out the post-mortem on the dead woman was Dr Ralph Helford, who attested in court to the fact that Miss Bryant exhibited signs of having recently undergone an illegal procedure. That procedure being the termination of pregnancy.

He tapped the paper impatiently. 'The rest will be in the court records, what exactly was said on the day, but what is important is that Mr Connacht denied that he had ever procured an abortion for her. A woman who was accused of carrying out the procedure had been arrested and identified him. Lord knows what happened to her. She would have ended up in prison doing hard labour at the very least. If it could be proved that she had caused death by her actions, she could even have been hanged, but that's not important just now. What if Helford lied? What if there had been no abortion? What if pressure was brought to bear and he gave false testimony?'

There was silence for a moment as they absorbed that possibility.

'But the abortionist recognized him,' Malina reminded Henry.

'Did she, though?'

'Is it really likely that Connacht would have gone with her to see an abortionist?' Belle was scathing. 'Men might pay the bill but the rest is left to the woman involved to deal with. What man would go and hold a woman's hand through all of that? Especially a "respectable man".'

Henry raised an eyebrow.

'Oh, Henry, for goodness' sake, in my profession women who get into trouble have hard choices to make. No one will employ a woman whose belly is showing. And very few married ladies continue on the stage unless they are married to others in the same business. And a woman trying to raise a child alone faces Lord alone knows what prejudices,' said Belle.

'But if Sir Ralph Helford gave false witness in this case . . . if that was found out . . . if his name came under suspicion for this—'

'It would bring every case in which he ever testified into disrepute. The consequences could be terrible indeed,' Henry agreed.

'So little wonder he was open to blackmail. So the question is how did Russell Clovis know this? And why kill him if that is really what happened? Did he threaten to expose his blackmailer?'

'Perhaps so. Or perhaps he was simply bled dry and no longer of use. No, what we are missing here is a clear link between Clovis and Richardson and Connacht. The Connacht case was a sideshow to the main event. Richardson's trial was contiguous with this and it's likely that many of the witnesses gave evidence at both but—'

'We need to look for other names, don't we?' Malina said. 'See if anybody else gave evidence, like anyone from the Cranston family. See if we can build connections that way. Henry, you suggested that Connacht was suspected as the mastermind behind the blackmail and extortion racket. Maybe Richardson merely wanted him out of the way? What better way than to ruin the man socially and see that he went to prison? If Sir Ralph Helford was already gambling back then and had debts, then he would be open to the same coercion he was in later life. It's possible, isn't it, Henry?'

'Richardson knew he was facing prison.'

'Since when does imprisonment preclude criminal activity?' Malina said. 'He only needed to bide his time. You admit that not all the gang was caught. What if Clovis continued what he and Richardson began? Clovis married well, his wife was Irish gentry. From what I can see, her connections would have opened doors for him socially. Richardson might have served a longer stretch than he'd hoped, but he still got out of jail and, from what I can see, must have had funds waiting for him. To have set up all that he has since leaving prison, must have taken a deal of money.'

'And the London Stock Exchange crash followed by Wall Street must have simply fed into his plans,' Henry agreed. 'He must have felt that all his Christmases had come at once.'

Again, they divided the task between them, this time simply noting down the names that came up.

There was a large amount of paperwork. Once Mickey had

understood what his boss had been looking for, he had gone down
to the archives and pulled any records relating to the Richardson-
McCready trial. But eventually, Henry, Malina and Belle made another
rather sad connection. It was one short witness statements signed by
Geoffrey Cranston to the effect that Miss Elsa Bryant was a frequent
visitor to their house during her childhood, her family home being
little more than a mile away and the families often attending the same
social events. And that, yes, he believed that the laurel water with
which she had killed herself had been made from bushes on his estate.

'Laurel water,' Henry said. 'His brandy had been laced with laurel
water, but he hadn't actually drunk any of it. According to his wife
and sister-in-law, Geoffrey smoked his evening cigar but rarely took
a drink. Someone put that laurel water in his brandy. My money is
on Clovis. We know Clovis visited the house, laurel bushes grow
along the drive, the poison is easy to make. And who would make
poison from laurel bushes, but the inhabitants of the house where
the laurel bushes grow? This would be the reasoning.'

'You think he assumed that Geoffrey Cranston would drink the
brandy, and that his wife and sister-in-law would be blamed for it
because they had access?' Belle asked.

'I think it's likely that that was the thought behind this, though
I don't fully understand the motive. Spite, perhaps, or did Clovis
make the assumption that Geoffrey would simply sign the papers
he had been given, would finally agree to underwrite his son's debts?
Effectively this would make Clovis the immediate heir if Geoffrey
died; getting the women out of the picture in such an underhand
way would obviously be a bonus.'

'Presenting the son's murder as suicide and warning you of it in
advance ensured that you would be involved,' Belle added. 'Involved
and therefore vulnerable – though no doubt if you'd not taken that
particular bait, another way would have been found. This is a man
as fond of play-acting as any in the theatre, Henry. As fond of
deception and misdirection as any playwright.'

In a somewhat sombre mood, they returned to their search. Belle
had once more picked up the papers Sir Ralph Helford had hidden,
so it was Belle that made a final connection.

'Oh my Lord,' she said. 'So that's his game.' She flattened the
much-folded will and laid it on the table.

The will was so short as to look unfinished, but it had been signed
by two witnesses. One a solicitor's clerk and the other: Fred Parks,

Sir Ralph Helford's valet. 'So he knew how the land lay,' Henry said.

'Knew that Sir Ralph had effectively disinherited his family. So he tried to help them out. His methods might have been a little unconventional, Henry, but you can understand his motives if he did actually care for his employers.'

'"Item," Henry read. '"All my worldly goods, entire and without exception to Mr Russell Clovis, my good friend, in recognition of my indebtedness to him." It's certainly direct and to the point. His wife is left with nothing.'

'Or would have been, had it not been for Fred Parks staging the robbery and fencing her possessions. Henry, surely no one will be pursuing the man for what was only a good deed.'

'Clovis might, if he discovers what has gone on,' Henry said. 'Legally, all of those goods and chattels belonged to Clovis from the moment Ralph Helford died. His widow had no right to any of them. And had Geoffrey Cranston also signed, then his wife and sister-in-law would also have lost all they had.'

'There is a man deserving of the rope,' Malina said angrily. 'But how does this help with Richardson and with Melissa?'

Henry's heart sank. In truth it didn't, not really. True, the picture on the puzzle box was now beginning to emerge, but the puzzle itself was still in so many pieces that Henry could only guess how it might go together. And just now, guesswork was not nearly enough.

THIRTY-TWO

Mickey Hitchens turned up at Cynthia's house just after four in the afternoon. Henry thought he looked weary. He said he was much in need of 'a reviving cuppa' but he told them he also had news to bring.

But first he listened to what they had discovered, the two women doing most of the talking. Henry had slipped back into his black mood, having spent the last hour with his sister and brother-in-law. Cynthia had refused to take the draught the doctor had offered. How could she escape into sleep when her child was still missing? From what Henry could see, she had run straight into exhaustion and tears instead. This was so unlike Cynthia that Henry once again felt he was cut off from all that was normal and good, whereas Albert could not keep still; he paced the room like some caged beast. Henry had tried to tell them how he and Belle and Malina had spent their day, but he knew that neither Cynthia nor Albert could take it in.

'Grateful, of course,' Albert had said, more, Henry sensed, because he felt he should be saying something rather than because he was actually thinking about the words. 'But maybe leave it to the police, yes, old man?'

Henry tried not to let the words, or their inference sting, but the truth was he felt that Albert had driven the knife into an already open wound and had twisted it there.

'The house where Melissa was held,' Mickey said after Malina and Belle had finished their report, 'is, as you know, just at the corner of Swallow Gardens. Not that there is anything left of the gardens. A couple of hundred years ago it was orchards and market gardens, then cottages were built and in time grander houses. The gardens were starting to be swallowed up even before the railway cut through and now it's just a name and a short street, almost all lost beneath a railway arch.'

'Mickey, I do not need a history lesson,' Henry said impatiently.

'And I'm not giving you one. I'm telling you that the house was once a very desirable property. Fallen on hard times, it might be now, but the same family who built it still own it. The family name is Simmons.'

'Simmons. Like Mrs Green's maid.'

'Indeed so, and the daughter, Mary Simmons, is married. To Mr Russell Clovis. The house belongs to him or at least to his wife's family, which no doubt Clovis counts as the same thing.'

Mickey set a newspaper clipping down on the table and pointed to one of the women in a group of society ladies. 'Do you recognize her?'

'Simmons. Mrs Green's maid. More play-acting, Mickey.'

'Alias Mary Simmons, or Mrs Russell Clovis, if you prefer. There to keep Mrs Green loyal is my guess. I spoke also to Mrs Green's sister, the elder Miss Connacht. She's married now and is Mrs Taylor, and by good chance is living only a street away from where she grew up. I had constables walk their old neighbourhood, knocking on doors in case anyone should know where she had gone. She wasn't best pleased at me dragging up her unfortunate past, but she agreed to give me a little of her time. Jennifer Connacht, Mrs

Green as she became, took it all very badly when her father was imprisoned. She was sixteen at the time, worshipped her father by all accounts and when their lives fell apart, she blamed the poor unfortunate Miss Bryant for it. Her sister tells me that she somewhat fell off the straight and narrow and, as their mother had less and less time for her children with her involvement in the court cases and trying to clear her husband's name, Jennifer drifted into a life of crime. She didn't specify what, but I think we can probably guess.

'Then, when she was nineteen, she met Oliver Green, a minor civil service clerk due to take up a posting in Egypt. As you know, our civil service prefers their servants to be married men. They were wed only six weeks after meeting, though Mrs Taylor reckons he was a decent sort and that her sister seemed to be happy with him. She wrote regularly, postcards, in the main, but from what I've seen she led a settled enough life out there.'

'Then he died.'

'He died, she returned to London, and her sister says she fell back into her old ways, so the sister had no more to do with her up until six months ago. Jennifer turned up on her sister's doorstep, all "excited and rambling" – Mrs Taylor's description – about getting the family money returned to them. Well, Mrs Taylor sent her off with a flea in her ear. I think she'd had enough by then of her sister's schemes and as a respectably married woman with children of her own, you can see how she might feel less than happy with Jennifer.'

'So, we have our link between Clovis and Melissa's kidnapping,' Belle said. 'Don't we? It's his property. That must be why she was held there. This is proof that he's responsible.'

'Proving that he owns that house is one thing. Proving that he knew what went on there is quite another,' Mickey warned, but his attention was drawn to Henry who sat as though frozen.

'What have you remembered?' Mickey asked.

'The will. Helford left everything to Clovis. Including his properties. Including, presumably, that big house out near Ilford. Mickey, can you recall exactly where that was? It's not among these papers, I'm sure it isn't.'

'Maybe not, but it will be in those back at the office. I'll be back sooner than you can say "jackrabbit".'

'You think that's where Melissa is?' Belle said.

'I'm sure of it. And this time I'm not going to wait to be summoned like some whipped dog,' Henry told her angrily. 'I need a map, Malina. Where does Albert keep his travelling maps?'

When Mickey telephoned the house a little over an hour later, Henry had already gone. 'We couldn't stop him, Mickey,' Belle told him. 'You know what he's like when he has the bit between his teeth. He'd been studying Albert's road maps and he's sure he knows which house Sir Ralph was buying. He talked to Cynthia and she confirmed that the house for single mothers that they had been fundraising for was likely the same one. Albert wanted to go with him, but in the end Henry just took one of Albert's guns and left alone.'

'It's all well, my dear. I might have expected what he'd do. I'm on my way with reinforcements. If Melissa's there, we'll bring her home, Henry too.'

Belle set the phone carefully back on its cradle and turned to see Cynthia standing in the doorway. Her face was red and puffy and her eyes were swollen. Belle took her friend in her arms and hugged her tightly. 'Oh, Cyn, it's going to be all right. Mickey's going after him with reinforcements.'

'What if they arrive too late, Belle? What if neither of them come back? What if I lose both of them?'

THIRTY-THREE

A tiny speckling of light had filtered in through a grating when morning came, and as Melissa's eyes had grown used to the darkness, she was able to make out some features of her prison. Gradually, she had found the courage to explore, feeling her way around the walls and looking for anything that might be useful to her. The walls were rough and had once been plastered, but much of that had now crumpled away. The floor was concrete in the corner where she had spent the night but about half of the rest was flagged, the stone smooth and very cold.

A flight of wooden steps led upward to the door. She climbed them slowly, wary of the creaks and what she soon realized was rotten timber. The door, however, was solid and the timber smooth and new. There was no handle on Melissa's side of the door, no means of opening and when she tried to peer through the keyhole she found it blocked. By the key? Was there a way of turning it from this side?

Like what? Melissa thought. She put her ear to the door, listened hard but the door was thick and the timber solid – she could hear nothing at all. For a terrifying moment she wondered if she was alone in the house. If she'd been left in the cellar to die.

She pushed the thought aside. Her family would be looking for her. Mickey and the police would be looking for her. She would be found. Wouldn't she? Despairing, Melissa made her way back down the steps and back into the corner, wrapping the blanket close.

The night had seemed so long and Melissa had felt abandoned. She had no idea where she was, but from what little she had seen on arrival, the house had seemed remote. Who would possibly find her here? And what made it worse was that no one had come anywhere near her since she'd been shoved down the steps and had fallen on to the broken concrete floor.

The corner on which she had spent the night turned out to be the driest in the underground space. Below the grate the walls were wet and green with slime, the floor puddled with dirty water. Melissa was thirsty by now, but not *that* thirsty.

The light through the grating was starting to fade, so Melissa guessed it must be somewhere around four in the afternoon. Teatime. She tried not to think of tea in the nursery with Nanny and Georgie, and often Malina and her mother. Nothing fancy, just bread and butter and jam or a slice of cake to 'tide them all over until supper' at six, as Nanny always said. By rights, Melissa was too old to need a nanny – she was kept officially to look after Georgie – but she was so much a part of the family that Melissa could not imagine her not being there.

A sound caused Melissa to look up fearfully. She watched as the door opened at the top of the stairs and the big man came down – the first person Melissa had seen since they had brought her here the previous night and the one Melissa least wanted to see.

'Not so much of a loudmouth now, are we, girlie?'

Melissa turned her face away. She didn't want to say anything in case he hurt her again, but at the same time, she didn't want him to feel that he'd won.

She might have guessed that would displease him too. 'Look at me, girl. Did your family not teach you manners?'

Melissa turned her head. He was standing quite close to her now and she had to strain her head back to see his face. He lowered over her, a solid mass of anger and irritation. 'No, not so much of a smart mouth on you now, eh?'

He stepped away and was gone almost before she realized it. Melissa breathed a sigh of relief. She had begun to cry again and she wiped away the tears impatiently. She had to find a way out of here. She had to escape before the man came back again.

THIRTY-FOUR

Melissa had no idea how much time had passed. It seemed like forever, but it was probably a couple of hours later when the door opened again and an immediate panic rose within her. The panic prevented her from realizing that the footsteps on the stairs were different this time, not heavy and steady but light and swift, and the figure was almost at the bottom of the stairs before she understood that this was not the big man. It was someone who was whispering her name.

'Melissa, Melissa, it's me, it's all right.'

'Uncle Henry? Uncle Henry!' She almost shouted the name, and then realized she must keep quiet, so it came out as a kind of squeak. A moment later he had his arms around her and she was clinging to his jacket. Her face pressed against his shoulder.

'Hush,' he said. 'Now you have to be very brave and keep very quiet. Can you do that?'

She lifted her head and nodded and then stiffened as a large figure loomed over them both, and she wondered briefly how he could be so big and still be so quiet. She squealed and pushed Henry away from her. 'Uncle Henry, behind you.'

Warning prevented the full blow from landing on Henry's head. He twisted sideways and caught it instead on his shoulder. The weapon was something solid and heavy, and Uncle Henry, caught off balance, went down hard.

'Melissa, run!'

'Oh no you don't.' The man made a grab for her, but Melissa dodged away. She was incensed now and gone beyond fear. She had her floorboard tack in her hand and she leapt at the man, striking at his face. He had never expected her to fight back, that much was clear, and he cried out as her makeshift weapon made contact. She dragged the tack down his cheek and then struck again, this time going for the eye. Uncle Henry was making a grab for the man's legs with his one still-usable hand, and as the man toppled to the floor, the cellar door opened and a bright light shone down the steps.

'Henry! Are you down there?' Mickey's voice. And then a clatter of footsteps on the stairs and a half-dozen men piled into the cellar and the big man was seized. Uncle Henry was helped to his feet and Melissa's blanket was wrapped around her shoulders once again.

She still held the sharp tack in her hand. It was pressing into her palm, she was gripping it so tightly, drawing blood, but Melissa didn't care. She was shaking, head to toe, and someone scooped her up and carried her back upstairs and into the light.

'I want to go home. I just want to go home.' Looking up at her uncle, she could see that he was in a great deal of pain, one arm hanging limply at his side. She took hold of his good hand. 'I want to go home.'

'We're both going home,' he told her. 'It's all going to be all right now.'

EPILOGUE

I t was almost Christmas before Henry's shoulder healed enough to be of any use. The blow from Richardson's weapon had hit it squarely, breaking bone and pulverising flesh and muscle. If it had not been for Melissa's warning, the blow would have fallen upon his head, Henry realized. He was fortunate to be alive; they both were.

Russell Clovis had left the country precipitously, together with his wife, and was reportedly en route for somewhere in South America. Richardson was back in jail awaiting trial. He had been charged with the murders of Detective Sergeant Cole and Detective Chief Inspector Paul. It seemed possible that the man they had known as Ansel Peach might have been responsible for the murder of Robert Cranston and perhaps the death of Sir Ralph Helford, but as his arrest was still pending, Richardson was also charged with these crimes. He had decided that Henry should suffer before he died – Henry had no doubt that he would have been just as dead as Hayden and Cole if events had gone Richardson's way. Mrs Green faced prison time as his accomplice. Henry was still puzzled as to why Mrs Green would join forces with a man who had done her family so much harm. But what had Richardson promised her? Henry thought. Or what did he know that he had used against her?

Henry had heard from Lady Helford; she and her remaining family were well and appreciated the efforts he had made on their behalf. Henry had been told that Parks, the valet, had been released without charge. Although Henry had initially wondered if Lady Helford had been the woman in the taxicab, it transpired that this had been a disguised Mrs Green. She had given the letter to the young actress, knowing that Henry's interest would be piqued. He tried to imagine her in a grey wig and failed miserably.

Henry was convalescing at his sister's house in Bournemouth where the family had decamped now that the London house had been closed and was already on the market. An offer had been received and, although it was lower than they had asked, Cynthia had told him that she was inclined to accept it. They would not be going back.

Three days before Christmas, a visitor arrived and asked for Henry. It was Otis Freeland. Henry had seen him briefly just after Richardson's arrest, but had no contact since.

'I didn't know you made house calls, Otis.'

'It's not common. How are you?'

'Healing slowly, but healing nonetheless.'

'And the child?'

'Is quieter and unsettled. She has bad dreams. But she will recover, given time.'

Henry studied his visitor thoughtfully. 'So, what brings you here?'

'Good news, I hope. You are to be reinstated, Henry. Scotland Yard has need of you, as does your sergeant.'

'I'm suspended, Otis. It's only the fact that I've been injured that's prevented me from being dismissed precipitously. The assistant commissioner has had the decency to wait until I was fit enough to face a hearing, but the outcome is already decided.'

'And what if the charges were dropped?'

Henry laughed. 'I assaulted a man. Not only that, but a man with influence and power. A rich man.'

'Who has been persuaded to withdraw his complaint. He has been magnanimous enough,' Otis grinned as he said this, 'to allow that you must have been under considerable strain. That he realizes that this was an act to put yourself beyond the pale. To draw out this Richardson fellow.' His last words were a passable imitation of Bright-Cooper senior.

'Your doing, Otis?'

'In part. Not entirely. I just nudged a little. I hope you're pleased.'

Was he pleased? Henry thought once Otis had taken his leave. Mickey would be. He'd been a lost sheep these past weeks, attached to first one inspector and then another – knowing more than all of them put together, truth be told.

Cynthia opened the door. 'Oh, has your guest gone already?'

'Oh, Otis doesn't alight anywhere for very long.' He told her his news and she perched on the arm of his chair and kissed the top of his head.

'So you'll be starting again in the new year? It's where you belong, Henry.'

He nodded. He supposed it was.

'But tonight we decorate the tree. It's a smaller one this year, the hall isn't as high ceilinged as in the London house.'

'Will all the decorations fit?'

'Of course they will, even if we have to hang three on every branch.'

Henry followed her into the hall. Melissa stood halfway up the stairs with her brothers. She had a silver star in her hand, ready to put it on top of the tree. Already a quiet child, Melissa had seemed quieter still in the aftermath, but at least that haunted look had gone from her eyes and she was smiling more readily.

Albert was directing operations, telling anyone ready to listen where each decoration ought to go.

Cynthia handed him a long strand of tinsel. 'Put it anywhere you like,' she said. 'Albert, you old bossy boots. Melissa, are you ready with the start? Everyone make a wish.'

Henry stood with the tinsel in his hands, wondering what he should wish for. Richardson with a rope around his neck – didn't seem like too much to ask.

That thought held fast, Henry, smiling as Melissa placed the star, wound the tinsel on to the tree.